FRACTURE

Also by David Longridge

In Youth, in Fear, in War
Silence in the Desert
Polka Dots and Moonbeams

For information on these books, visit David's website:
www.davidlongridge.co.uk

Fracture

David Longridge

Matador
9 Priory Business Park,
Wistow Road, Kibworth Beauchamp,
Leicestershire. LE8 0RX
Tel: 0116 279 2299
Email: books@troubador.co.uk
Web: www.troubador.co.uk/matador
Twitter: @matadorbooks

ISBN 978 1803130 316

British Library Cataloguing in Publication Data.
A catalogue record for this book is available from the British Library.

Printed and bound in the UK by TJ Books Ltd, Padstow, Cornwall
Typeset by Mach 3 Solutions Ltd (www.mach3solutions.co.uk)

Matador is an imprint of Troubador Publishing Ltd

To those of my family and friends who want to
understand France

An opening word from the author

This story is set in the years 1961 and 1962, after the return of General de Gaulle to lead France. His appointment initially as prime minister was engineered by those believing he would retain Algeria as part of France. It was not a colony. Much of the electorate who then voted him president thought the same, in particular the several million Europeans and pro-French Muslims in Algeria. That perception proved to be incorrect when it became clear that the General intended to grant Algeria self-determination, and that the National Liberation Front, or FLN, would declare the country an independent state.

The two years 1961–62 were traumatic for the French nation. Algerian independence ran like a fault line through France, polarising the population like nothing else did in the twentieth century. It fractured society. The focus of opprobrium or adulation was General de Gaulle. His change of stance was regarded on the one side as genocidal and a betrayal of those who brought him back to power, and on the other as the master stroke that would unleash France into a period of unparalleled growth in the economy and standard of living.

Faced with these irreconcilable forces, how would General de Gaulle react? Join with the characters in this story, feel the tragedy and triumph of events that unfold around them. Experience how conscience can be assaulted by conflicting loyalties, when morality in human life is swept aside.

My characters are fictional apart from known historical persons. All descriptions of people and events are fictional.

David Longridge

1

Who was this? Surely a workaholic, the way he studied avidly what looked like engineering drawings. Without let-up, in spite of the train swaying and lurching at full speed. Black hair above a handsome academic face, wearing a brown corduroy sports jacket and no tie. Captured in his own world, oblivious of all else. They might have been a million miles away, not just the other side of the compartment.

Leo could sense Theresa's interest in their fellow passenger, as he felt her hand touch his. What was so special about him? He would stop her staring if he thought the man was conscious of the interest he aroused. So captured was he by his work, he wouldn't have noticed if the Pope was sitting opposite. Concentration was one thing, this person acted as though immersed in solving an equation that defeated Einstein.

Leo's gaze moved to the window, to large open fields stretching towards the Champagne country. A river wound its way first one side of them, then through a bridge to the other, probably the Marne.

The door of the compartment slid open. 'Tickets and papers, please,' the conductor announced as he looked in some surprise at Leo. Perhaps it was the pale grey tunic he wore, with gold parachute badge. Leo handed over his *carte d'identité*, a Captain in the French Foreign Legion. Theresa took a German passport out of her bag, and security pass for a nurse in the Legion's medical service, married to Captain Leo Beckendorf. Their first-class rail warrants followed, issued by Supreme Headquarters Allied Powers in Europe with a letter referencing Leo's new posting to SHAPE at Versailles.

The passenger opposite finally looked up, giving them all a smile as he showed his papers. The conductor steadied himself while the train swayed and jolted over points, saying, 'Thank you everyone, we're on time, Paris in –' He never finished the sentence.

A brilliant flash of light, and thundering explosion an instant afterwards, enveloped them. The compartment seemed to lift in the air as they were flung sideways, their carriage whipping and twisting as it ran into the one in front. Everything around them broke up. Flying glass, steel partitions driven into the roof bulkheads, the floor splitting underneath them, darkness.

Leo knew he was in shock. Not a sound except long tortured screams from further up the carriage. Where was Theresa? Impossible to see anything in the dust and wreckage. What was that he felt, out in front of him? A lightweight jacket – yes, that must be her. A sudden spasm of pain pierced his right arm. It was free but lifeless, his right hand wouldn't work. He must crawl forward to the jacket, Theresa would be underneath it.

'Leo, Leo.'

It was her.

'Hold on, darling,' he gasped. 'I'm going to get you out of here.' A sudden surge of pain, his arm, he must try to ignore it. 'Are you okay?'

'I think so.' Her words were faint. 'I can just crawl forward. There's a gash in the side of the carriage. Beyond that, I can see light.'

'Hang on. I'm coming up beside you.' He pushed himself forwards with his good arm. 'We must get out of here right away, before there's a fire.'

The conductor was motionless close by, head bent backward, probably a broken neck. There was no way he should try to move him.

He edged forward. He could just see daylight ahead of them, as they squeezed under a twisted bulkhead. The other passenger was already trying to clamber out. 'Follow him,' said Leo.

Somehow the three of them slid down the side of the carriage to the ground.

From the grass verge beside the rail tracks, Leo saw that part of the train was lying below in a shallow ravine. Beside them, alongside the track, was their carriage and several others, twisted and contorted at each end. There was no one else to be seen, just shouts from the wreckage, the noise of pain and fear.

They checked themselves over for injuries. Cuts to face, arms and legs were not a problem. His arm was what needed attention, the pain was hellish. Theresa tore a strip from somewhere under her skirt, creating a makeshift sling.

'That'll help,' she said. 'I've got work to do. The medics will be here soon, and will fix you properly. Your wounds aren't life-threatening, paratrooper.'

They both tried to laugh. 'Lucky it's not cold,' said Theresa. 'You'll be in shock, ask the medic for a blanket when he comes.'

'What about you? What do you mean, work to do?'

'You forget who I am. I'm trained to deal with the wounded,' she said, looking at the crumpled carriages derailed along the track and down in the ravine. 'There are going to be plenty up here, and below.'

'Okay. Be careful, my darling. There'll be terrible sights when you go inside all that,' Leo said, looking towards the horror of the carriage they just crawled out of. 'It'll be dangerous in there.'

Theresa kissed him, stood up and called out to the other passenger who was sitting on the ground staring at them. 'You all right?' she asked, receiving a wave back.

Leo watched her run towards the shouts and cries from the shattered train. How did she manage to look elegant even in a moment of such horror? Tall, even in the soft flat shoes, her skirt swaying under the simple blue tunic.

It was still vivid in his mind. Her hand moving into his, just before the explosion and crash. The gentle squeeze, a signal of love and belonging, reminding him of Saigon where she'd walked into his life a second time. After tracking him down from the other side of the world. Theresa never gave up. He didn't deserve it, not after abandoning her when Germany collapsed.

How long until help arrived? Leo could see a few buildings further up the line. Perhaps a village where the locals should be calling the emergency services. He moved towards the fellow passenger who was brushing dirt off his clothes, a bad tear in his jacket.

'I've lost some of my work in there,' the man said. 'Too bad, I can replace it when I get back to the works. Your arm must be painful.'

'We were the lucky ones, look at that mess,' said Leo, staring at the wrecked carriage. 'How did we get out of there alive?'

Suddenly, the wail of sirens as a red fire truck marked *sapeurs-pompiers* drove across from the nearby highway. He waved to them, shouting, 'Give us a couple of blankets, and go on in. There are other passengers in greater need.'

After some time, impossible to know how long, there was that familiar sound from Algeria. The thwack of helicopter blades and whistling sound from the jet engine of the Alouette. The other passenger seemed to be giving it his full attention.

'You know the Alouette, Monsieur?' asked Leo.

'Know it? I could describe every nut and bolt of it to you.'

'Oh, how come?'

'It's a long story.'

'I'm used to the Alouette, from North Africa.'

'Ah,' said the other. 'I understand.'

'I served in Algeria before being posted to Versailles, to SHAPE,' said Leo.

'That's interesting. I love Algeria. I'll give you my card,' the other said. 'I sometimes come to SHAPE.'

'When you do, just ask for Captain Beckendorf. Theresa, that's my wife, is going to work in Paris at the American hospital in avenue de Neuilly, close to the army quarter we've been allocated.'

Leo lay back, his thoughts returning to Theresa. She was mad. Flying as a *convoyeuse* into Dien Bien Phu to nurse in a field hospital, okay, that was brave but it was war. Here it was peacetime, but what carnage. How could something like this just happen in the middle of France?

There was something about the brutal shock of impact. What was it? Just before the train shuddered and broke up. Yes, that flash of light outside, the shattering explosion. Not just a derailment, mechanical malfunction, fault in the track. His experience told him it could only be one thing.

His thoughts were jolted by someone leaning over him, a paramedic wanting to help.

'Just give me a shot of morphine and re-fix the sling with a splint,' said Leo. 'Then leave me where I am. It's my wife who needs help. In there,' he said, pointing at the wrecked carriage with his good arm. 'She's a nurse, trying to help people trapped inside.'

While he was being tended to, Leo asked where they were.

'The village of Blacy, near to Vitry-le-François, Monsieur le Capitaine.' The paramedic looked up at the scene. 'C'est horrible. Quelle catastrophe!'

Leo wasn't going to leave the scene until Theresa re-appeared. Looking at the business card of the other passenger, now gone to hospital for a check-up, he read 'Lieutenant Colonel Jean Bertrand, Chief Designer, Nord Aviation'. The name sounded familiar. Surely, there was a lot more to him than that.

2

Kim lay half-awake after turning off the alarm. Her eyes followed the drop in the ceiling down to the small window of her bedroom in the attic apartment. The top of a tower belonging to the Église Saint-Sulpice looked back at her. She turned on the radio to stop herself drifting back to sleep. Early morning news on RTF marked the start to Kim Cho's day. Today it was all about a train crash. Twenty people dead and a hundred injured was the count so far. It would get worse.

As a full-time journalist on the *Paris Tribune*, most of Kim's time was in politics and investigative work. Right now, that meant the war in Algeria, and the return of Charles de Gaulle. She carried the wireless into the bathroom. As she washed and made up, it seemed the disaster of the express train from Strasbourg to Paris was the only news item.

What to wear? No meetings outside the office today, so a white blouse and short black woollen skirt would do, with the patent leather belt. She was about to leave the apartment when the phone rang. Taking it with one hand and finishing her coffee with the other, what she heard made her freeze.

'Is that Kim?'

'Yes, it's me.'

'It wasn't an accident.' Silence, and the phone went dead.

Her mind was racing as she ran down the three floors and out into the street. Who on earth was that? Could it be Françoise de Rochefort, Justine's great friend, it sounded like her?

Outside the *tabac* across the road, all the front pages carried the story. Some showed pictures of the appalling wreckage. She must get to the paper as soon as she could.

Coming out at Metro George V, she was into the building in a flash and up to the newsroom. Knocking on a glass door, she walked into a small office beginning to fill with cigarette smoke.

Art Buchwald looked up, his dark bushy eyebrows lifting as he gazed at her through heavy black-rimmed glasses. The bow tie suggested a certain difference from the norm in Paris journalism. There was no look of surprise at her uninvited entry. Kim was something else. Not just her looks. There was an intensity, almost brashness, about her. That was Kim's passport.

He knew she could get in anywhere, given half a chance, and waved her to the large upholstered chair facing him.

Kim dropped down into the cushions, crossing her long slim legs, and stared at the person she most looked up to on the paper. 'Sorry to barge in. This train crash, there's something interesting going on. RTF says it was a derailment. A contact called me just as I was leaving the apartment, saying it wasn't. I just wanted to bounce it off you.'

'Oh? There was nothing to grip me in the overnight tele-type from New York, so I'm ready for something interesting.' He was referring to content from the *New York Herald Tribune*, with which the *Paris Tribune* was syndicated.

Kim liked Art as a person. Several years before, he'd given her the lifeline she was desperate for. Just when her life was ruined and in danger, he opened up a new world to her.

'Who's your contact?' he asked. 'Maybe that elegant deputy friend of yours,' he sighed, referring to Justine Müller, the left-wing member of parliament. He knew the two had been close for some years.

Kim didn't respond to the reference to Justine. She was protective about her most valuable asset in the Assembly, and anyway, it wasn't her. She raised herself a little in the chair. 'My friend just said it wasn't an accident, but couldn't tell me more.'

There was a long silence. Art Buchwald's sharp mind was on the case. Stubbing out the remains of his cigarette, he leaned back and swivelled his chair slightly, observing the scene in the newsroom outside. 'So, what is it you want from me, advice on how not to ruin your career?'

'That's about it,' said Kim. 'There are things that the government likes to keep quiet, particularly now General de Gaulle's back. They say he runs the country through a small number of trusted mates from the war days. Step outside that circle, and risk their wrath.'

'You're afraid of being censored?' he said.

Kim thought back to that day she showed Art a piece she'd written, just before French and British troops parachuted into Port Said. She'd picked up that there was a third dimension. 'You're remembering that conversation we had before Suez?'

'I certainly am. You said you had information that Israel was in a secret pact with France and Britain.'

'Yes, and you said Mendès France was a Jew. He must have a soft spot for Israel.'

'You've a good memory, Kim. Most of the left in France admire Israel as a young country building its society on socialist principles.'

'Yes. But what did we do? Not much, just a small piece when we could have boosted our circulation by blowing the whistle before the paras dropped into the Canal Zone.'

'Or they could have closed us down.'

Kim reflected. Art Buchwald was above all a satirist. He liked to show that off. She also knew that floating an alternative to the government stating the train crash was an accident, ran the same risks. At what point should the *Tribune* and its big brother in New York, run the story? The American paper would have to publish first. The French authorities would more than likely take the *Paris Tribune* off the streets if it accused the government of covering something up.

'We must be dead careful,' he said. 'First, we must learn more about the accident. We can't just run a speculative piece. How soon can you find out more?'

'Right away. I'll go and see the person who called me. If the crash was a deliberate act, we must ensure *L'Express* doesn't beat us to it.'

Art Buchwald nodded. 'I can't believe they would risk it. They'd have to run the story through the government. Prime Minister Debré would immediately silence them if he didn't like it.'

'Yes.' Her mind was racing. She must follow up that call from Françoise immediately.

He broke into her thoughts. 'See what detail you can uncover. At this stage, let's keep it between you and me. You're justified in protecting your sources at this early stage.'

As she was about to rise, Art Buchwald suddenly said, 'Kim. How are your family managing? I've heard the Communists are a problem for your king, Sihanouk.'

'Sihanouk is a capable ruler,' she replied. 'The Communist dissidents are dangerous, he calls them the Khmer Rouge. For the present, don't worry. Cambodia's safe in his hands.'

3

Paris, 20th arrondissement

Kim focused on how to develop a story out of a tragedy. That was Françoise de Rochefort's voice on the phone, just before she left for work that same morning. No mistaking it. Where to find her? Probably still at headquarters of the secret service, what Françoise called the *piscine*, doing her undercover work.

Kim didn't know Françoise well. They'd met a few times when Justine was bringing opium in from Vietnam. Did she have her phone number? You couldn't just telephone someone in the secret service and expect to be put through.

Yes, there was a private number, in some notes made ages ago when the three of them met at the Café Flore. How to make the approach? Best go straight in, that was her style. Did she have something she could offer her, information from another direction that might unlock the natural reticence of a secret service agent? It was Françoise who'd rung her, so she wouldn't be surprised.

'Françoise de Rochefort? It's Kim Cho, Justine's friend. Could we meet, today if possible?'

There was a short silence. Then, from the other end, 'There's a bar near the Metro in boulevard Mortier. See you there at twelve today.' The line went dead.

I'll take the bus, thought Kim. On a lovely spring day like this, so much more agreeable.

It would take half an hour, heading east towards the 20th arrondissement. One of the old green and cream buses, the driver sitting partly in the open, changing gear with a giant crank outside his door. How she adored this city. Beginning at the junction with the rue de Seine, fresh fish and vegetables brought overnight from Brittany and laid out on the market stalls. Over the *Boul'Mich*, past a brasserie with the chef in black smock and long white apron, opening oysters over a mound of crushed ice. On along the Left Bank, fascinating sights everywhere even as the bus entered the poorer districts.

There was the bar in boulevard Mortier with a few tables outside. Kim went in, recognising Françoise at a small round table in the far corner.

Shaking hands, they sat down facing one another as Françoise called the waiter. Both ordered beers and *croque-monsieurs*.

'So, Kim, you recognised my voice this morning. I didn't want to identify myself. Too many people listening in these days.'

'I guessed that was why you rang off before I could ask what it was about. I just assumed it was the train crash.'

'Tell me first what you're up to in the media world these days,' said Françoise.

Kim brought Françoise up to date on her work at the *Tribune*. 'I'm what the Americans call an investigative reporter. What you said about it not being an accident really fired me up.'

'I can imagine.' Françoise was watching her closely. 'That's why I rang you.'

'How did it happen, if it wasn't an accident?'

'I have to be circumspect in what I tell you, Kim. There isn't anything concrete as yet. No one's claiming responsibility, or pointing fingers. In fact, the only hard information so far is that the Ministry of Interior has taken tight control, and are not saying anything. That's what makes me suspicious.'

'Oh, thanks, Françoise. That does sound fishy. I must do some spade work of my own. I'm not sure where to start.'

Françoise was quiet for a moment, evidently thinking it through. 'Why not start with the passengers on the train. You might know one or two. I guess journalists like you know a tremendous number of people.'

Kim smiled. That was a sensible place to begin her investigative work. 'Good advice, thanks. Now, Françoise, you should always come to me if you think I could help you. I'm on the payroll of the *Tribune*, but the paper's not really a competitor of the main Paris press. I have some independence and can write feature pieces for magazines like *Match* and *L'Express*.'

'Yes, and you're very good at it,' laughed Françoise. 'I remember features you did on Justine. It's good of you to come over, Kim. Contacts like you are invaluable, aside from you being a good friend. I like to have sources outside the *piscine*.'

⇥⊷⊶⇤

Kim didn't waste time. She knew where to go for the names of the passengers. If she could identify any of them, she might learn more about what happened. What the conditions in the train were just before and just after the crash. The rumours flying around afterwards. Stories coming out of the hospitals where they took the injured.

A friend in the SNCF owed her a big favour, that was the great thing about being a journalist. You traded information and did favours, not just for the moment but for pay-back when another story came along. The *Train rapide No. 12* was an express, it would have a passenger manifest of the pre-booked passengers and seats assigned.

⋄⬤⬤⋄

The teleprinter outside her office clattered into life. This was it. She tore off the sheets and took them back to her desk. No indication shown against the names as to the twenty-five who had now lost their lives, nor of the one hundred and fifty or so reported as injured. At first, the names meant nothing to her. Then, suddenly she saw it. Someone she recognised dimly from the past. The name of a Captain in the French Foreign Legion, Beckendorf, first name Leo. Her job was to remember names. Where did this one come from? Army, Vietnam, yes. Her memory clicked in. A close friend of Françoise de Rochefort's brother, Henri.

The lady who brought round the coffees was beside her. 'Grand crème, mademoiselle, comme d'habitude?' Kim gave her a lovely smile in return and nodded yes to her usual café au lait.

She took a sip, and sat back to stretch her mind. Yes, she remembered Françoise saying he was something special, German, and knew the de Rochefort family. He and Henri were at school together in England, both having English mothers. On opposite sides in the war, Henri in the Legion, Leo a Luftwaffe paratrooper. How to get hold of him? She must call Françoise at her home. She had the means to find out. Her office at the *piscine* had lines into everywhere, the Paris police, the army, the Gendarmerie.

4

The answer came back quickly. Captain Beckendorf was at SHAPE, just posted there as part of the French army's contribution to what was originally Eisenhower's headquarters. When she phoned, she was put straight through to him and they arranged to meet at noon the next day.

Kim dressed smartly and drove her Simca 1000 out over the Pont de Saint-Cloud, heading west to Versailles. Twenty minutes and she was at the barrier guarding entry to the headquarters complex, looking like a prefabricated army camp. Her press pass and a phone call from the guardroom to confirm the appointment with Captain Beckendorf was enough. She was told to follow the signs to the US Army mess hall. The barrier swung up to let her in, and she drove past a series of long single storey buildings on either side.

That must be Leo Beckendorf waiting for her outside the mess hall. She took him in at one glance. Short and broad-shouldered, but a friendly battle-scarred face. Behind him was a tall, slim woman, presumably his wife.

'Mademoiselle Cho?' he called out, removing his green beret. 'I'm so pleased to meet you. This is my wife Theresa,' he said as the two women shook hands. 'Since it's the weekend, I thought Theresa should join us. Let's go and find something to drink. The Americans let us use their bar and restaurant here.'

They settled down at a table in the open. Service personnel in the uniforms of different nations walked smartly past, with a lot of saluting.

'Forgive me for calling you out of the blue. It's rather my style,' said Kim, jokingly. 'I have a contact in the SNCF and got hold of the passenger list for the train. I'm sorry you were hurt,' she said, looking at Leo's arm in its sling.

'Oh, that's okay,' he replied.

'It was a traumatic experience, the crash I mean,' said Theresa.

Kim turned to the elegant woman who looked like she'd seen a lot in life, yet kept her good looks. 'It must have been horrific. I won't ask for the dreadful details.'

'Theresa went back into the wreckage and did what she could until the rescue teams took over,' said Leo. 'She was in the Legion's nursing service and now nurses at the American hospital in Paris.'

'That explains why you did such a brave thing, Madame,' said Kim. 'Going back in to help the wounded, that was really something.'

A slightly awkward silence, before Leo said, 'I gather from our phone call that you write for the *Paris Tribune*. Many of your readers will be Americans in Paris?'

'Yes,' said Kim. 'Let me explain how I tracked you down. I think you know Françoise de Rochefort and Justine Müller.'

Kim took them through the background of the promotional work she'd done to help Justine when she was launching herself into politics.

'Justine's a larger-than-life character,' said Leo. 'I only met her in Bordeaux, when we were staying with the de Rocheforts. First of all before the war, then much later, after Dien Bien Phu. But I picked up what she was up to with her friends and enemies in Vietnam.'

'Yes, she's not flamboyant, but to be a top model and then get elected as a deputy, is remarkable.' Kim paused. 'And all that after the horrors of Buchenwald.'

Kim accepted their invitation to lunch, and the three of them headed for the cafeteria. She took an immediate liking to the couple. He was the archetypal tough paratrooper, yet somehow kind as well as hard. She was taller, with a steady look in her dark eyes.

'I'll be open with you,' said Kim when they were settled back at their table. 'I'm looking for an angle on the train disaster. I have that kind of inquisitive mind that looks for something else. Either something the authorities have missed, or something they want to cover up. There's been no statement yet on the cause.'

'Have you got any clues yet?' asked Leo.

'I was hoping you'd start me off.' Kim's sparkling laughter, perhaps from her Cambodian roots, was infectious.

Leo and Theresa looked at one another. There was something passing between them, eye contact only, but they were communicating. At least, that was what Kim's experience in years of digging out people's secrets signalled to her.

The couple clearly agreed on whatever it was. Leo did the talking.

'Kim, we're off the record. No reference to us or our regiment, should you go to print. Is that clear?'

'Absolutely.' Kim felt that intoxicating thrill when she was edging towards a big story.

'Theresa and I both heard it,' said Leo.

'Heard what?'

Theresa said, 'Just before the crash, before we felt the carriage leap into the air.'

Silence for a second.

'There was a flash, loud explosion.' Leo's voice was steady and convincing.

Kim sucked in what oxygen remained around them. 'What sort of explosion?'

'I've heard a lot of large bangs in my time,' said Leo, with half a laugh. 'It sounded and felt like … ' He paused. 'Like a bomb.'

Driving back into Paris, Kim was thinking about Justine. There was a strong friendship between the two, ever since the article Kim wrote on her in *L'Express*. That was when Justine won her seat in the Assembly. Could she help, through her political friends? If the authorities were keeping quiet on why there was an explosion just before the crash, someone in the Assembly would know why. Their relationship over the years was always professional. She admired Justine for her extraordinary career. And she valued the access she had to her as a deputy and influential left-wing politician. There was great chemistry between them. Justine clearly appreciated the advice Kim gave her on press relations, and the occasional articles promoting Justine's work for the deprived in society.

Kim was conscious though of more than that between them, that Justine felt an attraction for her which she couldn't reciprocate.

Years back, she observed the relationship Justine enjoyed with her seamstress friend at Schiaparelli, the lovely Vietnamese woman, Ka. She could only surmise at the time that there was something profound between them. How to describe it she didn't know.

Kim's attention in her normal life was always focused on men, as far as physical attraction was concerned. Men who sometimes were not right for her, and once a man who came close to killing her. Without Justine's intervention, he would have succeeded. The heroin addiction he forced her into would have put an end to it all.

She respected Justine enormously, what she achieved for the destitute of Paris, but she was hesitant about developing more than a professional relationship with another woman beyond a close friendship. Maybe the change in lifestyle would be more exciting, like an adventure to somewhere she didn't realise existed, but she wasn't ready for that. Aware of her sexuality and the effect it had on others, there was no shortage of attention men gave to her. Being Cambodian, she stood out to them as something different, increasing the attraction. No need to check on herself in a mirror to be reminded of her beautiful figure. She chose her clothes to add to the effect, people turning their heads wherever she went.

Justine was a secret person, Kim realised that a long time ago. Great to converse with, daring in what she was prepared to take on, and fun. Yet there was no way to penetrate under that calm and welcoming exterior. Inside the armour plating, felt Kim, lay other things. Maybe there was good reason why Justine wanted them kept locked away.

5

Paris, Palais Bourbon

Justine Müller made her way out of the *hémicycle,* the floor of the National Assembly, and into one of the corridors. It reminded her of her first day as a newly elected deputy, when they showed her around and explained the origin of the palace. How the magnificence swallowed her up, as did the faces of other deputies assessing her. That tall, slim newcomer with auburn hair tied smartly at the nape of the neck. She was no stranger to some of them. Female deputies could have seen her in the pages of *Vogue* magazine. Those rich enough might have glimpsed her in the salons of Schiaparelli.

That was seven years ago. Preparing herself now for the meeting with her mentor, Justine's mind flashed over the dramatic events that engulfed France since then. The tragedy of Dien Bien Phu. The break-away of France's colonies into independence. The farce and humiliation of Suez. The war in Algeria and the return of General de Gaulle.

She was heading for the room used by Pierre Mendès France, or PMF as they called him. Out of office since leaving the Radical Party, he was forming a new party focused on the intellectual left, the PSU. The two of them were close, it was he who encouraged her to run for selection as a Radical Party candidate.

He must have seen her through the open door as his secretary smiled and waved her through. 'Justine, hello there,' he called out. 'You need a drink, that must have been an exhausting debate. I'm not sure I miss being a deputy any longer.'

'It certainly was, Pierre.' When he was prime minister, Justine wouldn't have dreamt of calling PMF by his first name. Now that he was out in the political cold, they spoke to one another as close friends.

Taking the iced water and flopping down onto a sofa in the corner of the room, she remarked, 'General de Gaulle seems to be on a high since his visit to Algeria. Interesting how he missed out Oran and Algiers. Can't blame him.'

'I agree.' Pierre Mendès France stood there beaming, so short in stature. Black hair smoothed back, bushy eyebrows well apart, the intelligent round face and eyes always suggesting amusement not far underneath. 'What a change from the previous trip when they were adulating him in Algiers. This time, they would have bumped him off.' PMF clutched what looked like a scotch and Perrier. 'There's going to be a lot of trouble, Justine.'

'What sort of trouble? Where? In Algiers again?'

'The army out there, they could take Algeria over. I'm told the plotting started among a handful of colonels, now it's rumoured there are generals involved. They might even march on Paris.'

'What?' cried out Justine in astonishment.

'I know it sounds ridiculous, but we're beginning to hear things. There are army units here too, sympathetic to holding Algeria at all costs. They can't accept that after defeating the rebels, they're losing the political war.'

Justine knew what he meant. PMF had connections even into the heart of the new administration. Information must be seeping through, maybe via the *piscine*. Probably the army's intelligence people, the Deuxième Bureau, would be passing it back.

He sat back on the cushions. 'Justine.' He paused for a moment, a sign he wanted to change the subject. 'The Prime Minister tells me he wants someone in his team who holds sway with the working classes, acceptable to the unions. He's willing to take in a Radical-Socialist to join his government in a special "without portfolio" capacity. In effect to carry out special projects of a social nature. I think you would be the right person.'

Justine couldn't bring herself to respond, such was her surprise. Why her? Her political record was on the left, like PMF. Certainly, she would deal with the devil if it helped her cause. Yet, how could she be useful to a Gaullist government? She knew Prime Minister Michel Debré was originally in Mendès France's Radical Party. He had socialist ideals, or would have had at that time. How should she respond? It would be awkward. General de Gaulle's lot were ruthless, a tight clique going back to the Free French days. There would be conflicts, moral and practical. Her style, though, was to respond positively to an opportunity like this. It could be an important step up the political ladder.

'Pierre, you know me. If you think I'm the right person, I would trust your judgement. I'm one for accepting challenges.' She looked down as she laughed to herself, then raised her steady eyes to his. 'What would be the first step?'

'That's great, Justine. What the Prime Minister has in mind could be very interesting for you. I'll take you through what I know, a preliminary discussion. Michel Debré will want to see you himself.'

'Fine by me, Pierre.'

Justine's mentor in politics. ever since her decision to stand for the Assembly, explained the challenge facing Prime Minister Debré and President de Gaulle. They had to persuade left-wing leaders in France to recommend their followers to vote for General de Gaulle's proposals for granting Algeria the right of self-determination. Most would assume that would lead to the independence party, the FLN, taking control. That would come soon, when the question would be put to the public in a referendum.

The powerful Communist Party was another matter. If they refused to support the General's proposals, then the trick would be to get their members to abstain. Algeria was not a French colony. It was part of France, with its own deputies in the National Assembly. Deciding to cut the ties with a country integrated with mainland France over the past hundred years, with more than a million European inhabitants, would drive a wedge through the population. Violence and mutiny were in the air. Prime Minister Debré would tell her what he wanted doing.

Justine noticed the time. Oh Lord, she was due to be meeting Kim and Josephine Baker that evening at the Blue Note. Chet Baker was in town. 'Thank you, Pierre, for explaining. You've always been a wonderful supporter of my efforts. I'm flattered by your confidence in me.'

He showed her to the door. 'You've earned it,' the former Prime Minister said, with a broad smile. 'Come and see me when you can.'

She was meeting the others for a snack at Le Drugstore on the Champs-Élysées, then it was only a few steps to the rue d'Artois.

6

Justine adored Chet Baker's trumpet playing. She knew the club was a favourite of Kim's. And of course Josephine knew all the jazz places and *boîtes*. Wherever Josephine Baker walked in, they loved her.

The Blue Note was not a place for conversation, just somewhere to let the finest modern jazz flow through you. The three of them did it whenever they could.

Now late evening. Justine was almost through her second scotch and Perrier. Bud Powell was playing a piano solo, Kenny Clarke driving the rhythm on drums, Chet Baker and his trumpet taking a rest.

Suddenly a vibrating shudder, one that seemed to come up through the floor. The band kept playing, but Justine's training from a long time ago told her what it was. A hit somewhere close. She looked at the other two, and they were up and heading for the exit before the rest of the audience reacted. Outside, the sirens were already wailing as the special police rushed to the scene. The CRS were well practised by now, Justine thought, in four minutes they'd be there. Where was it? Probably in the Champs-Élysées nearby.

'Come on,' Kim shouted and in no time they were at the spot, close to where they'd been earlier that evening. A car bomb, someone said. No one found killed so far, but many injured.

Justine watched her friend swing into action. First, Kim dashed into a nearby *tabac*, asking if she could phone her photographer. Then they saw her pull out a notebook as she started to interview witnesses standing nearby.

The scene looked bad. The police were cordoning off the immediate area. A crowd was gathering, quiet and orderly. No one mixed it with the CRS.

'I don't want to hang around here,' said Josephine.

'Just a moment,' cried Justine. 'There's Kim. We should tell her if we're going.'

Inside the cordon, holding her press card and giving a tough-looking policeman her best 'We're in this together' smile, Kim was taking stock of the situation. It was a car bomb, the wreckage of the vehicle strewn a few metres from the entrance of Le Drugstore. Four or five wounded bodies close by were being attended to, the smashed glass from the front windows suggesting there could be more injured inside.

Onlookers suddenly cried out as a child was carried from the building. A woman was sobbing as Kim drew back for a second, a man's severed arm at her feet. The photographer arrived from the *Tribune* and she waved him over.

Outside the cordon, Justine turned to Josephine. They'd picked up a whisper coming back from the onlookers that one person was dead and at least a dozen badly injured.

'We're not needed here,' said Josephine. 'It's awful. We're just getting in the way.' She caught sight of Kim waving to them, shouting, 'Go to Castel. I'll meet you there later.'

As they settled in the back of the Citroën ID taxi, Justine turned to Josephine. 'Should we be doing this?' she said.

'Life has to go on. That's Paris.'

'I've never been to Castel,' said Justine. 'They do line dancing, don't they, what's that?'

'You'll soon find out. It's the latest with the smartest. Just perfect for a left-wing deputy,' laughed Josephine.

Justine didn't think a watering hole for the rich with the cliquey reputation of Castel would be her kind of place. As Josephine led her past the reception desk, and up to the maître d' to secure a table for three, the scene burst out before them. Plush and sophisticated rather than glitzy. Swing music pulsating everywhere, spotlights moving over the dance floor and the plush décor. Champagne buckets being re-stocked, smart food being served by smart staff. Everyone seemed to know one another, earnest conversation and laughter. Skirts were short and flared, tops sleeveless, hair up behind the head with a suggestion of velvet ribbon. If you sought a definition of 'chic', surely this was it. Cufflinks flashed on blue shirts as young men lit Camels with their Zippos.

The banquette enveloped Justine as they sat down in a far corner of the dance floor, the swing music engulfing them. The dancing was something else, everyone in two lines, one behind the other, in synchronised line dancing.

'That's the Madison line dance,' whispered Josephine in Justine's ear. 'We'll give it a go in a minute. Just get used to the scene.' Champagne arrived.

About an hour later, Justine spotted Kim being brought over to them by the maître d'. Why did she feel suddenly breathless as Kim approached, stunning in a cream silk dress hugging her figure, narrow shoulder straps, low in the front? How could she cover a bombing, file it in time for the *Tribune*'s late-night deadline, and then show up at Castel? She must have changed at her office.

In no time, the three of them were on the floor in line together, the disco belting out the Ray Bryant Combo playing 'Madison'. Justine followed the footwork as best she could. At least you could copy the person in front. Kim was beside her, exotic in the way she swayed and weaved in and out to the music. Someone came and pulled Josephine away to dance alone out in front of the two lines. Paris's greatest cabaret artist might be a bit above the age for this sort of thing, but she was everyone's star and they wanted her to lead them.

Justine saw Kim turn towards her, the soft and gorgeous smile said so much. She felt her senses running away with her, taking her to an unknown yet irresistible place.

⇔▸▩◉ ◉▩◂⇔

Unlocking the door of her apartment, Justine's mind was not its normal composed self. That champagne and dancing was a part of it, the tangible part. The other part was infinitely more complicated. The intangible was always like that. And when it was about emotions, it became complex. It was about her inner self.

Could she continue unattached, as though nothing was changed since the loss of her darling Ka? One moment they were together in Paris, as one. The next, Ka was in a race to rescue her family in Hanoi before Ho Chi Minh took over. The last Justine heard was that Ka was lost to the Viet camps. Places of brainwashing and re-indoctrination. There was no news, and Justine realised that the new Ka, if she ever emerged, would be a different person.

The time that evening with Kim was something she wouldn't forget, whatever the future held in store for the two of them.

7

Algiers, Hôtel Saint-Georges

Henri de Rochefort was sitting at the bar, square Moorish columns with their fine mosaics at intervals along it. Large fan-shaped lights above, clocks showing the time of the world's great cities facing him. He was very fond of this hotel, how it provided a magical escape from the harsh reality of military life in the rough hill country, the *bled*. The wilderness between the fertile coastlands and the world's largest desert, where the army fought to re-gain control over the rebel forces of the FLN independence party.

Even now that he was rooted to the home base of the Legion at Sidi Bel Abbès, Henri found the immense beauty of the city laid out below the Saint-Georges captivating and a relief. Walking to one's bedroom was an experience in itself, each door with a brass plate bearing names such as Dwight D. Eisenhower, Winston Churchill, Sir Andrew Cunningham, and General Marshall. A reminder of the Algiers visit of Allied leaders before the landings in Italy.

The note handed to him by the concierge earlier that evening was sudden, electrifying. Noelle Mercure was always in the back of his mind, from that time during the war when he thought he was in love with her. Ten years older than him, it was an experience he would never forget. Now she re-appears, and still he isn't married. He's in his early forties, meaning she is in her early – his thoughts froze as he felt the hand on his shoulder.

'Henri,' the soft voice said as he turned his head. Still the sleek black hair tied up behind the neck. Skinny as ever, older of course but no less striking. And that same scent as she moved towards him for a kiss on each cheek. The stern expression he first remembered her by, solemn but exuding warmth and attraction.

'You've grown up,' she joked as she squeezed his arm. 'Now it's Major de Rochefort, I'm impressed.'

Henri pulled himself together. 'Noelle, chérie. You're looking fabulous.'

There was a moment's pause as they looked one another up and down. 'Come on, let's go to a table on the terrace,' he said. The barman looked towards them, and they both asked for scotch with Perrier to be brought outside.

The hotel's famous terrace overlooked attractive gardens. Beyond, you could see the avenues lined with orange trees on the corniche leading down to the waterfront. Beyond that was the bay of Algiers.

To Henri it was unreal. How could this person he'd been so attached to just re-appear from nowhere? Someone he'd been very close to in Cairo, who'd disappeared when he returned after months of pain and horror in the desert. She was always something of a mystery. Was this another episode or would it be different this time?

'What brings you here, Noelle?' asked Henri as they sat down in the evening sun as it prepared to disappear. 'Are you still a correspondent with UPI?'

'Yes, believe it or not I'm doing the same thing I was back in Cairo days. I tried my hand as a concert pianist after the war ended, but missed the excitement of dangerous places,' she replied with a laugh. 'Algiers fits the bill.'

'That's understating it. How did you know I was here?'

'When I arrived last week and went to the UPI office, the staff were talking about what Foreign Legion units here would do if General de Gaulle went ahead with his strategy to grant independence. That reminded me of your Legion *demi-brigade* in the Western Desert, 13th DBLE. Was it here, and were you still with them? It wasn't easy to find out. The French army doesn't talk about the Legion, and when I asked around, all I got was that their headquarters were at Sidi Bel Abbès.'

'I shouldn't think they were very helpful either,' retorted Henri with a laugh. 'Even though that's where I am most of the time.'

'Dead right. Telephoning there was useless. I was going to give up when someone at UPI here said to try our people in Paris. I don't know how they found out, but they told me you were in charge of training at Sidi Bel Abbès. I tried that number again, saying that I was an old friend from Bordeaux, and they gave in and told me you were at the Saint-Georges this week.' She reached out for his hand.

He knew immediately she still had the same effect on him. What was going to happen? Last time, after the battle at Bir Hakeim, she'd left when he arrived back in Cairo. To another United Press International assignment somewhere else in the world. Just a brief letter, that was all he received.

'I'm so pleased you tracked me down,' Henri exclaimed. 'I'm still a lonely bachelor, you know. A lot has happened since we last met.'

'Dare I ask whether you were in Indochina during the war there?'

'Yes.' His perfunctory response showed he wasn't keen for the conversation to go there. At least not so soon after the wonderful surprise of Noelle walking back into his life. 'I'll talk about it some time, but right now, let's discuss happier things.'

'I understand,' and he felt her hand press against his. 'You used to talk about your twin sister Françoise, and the family in Bordeaux. Are they okay?'

Henri felt he could talk openly now about Françoise, and took Noelle through his sister's war years. Her espionage work in Vichy for the British secret service, and how she rescued her friend Justine after the round-up of Jews in Paris. He knew there were other things, a specific mission involving Justine and her sister Claudia in Berlin. She never told him what the mission was.

They dined out on the terrace. Noelle reminded him of her family background. That her mother, Annette Mercure, was a famous French scientist. The discoveries she made in nuclear physics made her a Nobel Prize winner. What she told him for the first time was that Annette died of radiation poisoning.

Suddenly, Noelle asked whether he knew of a place called Reggane, an oasis deep down in the Sahara.

'That's where the French nuclear tests are carried out,' he said.

Noelle leaned forward a little. 'I've heard something about it,' she murmured. 'What I was told by an editor back in the States is that the French are planning an atomic bomb test there any time now.'

Henri went on the alert, must watch what he said. 'That may be happening, but I know nothing about it. The place is shrouded in secrecy.'

'You see, those in the know, in the States that is, are asking what's going to happen to Reggane when the French leave Algeria. The US authorities don't want to see the equipment and know-how fall into other hands.'

'I can see that.' He paused, then turned towards her. 'You're very well informed.'

'Don't get the idea I'm out here spying, darling.' It's for the American newspapers.

Henri was thinking carefully, or as carefully as was possible under the circumstances he now found himself in.

'I can't go digging out information on France's atomic weapons programme, Noelle. I'm an officer in her armed forces.'

'I don't want you to.' She paused a moment. 'You see, I have a personal interest.'

'Oh, what's that?'

'My brother, who died three years ago, headed up France's research effort into nuclear energy.'

Henri was surprised. 'That's amazing.'

Noelle smiled at him, and went on. 'He always believed that the power of nuclear fission could be slowed down.'

'And so?'

'So that it could be harnessed for peaceful purposes, by generating electricity.'

'I've heard about that. There's a large project in the south of France somewhere?'

'Yes, at Marcoule.' Noelle hesitated. My problem is that the facilities there are primarily to produce plutonium.'

'To make atomic bombs,' he said.

'Exactly. I believe my brother was right. He insisted that atomic weapons should be banned, and they dismissed him.'

Henri saw Noelle into her taxi, back to where she was staying. 'This has been the best evening for a long time,' he said as he opened the door of the Citroën and gently pulled her towards him. She put her hand behind his neck and kissed him lightly on the lips.

8

Algiers, air force headquarters

'To give you some idea of the distance, think of driving from Berlin to Moscow. Reggane oasis is one thousand six hundred kilometres due south of Algiers, desert scrub and sand most of the way.'

The air force Commandant turned back from the wall map of the Sahara, to face Noelle. 'How did you obtain permission to visit the test site, if you'll forgive me for asking, Mademoiselle?

'When I inquired, I was told permission was never granted,' said Noelle. 'There were two reasons why I was the exception. Do you really want the detail?'

'I'd be fascinated to hear.'

'The first reason is that my brother Jean Mercure was a high commissioner of the CEA.'

'France's Atomic Energy Commissariat?'

'Yes. He directed all scientific and technical research. He received the Nobel Prize for chemistry, like my mother did for research into radiation.'

There was a moment's silence before the Commandant reacted. 'Of course, forgive my ignorance. I remember the sad story of your mother's death from radiation. She was a gallant woman.'

'The second reason is that the United Nations just established an agency to promote the peaceful use of nuclear energy. My employer UPI offered my services since I was already here in Algiers. I'm to report on the steps France is taking in that direction.'

'Now I understand. Thank you, Mademoiselle. That accounts for the impressive instructions I have to show you around Reggane.' He paused for a second. 'We're confirmed for the daily flight tomorrow from Blida military airfield.'

'Good. Should I plan for an overnight stay?'

'Yes, please do that. It won't be the Ritz. Security is strict, including a ban on photography. I have a declaration here for you to sign, that you will not divulge any information about your visit to the Reggane test facilities to anyone.'

'That's understood,' she said as she signed the declaration.

'It'll be hellishly hot there, over forty degrees in daytime,' he said.

'As long as there are buckets of Perrier and scotch, I'll make it,' laughed Noelle.

⇒⟩⟨⇐

A car came early to pick her up. She heaved her soft bag downstairs and handed it to the military driver. The Minox was at the bottom of her make-up case, the small rolls of film tucked in amongst the underwear. Whatever the rules, she couldn't do without her miniature camera.

The car drove her directly to the air force Dakota standing on the tarmac, the Commandant already there at the bottom of the short steps up to the cabin.

'I'm afraid it's a long boring flight,' he said as soon as they were on board. 'We do it in one hop. It's at the extremity of our range, flying time over three hours. Once we're beyond the coastal belt, there'll only be the rough hill country, the *bled,* and then a lot of sand to look at.'

Noelle glanced around the cabin. Twenty or so other passengers, French civilians by the look of it, plus some military. The one other woman, in the uniform of an army medic, smiled at her.

Her attention was drawn to a bald-headed man who appeared to be ordering the cabin staff around. Although short in stature, he was behaving in the authoritative manner of a senior official.

'Who's that over there?' Noelle asked the Commandant as he sat down in the seat across the aisle from her.

'His name is Foccart, Jacques Foccart. I hardly know him, but apparently he knows a lot about French colonial Africa. The rumour is that he played an important part in bringing back General de Gaulle from retirement.'

She'd have a nap after the light meal, must be awake and attentive shortly before arrival. With luck, she could look down on the site and try to memorise the layout and structures.

The flight seemed endless. Although there was a window beside her seat, there was nothing to look at. 'Could I be on the side with a view of the site when we come down to land?' she asked the Commandant.

'The airfield at the Reggane oasis is fifty kilometres from what we call ground zero,' said the Commandant. 'Too far to see anything of the test site.'

'That's a shame,' said Noelle.

'Don't worry. You might get an aerial view tomorrow morning when we take a light aircraft to Hamoudia. We drive from there to the site.'

After a bumpy landing, they taxied towards a makeshift control tower and terminal building. The Commandant pointed out the scientific staff waiting for them, armed with

Geiger counters. 'The practice is to measure the level of radio-activity in each of us on arrival, also at the end of today, and before and after the tour to ground zero tomorrow.'

A wall of hot air pressed in on Noelle as she negotiated the few steps down to the concrete. Arab porters began to manhandle luggage and freight onto a trolley, as she and the others walked over to the reception party and a line of jeeps.

'Welcome to one of the hottest places in the world,' said the Commandant. 'Reggane oasis is just a few minutes' drive. Due south from here there's nothing until the border with Mali and Niger. Niamey is nearly two thousand kilometres away.'

Noelle looked beyond the barbed wire fence around the airfield. Dead flat desert stretched to the horizon.

'Is there anything unpleasant I should look out for while here, Commandant?'

'Not really. No rebels, just the odd horned viper.'

'Horned viper, my God.'

'One got into the MT vehicle park the other day, no one would go in there. The whole Reggane operation practically closed down. They seek out the cooler spots. Look twice when you go into an air-conditioned room.'

⇔⟩⟨⇔

Resting in the hut assigned to her, trying not to think about snakes, Noelle used the time to start on the written commentary the UN had requested. The instructions were to memorise as much as she could and put it on paper at the earliest opportunity. First of all, those in the party with her, the technical features of the Reggane camp such as laboratories, and the number and role of those working there and exposed to fall-out. At the test site the next day, it would be the layout of towers, bunkers, aircraft, and military vehicles. What were the various distances from ground zero of this matériel, positioned to measure the effect of blast?

Later, she joined a dozen others in a prefabricated building for a presentation. The heat outside was still intense and the air-conditioners were fighting a losing battle. The senior scientist at Reggane welcomed everyone, explaining that the first nuclear test took place in February last year. They'd called that test Gerboise Bleue, a gerboa being a desert rat found in the Sahara and 'Bleue' being for France. It was three times the explosive power of the Hiroshima bomb. Tomorrow they'd inspect the site being prepared for the next stage of the test programme.

The presentation complete, they were taken on a guided tour of the Reggane facilities. Noelle was able to take a few shots in the underground laboratories, with her Minox concealed inside a hairbrush. Back in her hut, she wrote everything down.

Over drinks later on with the others in the party, the bald-headed man from the plane came over to her.

'Mademoiselle, I am Jacques Foccart, could I ask for the pleasure of sitting next to you at dinner this evening?'

Noelle was somewhat taken aback. This man looked more like the abbot of a monastery than an influential Gaullist.

'Oh, that is kind of you,' said Noelle. 'I'm not sure what sort of a meal they're going to give us.'

'I've brought a bottle of red Burgandy. I bet we have lamb, nothing like the local produce.'

'As long as it's not couscous,' laughed Noelle.

'They make that with camel meat in the desert,' was his response.

They were seated at two tables, one chaired by the air force Commandant and the other by the head scientist.

Jacques Foccart waved Noelle over to join his table.

'Well, I never,' he said as one of the staff placed slices of tinned foie gras in front of them, with a purée of red fruit and basket of brioche.

'If you're confined to a place like this for long, the cuisine takes on a special significance,' said Noelle. 'I remember eating in the desert in Libya, with the British army.'

'Oh, well, no comment, Mademoiselle,' he replied with a laugh. 'Now all we need is a cold Sauterne.'

'Here it comes,' said the guest on his other side, and a bottle of Rieussec appeared as if by magic.'

After the delicious first course, Jacques Foccart said, 'You have an interesting career experience, Mademoiselle.'

'You must have done your homework,' laughed Noelle. 'UPI is a global press agency, one sees the world.'

'I must confess I did inquire a little into your background.'

'I'm flattered,' said Noelle. 'What's the reason for your visit here?'

He looked surprised. Perhaps he wasn't used to being questioned about his business.

'I'm on a mission for the Prime Minister,' was all he said.

'Sounds intriguing.'

'What's the connection between UPI and this place,' he asked.

'The United Nations borrowed me.'

'Oh, how come?'

'They have a new agency promoting the peaceful use of nuclear energy.'

'That's not exactly what's going on here, is it?'

'The UN agency's remit is also to monitor nuclear arms proliferation.'

He laughed. 'We French have already proliferated.'

'Evidently, but hopefully now France is in the club, the club can close its membership,' said Noelle.

They both laughed, as the lamb cutlets arrived, along with Jacques Foccart's Gevrey-Chambertin.

❧

The very short flight the next morning brought them to Hamoudia, close to the test site. Before landing, she spotted on the horizon the hundred metre test tower from which the last device was detonated. The Commandant explained the layout of the site. Its sheer size was remarkable, reflecting the need to space all the objects to be subjected to the heat and blast at varying distances.

The Commandant pointed out a fifty metre tower close to the higher one, which was to be used for the next test. Two smaller towers stood five kilometres away, used for wireless signals relay.

Driving in ever increasing circles out from ground zero, they passed by military aircraft in their individual bunkers, tanks and other vehicles positioned at varying distances so the degree of damage could be assessed. Finally they came to the command post blockhouse one and a half kilometres away. Dotted around were small bunkers for optical instruments.

No explanation was offered on the supply and storage of material for priming the bombs, but Noelle knew the plutonium was produced at the Marcoule plant in the south of France. Security was paramount, given the volatile political status of Algeria and the threat from hostile military forces.

Taking photos undercover was not easy, and she decided to memorise the layout and distances as best she could, to reproduce later.

Sitting beside Jacques Foccart on the long flight back to Blida, Noelle learnt a lot about what he'd done in the resistance and what General de Gaulle would now do for France. Dropping her off at the apartment, he wished her luck with her report for the UN, and said he'd be in touch on his next trip to Algiers.

To Noelle, it was obvious that Jacques Foccart was someone to be reckoned with. She was sure they'd meet again, and wondered whether he'd bought into the explanation of how she worked her way into visiting something as sensitive as the Reggane nuclear site. That reminded her that Henri knew nothing about her trip. The Commandant was forthright about secrecy.

9

Henri de Rochefort was conscious of momentous events threatening to envelop him, as he sat under a canopy at the café beside the famous barracks, built by legionnaires a hundred years ago. He'd chosen a table well out of other people's way. Removing his *képi*, running a hand through the remains of his hair after the military barber's best efforts, his mind went back to this same place in autumn '39.

Fresh out of Saint-Cyr military college, his arrival in Algeria coincided with France declaring war on Germany. The parade ground unfolded before him, as hot and dusty as it was then. He remembered those marches, the distances they covered across the punishing terrain, the songs of the Legion all part of it. Henri knew he could no longer do that.

The five hundred kilometres forced march of the Dien Bien Phu survivors to the POW camps in the north of Vietnam had weakened his legs for ever. Forty days of torture, knowing that more Frenchmen were dying on the march than were killed in the battle. No doctors for the wounded men who dragged themselves along. Doctors for the officers only was what the Viets insisted on.

Now Algeria, another world, and here was Hélie de Saint Marc striding towards him. That call last night left Henri in little doubt as to what Major de Saint Marc wanted to discuss. He was an extraordinary man, even by the standards of the

Legion's officer corps. When Henri was fighting to liberate France in '44, Hélie de Saint Marc was a slave labourer in the Dora tunnels where V2 rocket bombs were being produced.

The two of them embraced, as was the way among fellow officers. Major de Saint Marc, second in command of 1st Legion Para Regiment at Zéralda and Major de Rochefort, head of training at the Legion's home base at Sidi Bel Abbès.

Still mid-morning, Henri poured cognac into his coffee, pushing the bottle over to his friend who did likewise.

Lighting a Gitane, the para officer seemed agitated. 'Henri, my friend. I'm taking you into my confidence. I need to know where your allegiances lie in the crisis we're on the edge of.'

Normally that would have raised a laugh between them. This time the mood was deadly serious.

Henri was pretty sure what was coming. 'Go ahead, I can keep my mouth shut.'

Hélie appeared even more intense than usual. To Henri, he was a purist, popular in the Regiment as someone clear and sincere in his beliefs, straightforward in what he expected of his men. Now was to be no exception.

'General de Gaulle's been back in office for two years,' said Hélie de Saint Marc. 'We all supported his return.'

'Yes,' muttered Henri. 'There seemed no doubt then that the General subscribed to *Algérie française*, keeping Algeria French. At least, that was the perception. Looking back, one realises he was careful not to be adamant on the subject.'

'We had the FLN beaten militarily and pushed back to the frontiers.' He stopped, raising his arms in frustration. 'That's what the army is furious about, at least us officers. Yet the FLN's winning the political war.'

'True,' said Henri. 'Not only Russia and China support them, even the United States is sympathetic.'

Hélie de Saint Marc leaned forward. 'Dead right. Having changed his stance on Algeria, the General will take an irrevocable step anytime now.'

'That being?'

'He'll put it to the French nation in a referendum, to approve his decision to grant independence.'

There was a heavy silence. Henri knew the consequences. It was like the end in Indochina, but worse. The hatred built up over years would unleash terrible forces. The pro-French Muslim would be turned on by the pro-FLN population. The Europeans, the *pieds noirs* as they are now calling them, would have their property grabbed.

'There's only one thing that can stop that happening,' continued Hélie.

'The armed forces,' said Henri, with some finality.

'Precisely. Crucially, that means the army in mainland France as well as in Algeria.'

Another long silence. Neither wanted to mention the word. Finally, Henri said, 'That could be treason.'

'It would have to be fast and effective.' Hélie paused. 'Control of Algeria and a positive response by the army in France. It must be a military statement, not a political one.'

Henri thought hard. General de Gaulle had tricked them. He was clear where his own feelings lay. It was he who supervised the training of Muslim auxiliaries for the French army, the *harkis*. They were fine men, his men. It was becoming clear that the *harkis* would be abandoned to the FLN. Murder would follow. He was not going to let that happen.

'I'm with you, Hélie. What is proposed?'

The Major's relief was obvious. 'That's marvellous. We must have you with us. General Salan is ready to return from retirement. He's in Madrid, keeping his head down. He would be in charge overall. Here in Algiers, it will be General Challe. I know he's air force, but the army loves him. His counterinsurgency campaign out here was nothing short of genius.

'I agree,' said Henri. 'What about the officers generally?'

'There are very few who would disagree. My predecessor, Henri Dufour certainly wouldn't.' He was referring to the former commanding officer of 1st Legion Para Regiment, ordered back to France after a speech he delivered. 'You know what he said at the funeral of the ten paratroopers?'

'Remind me of his words.'

'It is not possible that your sacrifice was in vain. It is not possible that our compatriots in metropolitan France remain deaf to our cries of anguish.'

Henri knew that was only half the story. 'The reaction of the army in mainland France will be critical. Are there units there that we can rely on at the critical moment?'

The Major showed signs of nervousness, not sure where to put his hands, looking away from his friend. 'We're not out to overthrow the government, least of all the President. We want to change his mind.' He paused, seeming to want to remember something. 'Incidentally, isn't your German friend now at SHAPE?'

'You mean Leo Beckendorf. Yes, he's French now, of course. He'd be sympathetic to our views, but I doubt he's in touch with other army units in the *métropole.*'

Henri began to feel uncomfortable about the magnitude of what was planned. How long could a takeover of Algeria by the army withstand local and international pressure to relent? He wasn't going to argue. He'd given his word to Hélie because he couldn't conceive of Algeria and its people being handed over to the FLN.

They parted. Hélie de Saint Marc would keep him posted on the timetable.

Henri's mind switched to something else pressing in on him. He was due to see Noelle that evening. God help them if she sensed something like this was going to happen, and broke the news in advance through UPI.

10

Algiers, Hôtel Saint-Georges

He recognised that stern expression Noelle put on when she was working up to something important to her. They were back on the terrace of the Saint-Georges, and the waiter was arriving with the coffee after another excellent dinner. Henri ordered them both Armagnac.

Noelle was talking about her journalism, but he sensed it wasn't the most important thing on their minds. They were alone together, the magic of the relationship alive in them. How was the evening going to end? Should he let it run as he secretly hoped it would, or should he hold back? Was he questioning himself because of some doubt in his mind?

'When I'm writing a piece for the wire service,' she said 'I have to think of the editors of top newspapers. Their readers are Americans in the professional classes. They know something about the issues here, and they want more.'

'So, what are you going to give them?'

She didn't laugh. 'I don't want to upset you, Henri, but there have been these stories about the interrogation techniques used by the French army in Algeria.'

There was silence for a moment.

'I suppose you mean ...' He paused mid-sentence. 'You're going to ask about torture?'

She felt his arm gently. 'I don't want to embarrass you, my darling. I know dreadful things happen in war. You must be faced by difficult choices. Worse still, you may have no choice in certain situations.' Noelle paused. 'The fact remains that stories of torture by the French here continue to surface in the American press.'

It was now almost dark. Henri looked out across the lights of the corniche, winding its way down to the port. He was playing for time, uncertain how he was going to respond. Why couldn't they talk about the two of them, not about the bad things in his life.

Noelle continued. 'One of the editors referred me to a guy called Aussaresses, Colonel Paul Aussaresses, who apparently operates an interrogation centre near Algiers.'

'I know him,' said Henri, 'though not well.'

'I'm not going to press you to tell me what's been going on. I just wanted you to know that while I'm here, I'll be seeing what I can find out about torture inflicted by the French army. I'll try to reach Colonel Aussaresses.'

Henri was only too aware what she was talking about. The issue arose periodically in the French press, although with editorial restraint. Torture was against French law. Outright accusations would have to be substantiated. The intellectual left were becoming vocal, the likes of Sartre and de Beauvoir, but newspapers such as *Le Monde* were careful what they printed.

'That's your business, Noelle. Maybe I can help you in general terms. But we'd have to have an understanding that there would be no specific reference to my regiment.'

She nodded and whispered, 'Of course.'

Henri knew he'd reached his limit on the torture issue. He supposed that was why he was moved from front line duties to become head of training at the Legion's base headquarters. He didn't want to go near the subject, and wouldn't with anyone else. Noelle was different. The dimension she added was suddenly central to his life.

'Noelle, my darling, I didn't think I was going to discuss this subject with anyone.'

Noelle was silent, attentive, anticipating. She smiled encouragement.

'Three years ago, the paras conducted a major campaign to liquidate the FLN in this city, including the Casbah. General Massu and Colonel Bigeard moved fast and ruthlessly. Information was key. They needed to find out where the FLN operatives were hiding out, who was supporting them. It followed a series of outrages, bombs in restaurants, civilian officials gunned down in the street.'

'I heard. The press called it the battle of Algiers. A convincing victory for the French army, wasn't it?'

'Yes, it was.' Henri paused. 'The paras did use torture. You couldn't hide that although no one talked about it.'

Silence for a bit until Noelle said, 'I suppose that for every FLN agent who did have information, there were many innocent people arrested and interrogated. Those who didn't cooperate, or couldn't, were tortured.'

Henri nodded. 'Yes, I guess that figures. Being in the Legion infantry, 13th DBLE, I wasn't directly involved. The fact is, though, that beatings, water treatment and use of the *Gégène*' have become a feature of this war.'

'The *Gégène* being the apparatus for electric shock treatment?'

'Yes, some try to graduate torture by degree of necessity, arguing that it's the only way to prevent terrorist attacks on the civilian population. Personally, I don't try to justify it with that argument.'

'You mean you have a moral problem with torture?'

'Yes, you could put it that way. I'm not the only person, although only two officers have resigned. One was a wartime hero and out here became the youngest general in the French army. Yet after the battle of Algiers, he requested to be relieved of his command, and was sent back to France.'

'That's astonishing.'

'I came to similar conclusions as he did and spoke out about them.'

'And?'

'It's probably why I'm still a major, parked in a training role.'

Noelle was visibly moved. 'I'm proud of you, my darling. For what you stood up for.' She paused. 'And for telling me.' With a quick look round the terrace, choosing the moment when no one seemed to be looking their way, she kissed him. 'I think we should talk about you and me.'

Henri looked into the dark enticing eyes that somehow drew him into her. He'd hoped, maybe knew, this would happen. Yet, there was hesitation in his mind. Could he handle Noelle if they allowed themselves to fall into a relationship at this moment? He could be committing to something that would take precedence over all else in his life.

'Yes, it's about us two,' said Henri. He felt the power of her attraction.

She seemed to sense his thoughts. 'I have a suggestion. Why don't you come back with me to the apartment I rented for my stay?'

Henri said nothing. The look in his eyes was enough.

They hardly talked on the way. Just being close to her in the taxi was erotic in itself. Following her into the apartment block and up to her floor, he noticed once more the slightness of her body. A narrow silhouette moving in almost darkness.

Inside the apartment, Noelle walked through the small hall
and into a salon with broad windows overlooking the ocean
frontage across the rooftops. With no lights on inside, the
view over the corniche lined with orange trees was breath-
taking. Opening the double windows, she turned around and
faced him. 'Come over here, my darling,' she said.

Everything seemed to happen in slow motion. He watched
as she took off her light jacket, showing him the tight white
vest underneath, the outline of her breasts pressed against
the thin cotton. He let her take one of his hands and touch
it against a breast. He came alive, feeling the softness and
warmth underneath as he worked his hand over the thin
material.

11

Versailles

'Been in a fight, Leo?' Roger Trinquier was watching how carefully Leo sat down, lifting his heavily plastered arm so it rested on the restaurant table.

'No, a train crash,' said Leo, grinning at his old army friend.

'What, you're joking. You don't mean you were on the Strasbourg to Paris express?'

'Yes, unfortunately. The arm's been playing up but should be on the mend, the medics tell me.'

'Lots of American penicillin, I guess, given you're at SHAPE.'

Roger Trinquier had been an important person in Leo's life, a mentor to him at Saint-Cyr during his commissioning course. A counterinsurgency specialist in Vietnam, he was now back instructing at the military college.

They'd come together again at the Trois Marches restaurant, the conversation veering inevitably towards Algeria.

'So, why has France reached this impasse?' said Roger Trinquier. 'The rest of the world backs the FLN. General de Gaulle is caving in.'

'We'll ruin our dinner if we get into that!' exclaimed Leo emphatically.

Eventually, coffee and Armagnac on the table, his friend brought them back to the subject. 'You know, Leo, I'm wondering if the General's going to make it.'

Leo was unsure where the conversation was going. He said nothing, just looked at his friend in surprise.

'The General thinks he's free to give Algeria away. Those million French people over there will want to escape to mainland France.'

'You're right, it'll be bad,' said Leo.

Roger Trinquier was getting up steam. 'They're desperate to stop the President. First choice will be to get the army to take control of Algeria, and force a change of heart in Paris.'

'And the second?' asked Leo.

'Bombs and assassination.' He said the words almost as a matter of fact.

'Have you heard something?'

The other avoided the question, saying, 'There are rough guys around who loathe General de Gaulle and would do it without another thought. Even do it on principle rather than for the money.'

'I suppose so. Although, you'd need an organisation behind you to succeed. I've not heard of any.'

'That's true. In the meantime, option one seems a real possibility, the Generals taking control. I'm no part of that, but it could happen soon. Algeria is behind me and I'm thinking of retiring,' he said. 'I've had approaches from other countries wanting advice on counterinsurgency.'

Leo was surprised. 'I'd be sorry to see you go, Roger. A big loss to the army.' He paused for a moment. 'Getting back to a take-over in Algeria, who's going to lead such a plot?'

'Raoul Salan has retired. I think he's in Madrid right now. He'd step up when the moment was right.'

'It'll have to be soon,' said Leo. 'The President's going to agree peace and independence with the FLN within months. I hope I'm here at SHAPE when that happens. I don't fancy being charged with treason after my efforts to become a Frenchman.' He hesitated, thinking. 'You know, Roger, it would only work if the army here in France *métropole* supported a coup in Algiers. In my view, that wouldn't happen.'

'Why wouldn't it?'

'The army's changing, none too soon. The younger officers look more towards military integration with other countries in Europe.'

'You may be right. But I do think there'll be a final big effort to persuade the President otherwise. 'If the Generals in Algiers can't persuade him, others will try.

'Who are you suggesting?' asked Leo.

'You know Henri Dufour and Hélie de Saint Marc. There are younger officers with them like Pierre Sergent and Roger Degueldre. All from 1st Legion Paras, your regiment. They're totally committed to *Algérie française*. If they have to, they'll take the law into their hands.'

Leo nodded.

'Are you still in touch with your old schoolfriend, Henri de Rochefort?'

Leo wondered why he was asking. 'Not regularly, now that I'm at SHAPE.'

The two were now watching one another closely.

'Leo, someone was speaking to me about Henri the other day. He said he was very uptight over what is going to happen to his *harkis*, the Muslim auxiliaries he's been training. General de Gaulle couldn't care less about them. Once an armistice is signed and the FLN takes over, the *harkis* will be first in for the chop.'

Leo looked at his friend and mentor carefully. 'Are you implying that Henri de Rochefort might join these Generals in grabbing control in Algiers? I just can't see it,' he said, shaking his head.

'Well, if Major de Saint Marc joins them, why not Henri?'

'I'm not convinced Hélie de Saint Marc would take such a drastic step.'

'Nor am I, Leo, but from what I've been told they might be on the point of doing so.'

They were about to call it a day, when Roger Trinquier said, 'That train crash you were in, Leo, I heard a muttering.'

'What do you mean by that?'

'The suggestion is that it might be the first statement in mainland France by the OAS.'

'The *Organisation armée secrète*? I don't know anything about the OAS,' said Leo.

'I'm told there was a warning telephone call to the station manager at Vitry-le-François a couple of days before the crash, saying the line was going to be mined.'

'That's a drastic way to make a statement, Roger.'

'They're wild people, but deadly serious.'

12

Paris, Hôtel Matignon

I bet they're surprised to see a woman in a small private meeting at the Prime Minister's residence, Justine was thinking as Michel Debré strode into the magnificent salon. He beckoned to her to sit next to him at the large highly polished oval table, a vase of spring flowers in the centre. He welcomed everyone, and turned towards Justine.

'Today's special session of the security committee will focus on Paris. I have asked deputy Justine Müller to join us. Mademoiselle Müller will be helping the government win support from the trade unions when the President presents the final terms of an agreement on Algeria. In the meantime, she'll be observing and advising on demonstrations in Paris linked to the Algerian emergency.' There were some nods towards her and a few smiles.

'Now to the subject matter of today's session.' There was a moment's pause as the Prime Minister shuffled his papers. Justine was conscious of Maurice Papon's stare in her direction. Could he be aware of what she knew about his past? How did he get where he was now, Préfet of Police in Paris, head of the *Sûreté*?

'Recently I was visited by a Colonel Argoud who spoke of the army marching on Paris if the President didn't change his policy on Algeria,' said Michel Debré. 'The intention is probably to coordinate a military takeover in Algiers with a move on Paris. It would likely take place in the coming month of April when talks with the FLN are due to start.' He paused to let the threat sink in.

'Arrangements need to be in place to protect key locations, in particular the Palais Bourbon, in the event the National Assembly is threatened. Army units loyal to the Republic and the government would operate in tandem with the police,' he said, looking towards Papon. The room was silent, each person gripped by the gravity of his words.

'Provided we lead from the front, the popular mood in France should remain with us and behind the President. Time would be on our side. If an effective blockade on the Algerian ports can be sustained, the plotters and their forces would run short of essential supplies within three weeks. The navy is expected to side with us, both here and at Mers-el-Kébir. Provided the air force do the same, transport aircraft would be moved back to the *métropole* to eliminate the risk of an attack by airborne forces.'

Pierre Messmer, Armed Forces Minister, raised an arm, apologising for the interruption. 'Please recognise, everyone, that an airborne attack on Paris could be disastrous. By its nature, it would be rapid, and key locations would be taken in no time. We don't have army units close to Paris that we can rely on. We could count on an uprising of a few thousand citizens in our support, but they would not be armed, and have no effect against highly trained close combat troops. That could be the signal for the army here to switch allegiance to those in control in Algiers.'

Silence reigned.

'Thank you, Minister,' said Michel Debré. To everyone, he added, 'I'm open to questions, and let's speak freely about what we think.'

The discussion focused mainly on how to prepare and respond to a putsch. Justine watched each person closely. Several emphasised that General de Gaulle's reaction would be crucial, his handling of the threat would have the greatest influence on the outcome. He must address the people of mainland France to urge them to block any military interference in Paris and the other large cities.

The Prime Minister continued.

'Should an insurrection in Algiers mean that the leaders take control of the whole territory, that would include the Sahara.' He paused. 'So far there were two nuclear tests near the Reggane oasis. There are materials there that must be protected from falling into other hands. We're sending out today a small team with instructions to dispose of surplus materials. A minor nuclear explosion may be necessary.'

All Justine could hear in the room was the tick from the fine Boulle clock on the pedestal behind her.

Pierre Messmer interjected. 'Is the so-called *Organisation armée secrète* likely to be a factor in terms of moving public opinion?'

'Perhaps I could give my views on the OAS,' said Jacques Foccart, the only person present whom Justine didn't recognise. She was immediately conscious of the man's confidence and charisma, in spite of his modest stature and lack of hair.

'You may be aware of the Service d'Action Civique. The SAC will be standing by to monitor OAS commandos, should they present a serious threat in the *métropole* as well as in Algeria. It makes sense to employ the SAC since, to be honest with you all, the secret service and Deuxième Bureau have on their staff a fair number who would support a military take-over.'

Not a sound from anyone.

Justine waited for the right opportunity to say her piece. It came when the Prime Minister said, 'When the next referendum arrives, probably after terms for the armistice are agreed, we need a solid vote from all sections of society to back the President's negotiated solution.'

She picked it up there, everyone switching their attention to her. 'The electorate, whatever their political colour, will back the President and the government when they become frightened. That's the moment when organised labour and the armed forces can swing the balance of popular support. The worse the threat to the stability of their lives and families, the more they will look to the President.'

There were some nods of approval from around the table.

Justine continued. 'I believe we can persuade the unions to back the President's position. They know that peace in Algeria should be a springboard for strong economic growth and investment. That will create jobs and the infrastructure to go with them.'

'What about the Communists, the CGT union is affiliated to them?' It was Maurice Papon, the one whom Justine felt on edge with. The public didn't know of his wartime crimes against humanity in German-occupied Bordeaux.

'That's the tough question,' she responded, allowing him the satisfaction of scoring a point. 'It's hard to see the Communist Party outwardly supporting the President and a Gaullist government. Yet the Russians are longing for a liberated Algeria, another step to increase their influence in Africa and voting power in the United Nations. I'm hopeful the Communists and CGT will at least take a neutral stance.'

No one took issue with that, and she went on. 'We have to look to the point where the OAS might extend their terrorism to the mainland. In particular, if an insurrection in Algiers fails, we can expect a backlash here. Monsieur Foccart's comments are reassuring. As long as the government are seen to be maintaining order, the unions and Communist Party will keep out of it. Should the OAS, however, be seen to assassinate and bomb at will, the people of Paris won't stand for it. That's a real risk for the government and the President, in my view.'

'Absolutely right,' said Michel Debré and several others nodded in agreement.

Justine breathed more easily. Nothing like a common enemy to bring us all together, she thought.

The Prime Minister asked everyone to phone in at the start of each week and give their itineraries and contact telephone numbers to the Chef de Cabinet. The call to attend would take priority over all else.

The tension in the room was tangible. Little was said as people rose to leave. The realisation that France was facing events that could decide its future weighed down heavily on everyone. Justine sensed the challenge before her, how to protect the interests of the ordinary people.

13

Durban, South Africa

Bill Lomberg watched the airfield teleprinter clattering away. Yesterday's cable from his old school pal Henri de Rochefort intrigued him. All it said was to expect a teleprinter message at 11am Paris time the following day. As the machine went silent, he tore off the paper, and read:

The last message from you six months ago spoke confidently about your airfreight business. Well done. I have a special request on behalf of French Air Force Command, Algiers. Requirement is for three, repeat three, C47 Dakota aircraft fitted out as troop transports. To be contracted under wet charter. Area of operation: Algeria and mainland France. We require you personally and two of your staff pilots to accompany these aircraft. Payment to be made value the date of delivery Algiers. Currency of payment: US dollars. Term of charter: 30 days. Please submit your proposed terms within 24 hours.

That was surprising, to say the least. Bill re-read the message. Sure, the French moved forces around in large numbers, most recently the drop on Port Said. But to charter in additional capacity from commercial sources was unusual. The request came from Henri de Rochefort, Major, French Foreign

Legion. That was reassuring. They'd worked together often enough, since school together in the west of England.

Taking three Dakotas out of his fleet meant almost all the available aircraft in his freight airline. The fourth was in major overhaul. He'd have to find sub-contractors to handle his regular business. Henri's deal would have to be highly lucrative to make it worth taking the risk. The logistics were challenging. Flying three Dakotas from Durban to Algiers meant refuelling stops, probably Nairobi and Cairo. No, not Cairo, he suddenly realised. President Nasser of Egypt was said to be supplying arms to the FLN in Algeria. If he discovered Bill and his pilots were helping out the French, it would be curtains. Khartoum should be possible.

He would reply the next day. There was a lot of work to do between now and then. He'd start by sounding out two of his best pilots. Then fitting out the aircraft for troop use, and route and logistics planning. It was obvious something highly unusual was about to break. General de Gaulle seemed to have set his mind on an independent Algeria, he'd noticed that much from local newspapers and those which arrived several days old from London. Over a million French citizens were about to be uprooted, some said. Three Dakotas were not going to make much difference. Henri must need me for back-up to something much bigger, was Bill's best guess.

14

Some around the room looked enthusiastic, others appre-hensive. The military hierarchy were ready for anything, the key government officials more cautious. To Henri, looking around the room, they all shared a common resolve.

Retired army chief of staff, General Zeller, was leading the meeting. All were pledged to secrecy, Henri hoped.

'Here's what we should agree upon.' André Zeller passed an agenda round the table and remained standing as he presented the plan for what everyone knew was the take-over of Algiers.

'General Salan is ready to fly in from Madrid. General Challe is giving his full support and will lead the putsch, along with Air Force General Jouhaud and myself.

'Tomorrow, April 21, the army commanders of Oran and Constantine will be asked to lend their support. As will be the naval commander at Mers-el-Kébir.'

General Zeller looked around the room. There were a few nods, and he continued.

'Saturday, April 22. Shortly after midnight, 1st Legion Para Regiment, Major de Saint Marc in command and backed by Major Robin's parachute commandos, will move into the city and take over the key locations shown in the annexe to the agenda. Major, please explain,' he said looking towards Hélie de Saint Marc.

The parachute commander stood up. 'The main objectives in the early hours of Saturday, are the army headquarters at Caserne Pélissier, Government Building, and Ouled Fayet radio station. Resistance should be minimal since the city is essentially free of FLN, and the European citizens should be one hundred per cent with us. The Muslim population won't react as long as we maintain a show of force.'

Around the room, there was a palpable fall in tension at this show of confidence by such a well-known and respected officer.

General Zeller took over again. 'Also Saturday morning, Radio Algiers will announce that army units have taken over the city and that Algeria and the Sahara will remain part of France.

'Sunday, April 23. 2nd Legion Para Regiment will truck in from Philippeville, and take control of Maison Blanche airport.

'Colonel Argoud in Paris will coordinate army units willing to support us in the *métropole*. He'll communicate with General Challe here on whether we proceed with para drops on key locations in mainland France.'

The magnitude of this last step struck home among everyone. Not a word was said, as General Zeller paused before continuing.

'Our undercover network in Paris will mobilise on-the-ground support, standing by at an assembly point in Fontainebleau forest.

'Transport and logistics. Troop-carrying aircraft to be on stand-by at Blida, as well as Maison Blanche.

'Immediate assessment to be made of fuel and supplies.' This was to be Henri's responsibility. He would have Bill Lomberg and his aircraft as back-up to air force transports.

Sitting down, General Zeller said, 'Now, let's take each item in turn. Your comments, please.'

Henri knew he was entering something he didn't feel entirely committed to. His decision to join in the putsch was emotionally driven. His personal judgement told him there would be little support in the National Assembly. It would need broad support from mainland French people. These voters already backed General de Gaulle in the recent referendum. Why would they change their mind? Would fear of an insurrection, maybe of civil war, sway them?

If the putsch failed, it would be disastrous for him. He'd probably be dismissed from the army. General de Gaulle wouldn't take prisoners, the French courts would do the dirty work for him.

He couldn't turn back at the eleventh hour. Hélie de Saint Marc only just made up his mind to lead the army into the city. There was no-one Henri respected more. No way he could withdraw his support. The dice were thrown.

15

It started like the perfect war game. At midnight, 1st Legion Para Regiment climbed into their trucks to make the short distance from the Legion para barracks at Zéralda to the city, paying no regard to police roadblocks. The first company of paras to arrive was led by Captain Pierre Sergent, his initial objective being the army barracks at Caserne Pélissier. A brief conversation between Captain Sergent and the officer of the guard, and in they went, capturing the general commanding Algiers.

Then on to Ouled Fayet radio station which was taken after a fire fight with the one French NCO who rose to its defence, followed by the police academy.

The headquarters of the French government in Algiers, the remaining critical location together with two generals, was soon in the hands of the paras. At 3.30am, Hélie de Saint Marc informed General Challe that all strategic points were in their hands.

So far, so good. Henri knew the next twenty-four hours would be crucial. They must win the support of the commanders of Constantine and Oran, not to mention the rest of the Legion in Algeria.

Sleep could wait. He stood by, using the time to review supplies and their protection. Suddenly, the phone rang. It was Noelle, from her apartment. She sounded breathless, anxious. 'Chéri, I just heard on the radio that the army has taken control of Algiers.'

Henri couldn't bring himself to answer clearly, given they were on an open line. Finally he said, 'Okay, thanks. I'll call you later.' He could already hear the first car horns strumming out *Al-gé-rie fran-çaise*. Turning on his wireless, he heard General Challe speaking from the captured radio station.

'I am in Algiers with Generals Zeller and Jouhaud, in contact with General Salan, to keep our oath. The oath of the Army to guard Algeria because our fallen soldiers are not to be victims for nothing.'

At the Villa Poirson where they gathered after breakfast, General Challe looked pensive. 'General Gouraud in Constantine seems to be turning against us,' he said, 'And General de Pouilly in Oran is only lukewarm,' he added. 'They're not coming out in open support of us. They're sympathetic, but that's not enough.' He paused. 'In Mers-el-Kébir, the navy don't want to know.'

'I may have to go and try to convince Gouraud and de Pouilly,' said André Zeller.

'Good, it looks like face to face is the only way,' said General Challe. 'At least, the two Parachute Chasseurs regiments are streaming into Algiers to join us, and 2nd Legion Paras are on the way from Philippeville to Maison Blanche airport.'

Major de Saint Marc spoke up. 'I've spoken to Colonel Brothier.'

There was an expectant silence. All knew that Albert Brothier was key to swinging other Legion units their way.

'I bet you didn't get a straight answer,' said André Zeller. They knew what he meant. Brothier commanded the French Foreign Legion's home base at Sidi Bel Abbès. His position was crucial in that Legion units throughout Algeria looked to him as their guiding hand. So far, he appeared openly supportive of the take-over. Underneath he was suspected of doing things supportive of General de Gaulle's position.

'He sounds okay,' said de Saint Marc. 'We have to see. The next twenty-four hours will tell. Any news from Paris?'

It was General Challe who replied, 'I was just in touch with Antoine Argoud. The President has already called a state of emergency. He's bound to talk to the nation, probably a television broadcast.'

At that moment, Pierre Sergent entered the room. Everyone fixed their gaze on him. A junior officer wouldn't normally enter a conference of his seniors without being called for, but his Company just headed the successful takeover of Algiers. 'There's a teletype just in from Paris,' he said. 'Tanks on transporters are arriving at the National Assembly. It seems someone tipped off Prime Minister Debré that we were about to fly in paras.'

Suddenly, tension filled the room.

'Damn it,' shouted General Zeller. 'It probably got out via the Deuxième, army intelligence is looking both ways on Algeria. Some of their people here are on our side, some are not. We must move quickly. Algiers is ours. You only have to hear the *pieds noirs* out on the streets.'

Maurice Challe looked tense. 'We need to know from General Zeller the latest from Constantine and Oran. Let's meet back here at five this evening.'

Henri and Hélie went out together. 'I don't have a good feeling,' said de Saint Marc.

'I might try and reach Pierre Messmer, to get a feel for the thinking inside government,' said Henri. Both of them knew the armed forces minister, a wartime Legion officer, now in Michel Debré's Cabinet.

⟶⟨●⟩ ⟨●⟩⟵

Henri was unsure how to approach Pierre Messmer. He would remember when both were with the British 8th Army in the Western Desert. At Bir Hakeim, Pierre was a company commander out on the northern perimeter when they were confronted by the Afrika Korps. It was to him that General Rommel's ultimatum to surrender was handed. On the other hand, how could Henri now disclose to a senior minister close to the President, that he was on the side of the rebel generals?

Maybe he should have someone do it for him. That would avoid Henri being asked directly which side he was on. What about his sister, Françoise? She or one of her close colleagues at the *piscine* ought to be able to sound out the Armed Forces Minister on whether General de Gaulle was feeling the pressure. Would the Generals taking over Algeria and the threat of civil war in France, make him re-think his plan for independence?

He gave the operator Françoise de Rochefort's home telephone number in Paris, and sat back and waited. It would be an open line, but there was nothing he could do about that.

The connection came through rapidly, his sister's voice was cracked by the static.

'Henri, so good to hear you, how are things? I heard the news this morning.'

'Françoise, I'm doing fine, thanks. Sorry to pressure you but there's something I need help on.' Henri explained a little more about what was going on than she would have heard on RTF. Crucially, was there a way she could find out the attitude of the President to what was happening? Whether there was any indication he would change his mind.

'Henri, you're not in with these Generals, are you?'

Henri avoided the question. 'There's enormous pressure here for the President to re-think his policy.'

'That may be. But the referendum asked the people to back General de Gaulle on Algeria and that's what they did.'

There was a pause before he said, 'If General de Gaulle changed his mind, most people would surely follow him, wouldn't they?'

'That's a hypothetical question,' said Françoise. 'Personally, I can't see him changing course. It's not in his nature.'

Henri ignored his sister's remark. 'Is there a way we could sound out someone close to him, Pierre Messmer for example?'

Silence, presumably while his sister thought through the possibilities. 'Well, there's Justine Müller. We're lunching together today. Although she's on the left, Michel Debré has brought her in to help him get closer to the unions. If she was willing to help, she could have a word with Pierre Messmer. I agree, he's closest to the President.'

'Interesting,' said Henri. He remembered Justine. She was bold enough to have a try.

Françoise added, 'That way, the name de Rochefort wouldn't come into it. You wouldn't want to risk being contaminated, nor would I, whatever it is you're up to.'

'Okay, thanks. Please try Justine right away. Needless to say, it's urgent. I'll give you a private teleprinter line you can use to get back to me, as soon as possible.'

Henri was back that evening with General Challe, Major de Saint Marc and others. He must give them some bad news. Not from France, but right from where they were.

'General Salan arrives from Madrid this evening,' said Maurice Challe. 'He may bring some of his OAS pals with him. We need him, but as far as I'm concerned we should keep the OAS out of it. I can see us fighting them as well as the FLN in due course.'

Everyone seemed to agree.

André Zeller interjected. 'I've made some calls. General Gouraud in Constantine is taking a lot of persuading, but I think he's with us. As for Oran, de Pouilly is threatening civil war if our troops turn up there. Not good.'

Hélie de Saint Marc reported next. '2nd Legion Paras have taken Maison Blanche airfield. It was messy.' Attention was all on him. 'It was guarded by marines, mainly conscripts. They resisted, and the paras pushed their way through, clubbing the marines and beating them up. And that's not the end of it.' He looked across at Henri.

This was it. He must give it to them straight, they would blame him anyway. 'When 2nd Legion Paras arrived,' said Henri, 'the Noratlas transport planes were no longer there. The air force high command in Paris must have made a fast decision to withdraw our airlift capability. The potential for dropping paratroopers is now limited to the three Dakotas I brought in from South Africa.'

Silence. Henri braced himself. No one cursed him. They realised that the implied threat to drop paras at key locations on the mainland was lost.

16

Justine was finishing her lunch with Françoise at the Café Flore, having heard the news on RTF that morning. Coffee was just being placed on the table when there was a sudden commotion outside. The first copies of *France-Soir* just hit the pavement, with the headline *COUP DE FORCE MILITAIRE À ALGER*.

'So, what next?' said Justine as she brought in a copy.

'What you told me about the government bringing army units into Paris is about to happen, I guess.'

'They're probably on the way.'

Françoise realised this was the moment. 'Justine, I have a favour to ask you.'

'Oh, and what's that?'

'My brother, Henri, called last night from Algiers. He wants to know whether the President will now be open to re-considering his policy for Algerian independence. Henri served with Pierre Messmer in Libya in '42, and we wondered whether you could sound him out.'

Justine was silent for a moment, thinking it through. 'Well, I suppose I could.'

'I don't know what side Henri's on but, if I had to guess, I'd put him in with the plotters,' said Françoise. 'He's passionate about the way the FLN would go after his Muslim auxiliaries after the armistice. General de Gaulle has implied they'll be left to fend for themselves.'

'Okay, I'll see what I can find out. I suppose Henri wants to know right away.'

'That's right,' said Françoise. 'You're a friend for ever, Justine.'

I've heard that before, thought Justine. But she was right.

Algiers

The teletype from Françoise came through late in the day. She was disguising the content in a way that her brother should be able to decipher.

> *J has approached M. His view is the action is against the law. He'll have no part in it. The feeling here is that it's an aberration, reflected in the press across the country, and that the boss is unlikely to change.*

Not good at all. Henri felt uneasy, to say the least. Even Maurice Challe was showing signs of doubt.

General de Gaulle's address to the nation was about to start that Sunday evening. How many would see it in Algiers? Certainly, throughout mainland France many would. It felt like the defining moment. Noelle was beside him, in the lounge area of the Saint-Georges.

There, suddenly on the TV screen, was the familiar profile, this time in uniform.

'That's the brigadier's uniform he wore when he arrived in London twenty years ago,' said the manager of the UPI office, standing behind Noelle's chair.

*'Françaises, Français, aidez-moi. In the name of France,
I am ordering you by all means possible to block every
route to these men. I forbid every Frenchman, and in
particular, every soldier, to obey any of their orders.'*

'The French on the mainland are going to back him,
surely,' said Noelle quietly as she pressed her hand into his
after the speech ended.

'I know,' said Henri, in just a whisper. The full impact of
what was happening caught up with him. There were already
indications that the national service conscripts in the army
in Algeria, let alone in mainland France, were for standing
behind the President and the law. After such a powerful
speech, these young men were all the more likely to refuse
orders from the rebel Generals.

More positive for Henri, Algiers TV confirmed that the
Generals including Raoul Salan would address the public the
next day at the Forum. Massive crowds were expected.

17

Sidi Bel Abbès

Very early the Monday morning, all was quiet on the streets as Henri drove fast out of Algiers, heading west along the main road towards Oran and the Legion's headquarters. It gave him plenty of time to think as he passed mile after mile of richly cultivated farmlands and vineyards, the wealth of the country, indeed of French North Africa.

He wanted to test the temperature, consult with his colleagues and staff following the putsch, particularly since the Legion's commander, Colonel Brothier, was now said to be absent 'on leave'. The success of the putsch was in doubt, and the level of support from other army formations would prove crucial. Aside from the consequences of failure for the European population of Algeria and France's Arab supporters, his own future would be in jeopardy.

Three hours later, just before the great naval base of Mers-el-Kébir, he turned inland and approached the town of Sidi Bel Abbès. Beyond it, the Atlas mountains stretched across the horizon from Morocco in the west towards Tunisia in the east.

Passing through the high gates of the entrance to the Legion's historic depot, and saluting legionnaires, he parked by the Foyer des Légionnaires, and went looking for a late breakfast.

Sipping a second coffee on arrival, he spotted the orderly room sergeant marching towards him.

'Sir, there's been an unusual telephone call from Sétif. She just rang a second time.'

'She? Who is the woman?'

The sergeant was having difficulty explaining himself. 'Sir, it's a girl, sounds very young. She says you know her father, insists on being put through to you.'

Henri was surprised, this was something highly unusual. 'Very good, Sergeant, I'll come and find out what it's about.'

Returning to the office, the sergeant passed Henri the phone.

'Is that Major de Rochefort?' the little voice came through. 'My name is Taouès.'

'Taouès? Taouès who?'

'If I tell you, you must not tell my father.'

Henri almost laughed. Should he continue the call? The girl must have a real problem if she's come through to him, someone so young. 'All right, I won't tell your father.'

There was silence on the line. Then the little voice said, 'My father is Sergeant Titraoui, he used to work for you.'

Henri thought hard. Yes, he remembered Titraoui, a *harki* who was on one of Henri's training courses. A good man, 'I remember your father. Why are you calling me?'

'His unit is now disbanded,' said the young girl. 'My father says we must go to France, but doesn't want to ask for help. I know because Mama tells me everything, now I'm twelve. She says the FLN soldiers coming here from the frontiers will kill us.'

'Why does she think they want to kill you?' Henri asked, although he knew the answer.

'Because my father was in the French army.' Silence for a moment, before she continued. 'One of my father's friends, another sergeant, was killed and his body was cut up and put on show in the market.'

Henri took a large breath, disgust and shame sweeping through him. How could a child be exposed to these atrocities? He'd heard about a *harki* sergeant being castrated and cut up alive. The regular army was under orders from Paris to do nothing pending the start of the peace talks at Évian.

He heard himself saying down the phone, 'I'm going to try to help you, Taouès. You must tell your mother that I will send instructions to your family. Tell her and your father that they must collect the names of other families who want to escape to France.'

The voice at the other end was solemn. 'Thank you, sir.'

'Now, listen carefully, Taouès. I want your father to telephone me tomorrow, in the morning.'

The line went dead. Henri dialled the Blida airfield number and asked for Bill Lomberg.

Back in Algiers late that evening, Henri could see Hélie de Saint Marc was worried. As commanding officer of the regiment which led the seizure of the city, the hour of reckoning was fast approaching. He was a wonderful man and friend. How could he be in this predicament after what he'd suffered for is country? Worked almost to death by the SS as punishment for his work in the Resistance, followed by years of service as a fine Legion officer in Indochina and Algeria, he now faced public disgrace for following his conscience in the Generals' putsch.

'I've decided to give myself up,' he said.

'What?' exclaimed Henri.

'I realise now there's no hope of carrying the whole of French Algeria behind what we set out to do. Not only that. It's clear from the President's speech and from the response of the press in France, that what they are calling the Generals' putsch has failed to win meaningful support in mainland France.'

Henri was shocked, if not surprised. A much better Catholic than he was, Hélie never wavered from his strict moral principles. A perfect example of what the Jesuits set out to make of a boy they launched into manhood.

Hélie de Saint Marc continued. 'My immediate priority is to take responsibility for what has come to pass. I must distance the 1st Legion Paras from the consequences, convince the court martial which will follow that my men, trained as they are in the absolute duty to obey, followed my orders and played no part in planning what happened.'

'You were one of several,' said Henri.

'Some may take the same course as me, others will disappear, go underground. Probably they'll fight on with the OAS. I cannot countenance that. Our mission was to make a military statement in the hope the politicians would re-think their strategy. That hasn't happened.'

'I agree with you on that.'

'Henri, it's essential that your involvement in the putsch be minimised. You can save your army career if you can be regarded as drafted in by me simply to assist with the logistics.'

'I appreciate your concern for me, Hélie, but that means you'll be taking responsibility for what I determined for myself.'

'You were driven to join in at the last moment by the same concern for the *harkis* that I have.'

'Yes, but I'm not giving up on doing something for them.'

Hélie de Saint Marc looked surprised. 'Such as?'

Henri reminded him that his friend Bill Lomberg flew three Dakotas in last week, as back-up for any para drops on the mainland. Two had flown back to Durban but he'd kept Bill at Blida with the remaining aircraft. He believed that he and Bill could bring in several plane loads of *harki* families before the FLN descended on them.

'That sounds daring enough, but Paris may take a dim view of what you're doing if they find out. The President's made it clear, he's not interested in helping them.'

'There's no time to lose,' said Henri. 'If General de Gaulle signs an armistice rapidly, the army will have to stand back and the FLN will start butchering the *harkis*. I just had a call from one family in Sétif. The father is an auxiliary I trained here a couple of years ago.' Henri recounted the drama of the daughter's telephone call.

18

Algiers

Henri had to see Noelle that evening. She had to be in the picture, what he was intending to do to rescue his *harki* auxiliaries. He would explain that other fellow officers felt the same. There was little time, he would need aircraft to bring them in from outlying towns and outposts, and Bill presented that opportunity. From Algiers, they would have to be evacuated to France. Otherwise, torture and death awaited them.

Noelle wouldn't be surprised. She must have sensed that he was preoccupied with something. After the failure of the Generals' putsch, both knew the game was up for him, and his military career threatened. She appeared relieved when he came out with it, and said to him, 'Where does that leave you with General de Gaulle and his crowd, my darling, if they find out you have helped the *harkis* escape to France, against orders?'

Henri tried to sound positive. 'I have friends. Pierre Messmer made it clear he regarded the putsch as illegal and out of order. But I know he worries the same as I do for the safety of the *harkis*. He's Cabinet Minister for the armed forces and has been trying to convince the President something has to be done for them. We have the opportunity if we move now.'

At UPI, they say some *harkis* have been finding their own way over to France,' said Noelle. 'Apparently, the International Red Cross is involved.'

'Yes. We think we can find ways to send them over. The problem is to bring them in from Sétif and other outlying points. I'm going to see Bill. He still has a Dakota here at Blida.'

'I hope he can find a way to help them. I'll see what I can do to draw attention to the *harki* situation in the American press. Meantime, watch your back. General de Gaulle is going to be after those Generals, and you're only one step away from them.'

⊷⊷⊶⊶

Bill Lomberg saw Henri parking his jeep outside the crew building at Blida military airfield, and was waiting for him at the entrance.

Henri explained what he and some other officers were planning. That a transport plane was needed for unofficial flights along the north coast, to bring in *harki* families. Could Bill help?

'What's security like in these places?' asked Bill. 'Is it high risk, landing and taking off with trigger-happy FLN breathing over us?'

Henri explained the procedure, the plan for an armed escort to pick up the families and transfer them to the landing ground. He or another Legion officer would accompany Bill on each flight. The aim was to bring in around five hundred *harkis*. There would be other crews doing the same. If trouble was expected, Henri's people on the ground would provide armoured vehicle support at the landing ground.

'Sounds hairy,' said Bill, grinning at his old friend. 'Let's give it a go.'

'I'll come with you on the first evacuation. It'll be at Sétif, about three hundred kilometres east of Algiers. If you could handle the route mapping, I'm obtaining a list of the families to be flown out. I guess you could cram in forty including small children?'

'Won't be the first time,' said the South African, with a broad smile.

⟶⟫⊙⟪⟵

'I'm flying to Sétif tomorrow with Bill.'

Noelle was lying close beside him. He felt her body tense.

'We're going to bring in a plane-load of *harki* families. It should be straightforward, or at least as straightforward as any plan can be in Algeria right now.'

'Oh, that's rather sudden. Does it have to be you, and what then?' Noelle sounded nervous.

'I have to accompany Bill on the first evacuation. He'll continue flying them in from other pick-up points, with one of my men.'

'What happens to the *harkis* when they arrive here?'

'We're in touch with the International Red Cross. They've agreed in principle to take custody of them and help to ship them to mainland France.'

'This will make a great story!' Noelle exclaimed.

'That would be tricky for me, darling. It runs contrary to General de Gaulle's decision not to "repatriate" Muslims to France, even those with French identity cards. Can you wait until the operation is completed, a week if all goes well?'

Noelle was silent for a moment. 'Of course, mon chéri, one week it is.' With that she pulled his head down to hers and kissed him.

19

Algiers and Zéralda

Noelle was at the UPI office first thing on the Wednesday morning, thinking of Henri and his flight with Bill Lomberg, when suddenly the phone rang. The voice said, 'If you want a good story, go to Zéralda right away. There's going to be trouble.' The line went dead.

She already knew of Zéralda, a few kilometres west of Algiers, where the Legion paras had their barracks. Noelle and her colleagues were aware the putsch was failing. There was a rumour that General Challe was giving himself up, that he'd spent the night with the Legion at Zéralda. She grabbed a photographer and they dashed out and jumped into a taxi.

Competing with the other rush hour drivers in exchanging curses, their driver swept past the magnificent edifice of the Grande Poste with its three great arches like a palace in *A Thousand and One Nights*. On arrival, the police and army were surrounding the barracks complex. This was no ordinary army base. She could still admire the structures and layout in spite of smoke rising from several of the fine buildings. Something unusual was certainly under way.

A police inspector was standing close to the entrance. Crowds were gathering.

'Inspector, my name is Mercure and I'm from the American press agency, UPI. Please could you explain what is going on?'

'Madame,' said the Inspector, 'you are witnessing history. Armed Forces Minister Messmer has issued orders from Paris to disband the 1st Regiment of the Legion Paratroopers, and to expel them from their barracks.'

'Looks like there's trouble?'

'They're destroying the place, burning records, blowing up ammunition stores. They are not happy, Madame. Soon they will have gone, for ever.'

'I need to go in. I want to speak with the commanding officer, Major de Saint Marc.'

'Impossible, Madame.'

'Why is it impossible?'

'He's not here.'

'Who's in charge then?'

'The Company Commanders, I assume,' said the gendarme.

Noelle thought quickly. Who was it Henri said led the first Company of the Regiment into Algiers on the Saturday morning? The name stuck in her mind, it was Sergent, Pierre Sergent, that was it.

'I need to speak with Captain Sergent immediately. Tell him Noelle Mercure of United Press International is here to speak with him.' She added for good measure, 'Tell him I had an appointment with the commanding officer.'

'Very well, Madame,' and the police inspector disappeared into the magnificent barracks from which the noise of destruction was coming. Five minutes later, Noelle saw a tall Legion officer approaching. He saluted smartly and announced himself as Captain Pierre Sergent, saying he only had a few minutes before his Company was due to drive out.

'I suggest you report to the world,' he said, 'that the 1st Paratroop Regiment of the French Foreign Legion has been dissolved and ordered to leave the famous Zéralda barracks, its home, built by legionnaires eighty years ago with their bare hands. I am sorry, Madame, but I can't say any more.'

With that, he saluted, swivelled in an about turn, and marched back into the closest barrack block.

Noelle scribbled in her notebook and waited, as the morning heat of the desert flooded in around her.

It was the singing she heard first. Somehow stirring, defiant, growing louder over the rumbling of truck engines as the convoy drove out into the streets. A roar from the *pieds noirs* in the crowd, their cheering a mixture of love and despair. Those words, it was Piaf, not what the Legion usually sang during its epic marches. No, this was different. This was Piaf's 'Non, je ne regrette rien', being sung by the paratroopers of 1st Legion Paras, proudest of regiments, expelled from their home and destined for oblivion.

What a story. She and her photographer must meet the late evening deadline. Her UPI report and pictures would be on the wires. The drama of it all flooded through her. She was doing what she loved, exposing to the world the reality of the moment.

⟨⟩

Back at the UPI office, news was just breaking that Hélie de Saint Marc was under arrest. The ultimate punishment of dissolution already inflicted on his regiment, the powers of state were now turning on him. Great for what Noelle was about to file to New York, but what did it mean for Henri?

20

Algiers, Hôtel Suisse

Something else was exercising Noelle's mind. Her report back to the UN's atomic energy agency, on the visit to the Reggane nuclear test site, was generating interest. Her name was beginning to circulate in that tight community that monitored the nuclear arms race.

Was this the reason for a strange telephone call to her office, from a Monsieur Jansson? The man wouldn't disclose the purpose of his inquiry, but said he did work for the United Nations and would Mademoiselle Mercure meet him at the Hôtel Suisse after breakfast in a couple of days' time?

She decided to walk the few blocks from the office to the hotel. The heat of the day was not yet insufferable. It was only when you walked in Algiers that you realised how up one hill and down the other the city was, with staircases of stone steps connecting the different levels. The old buildings with their wrought iron balustrades were a joy, and the buzz of the streets showed off the smells and noises of this remarkable city. The views to the hills above and the bay below were like nothing else she'd seen in her many adventures around the world.

The staff were polite and friendly when she entered the small hotel just off the city centre, taking Noelle over to the salon where Monsieur Jansson waited for her on a comfortable looking sofa. A uniformed butler arrived at the same time and poured them coffee.

'I apologise for taking your time like this, Mademoiselle,' he said as he rose and took her hand.

Noelle looked straight at him, smiled and nodded. He was not bad-looking, lean in stature with blond hair, face and hands showing him to be over fifty. His manner was on the cool side, in keeping with the ice blue eyes.

'You came to my attention via the United Nations.'

'Oh, that's interesting,' she responded.

'I am a geologist, and the UN ask me to do work for them from time to time.'

'I see,' said Noelle, now sensing where the conversation might be leading. The oil industry was in its infancy in the Sahara and was generating considerable international interest. 'How can I help you?'

'I am interested in the resources offered by the Sahara.' Jansson hesitated, pouring her some more coffee. 'With all respect, I was intrigued that someone like you could penetrate the heart of France's nuclear arms research.'

That was surprising. How could he have learned of her trip to Reggane? 'You must know the right people,' she laughed, rather half-heartedly.

'Yes. I have always been interested in nuclear research. Which led me to your family, and the award of Nobel Prizes to your mother and brother.'

'Ah, yes. That's where you came across the name Mercure.'

'Precisely. Your family are heroes to me.'

'They are to me, as well,' said Noelle, still wondering what this was about.

'What I found out is that your family, particularly those doing research into the atom, were Communists.'

So that's it. This Mr Jansson is questioning my motives.

'I guess it was the *Zeitgeist* of the twenties and thirties, the intelligentsia were sympathetic to the ideals of the Bolsheviks.' She paused, adding, 'Particularly when the alternative was the fascists.'

'Your brother was a Communist also.'

'True.'

'Did that have something to do with his dismissal from the French Commissariat of Atomic Energy?

'I think it did.' She paused, adding, 'He was also adamant that atomic energy should be used only for peaceful purposes.'

'I can see that was incompatible with the French government's aim that France should join the nuclear weapons club.'

'You are right, Monsieur Jansson.'

'Could I ask what your politics are, Mademoiselle?'

She thought of saying, mind your own business. 'Monsieur Jansson, I have worked for UPI on and off for twenty years. I'm almost an American. My life is driven by the capitalist ideals of our clients. If I'd been a Communist, Senator McCarthy would have had my guts for garters ages ago.'

He smiled at her for the first time. 'I like your style, Mademoiselle Mercure.' He waited for a moment. 'What about your views on the use of atomic energy?'

'I also believe passionately it should only be used for the good of man.'

'Well, that couldn't be more clear. I admire your ideals, Mademoiselle.' He smiled. 'You know, we should meet again when I have one of the intelligentsia with me,' he said jokingly.

That smile again, as she rose to go. Was it a smile, or was it verging on a sneer?

Noelle was pleased to be out of the place, the Swiss flag over the hotel entrance swinging limply behind her as she walked out into the searing heat of the street and called a cab. Who was this man, what was he really doing in Algiers? What did he want from me?

21

The two Pratt & Whitneys burst into life as Bill completed his pre-flight checks. Henri couldn't help wondering where this aircraft had been in its lifetime, dropping paratroopers over Arnhem, gun running in the Middle East, transporting avocados in South Africa. The 'Lomberg Air Transport' markings on the fuselage were painted over.

Would there be trouble at the other end? He'd been blasé in his response to Noelle's anxious questioning. It wasn't just FLN opposition, still active outside Algiers. The Organisation armée secrète or OAS was growing all the time. The organisers were said to be recruiting thugs off the street. Provided with weapons, they were shooting down anyone they took a disliking to.

At cruising altitude, Bill throttled back and it was possible to talk. Henri pointed out landmarks along the coastline as they headed east. He explained that Sétif lay at the heart of the area of massacres a few years before, when the authorities took vengeance on the Muslim population.

'Glad we'll have protection on landing,' grunted Bill.

Passing back a flask of coffee, he shouted back over his shoulder, 'Seatbelts on everybody, landing in ten minutes.' Banking to starboard and losing height, they flew inland. Fertile countryside and rolling hills spread out below, until the town and its airstrip approached from the distance. On board were two armed legionnaires and two nurses.

Henri looked across the airfield as they came down to land. Close by the simple terminal building was a Panhard AML armoured car together with several trucks and jeeps. All seemed quiet. Bill taxied the Dakota towards them, one of the legionnaires throwing open the door in the rear of the fuselage. A jeep moved forward, parking alongside as Henri climbed down the short steps to the ground. A young officer and much older NCO jumped out, saluting Henri and shaking hands.

'Any trouble expected?' asked Henri.

'We don't think so, sir,' said the officer, 'but we're taking no chances.'

'Good. Where's the cargo? Let's load up right away.'

The officer pointed over to two of the trucks, parked in the background, as the NCO signalled them to come forward.

Henri spotted the girl as soon as the *harkis* started to climb out of the trucks. That must be Taouès, looking serious and determined in spite of her twelve years, black hair everywhere in the wind. Her parents either side of her, the father coming forward with a military bearing although not in uniform. Yes, that was Sergeant Titraoui who attended the training course for army auxiliaries.

'Sergeant, I'm pleased to see you again,' Henri said as Titraoui came to attention and saluted smartly. 'Do you speak for the whole group in these two trucks?'

'Yes, sir. I have a passenger manifest showing names, ages, and provenance. There are thirty-six of us in total including the children.' Titraoui handed Henri some sheets of paper.

'Excellent, Sergeant. On board straight away, there's no time to lose.'

Both trucks emptied, everyone scrambling up the steps and into the aircraft. Suddenly the young girl, helping her father to organise the loading, shrieked out, 'Regarde là-bas' – pointing at figures running beyond the small terminal building. At the same moment a grenade exploded and rifle fire broke out, everyone diving flat on their faces.

Henri's two legionnaires ran behind the trucks and started to return fire as Sergeant Titraoui, hit in the leg, writhed on the ground.

Henri was beside Taouès in a flash, scooping her up and handing her to one of the nurses on the steps into the aircraft. Turning back to the father, he lifted the sergeant's arm up over his shoulder and helped him in the same direction.

Suddenly, a roar from the Pratt & Whitneys, Bill's warning that they must leave.

A wave from the legionnaires, telling Henri they were staying with their mates to fight it out.

Clouds of dust as the Dakota wheeled around and tore out to the end of the strip. Full throttle, and they were heading for take-off as Bill pointed out the armoured car using its heavy machine gun against the insurgents.

'First mission accomplished,' Henri shouted to Bill.

'I need danger money,' Bill snapped back.

⋆⊸⧫⊷⋆

A Red Cross vehicle stood waiting as the aircraft taxied towards the terminal building at Blida. Alongside it was a police car. To Henri, that was not unexpected. On the other hand, why were there three *gendarmes mobiles* standing apart from the group. A sense of unease crept over him.

First down the steps close to the plane's tail, he made towards the Red Cross staff, passenger manifest in his hand. A Gendarmerie captain stepped smartly up to him and saluted.

'Major de Rochefort, sir?'

'Yes, Captain.'

'You are under arrest, sir. Come with us, please.'

Surprise and anger welled up in him. 'I have brought thirty-eight army auxiliaries and their families with me, for transfer to the *métropole*. Their lives are at risk. This is a humanitarian mission.'

'That's not our business today, sir. I have orders to take you to police headquarters to answer questions which could lead to a charge of treason being brought against you.'

The full force of what was happening overcame Henri. Being detained because of his involvement in the Generals' putsch was not unexpected. The realisation that he could be charged with treason shook him rigid.

Bill was approaching from behind his right shoulder. For a wild moment he thought of grabbing his old friend and making a dash to escape in the Dakota. They would never make it. Even in his current state of mind, he could figure out it would be better to cooperate with the law rather than flee from it. Looking at Bill, he said quietly, 'Jump in and fly back to Durban as fast as you can.'

22

They were taking no chances. It was a real cell, bars on the door and one small window up against the ceiling.

Hélie de Saint Marc was in the cell opposite. They exchanged nods as Henri was marched into his. It flashed through his mind, the trick would be to exercise together so they could discuss their predicament. The accommodation was sparse. About three metres square with bed, chair and washbasin. Pyjamas and towel were provided, and he was told to call for the guard when he wanted to be escorted to the latrines.

After coffee and bread rolls the next morning, he was taken upstairs to be greeted by a smartly dressed middle-aged man, probably a civil servant or lawyer. No doubt he'd been flown over from the French mainland to conduct the preliminary interrogations before formal charges were brought. A cigarette was offered and declined.

'Major de Rochefort,' the interrogator commenced, 'my name is Dubois. What I'd like to do this morning is listen to your explanation for becoming involved in the insurrection a week ago. You will have the right to legal representation once we are past this preliminary stage.' He paused. Henri said nothing.

'I understand you were asked to join the Generals plotting to take over, to assist with logistics.'

'Yes, that's correct.'

'What did that involve?'

'Essentially supplies. Supplies already available in Algiers, and the procurement of whatever was in short supply.'

'Did that include transport aircraft?'

'Not directly. The air force remained in control of their troop-carrying transports, mainly the Noratlas.'

'Is it correct that you chartered three C-47 Dakotas and crews from Lomberg Air Transport in Durban, South Africa?'

Clearly Dubois had done his research, and in a very short space of time.

'Yes, that's correct.'

Dubois was silent, waiting for Henri to elaborate.

'I took the decision on my own judgement,' said Henri. 'I felt we should have back-up in case there was a problem.'

'What sort of problem?' asked Dubois.

'We could have been left with no means of air supply if the air force withdrew support and flew their planes out.'

'Which they did.' His tight-lipped mouth broke almost imperceptibly into a smile.

'Yes.'

Dubois paused, giving Henri the feeling a big question was about to be asked.

'Was part of the plan to drop airborne forces at key locations on the mainland?'

In a flash, Henri knew his reply could be used in charges brought against the leaders of the putsch. He must take care, but not suppress the truth. That could rebound on him.

'I once heard reference to a drop of para formations into mainland France, but I don't believe it was regarded as a serious option.'

'And what about Lomberg Air Transport? It is owned by a Squadron Leader Bill Lomberg, ex-RAF. What do you know about him?'

'I was at school with him.'

Not the reply Dubois was expecting. One eyebrow went up briefly. 'At school together. Where was that?''

'St Gregory's, a Benedictine college in the English west country.' Observing the sceptical look Dubois was giving him, Henri added, 'We both had English mothers.'

The interrogator seemed satisfied.

'You were brought here from Blida airfield, having landed in a Lomberg Air Transport Dakota with thirty-eight army auxiliaries and their families. What was that about?'

Henri suddenly realised, here was his motive for supporting the putsch.

'I was bringing them to safety. Following the referendum and the President's decision to negotiate independence with the FLN, my overriding concern has been for the *harkis*. How they will be treated by the new administration in Algeria.'

'Why do you believe they're at risk?'

Henri explained the situation of Sergeant Titraoui and his family and their auxiliary army friends, the saga of the telephoned plea from the daughter and later the call from her father. How he instructed that the group be brought together, and Bill Lomberg agreeing to fly out to Sétif and bring them to safety.

Dubois made no comment, looking at his watch. 'We'll take half an hour's break. You can go out into the exercise yard.'

⇢⊱◉⊰⇠

Hélie de Saint Marc was out there already, still awaiting his interrogation. They were not stopped from walking round the yard side by side, Henri reporting on his session with Dubois. Hélie de Saint Marc urged him to be frank in describing their relationship and decision to join the group of plotters, urging him to use that and their mutual fears for the impact of independence on the *harkis* to justify their involvement in the plot.

Back in the interrogation room, Dubois asked, 'Tell me how you were recruited into the rebel group.'

'I didn't keep secret my views on the likely consequences of a French withdrawal from Algeria. These were known generally, but I didn't attempt to influence others. My colleagues also knew of the problems I had.'

'What do you mean by that, Major?'

Henri wondered how much he should say. Deciding to be as frank as his predicament demanded, he explained to the interrogator his removal from front line command to head up training at Legion HQ. That, he assumed, was a consequence of him speaking his mind about the army's widespread use of torture in Algeria.

'So, you think your position on torture affected your promotion prospects?'

'I graduated from Saint-Cyr as an aspirant in 1939, fought through the war with the Free French forces, and afterwards was posted to Indochina. Then five years here, and I still haven't made Lieutenant Colonel.'

'I see.' Dubois paused, thinking. 'What influence did Major de Saint Marc have on your decision to join the plotters?'

'We think alike as to what will happen here after independence. We've both been heavily involved with the recruitment and training of the large auxiliary army assembled in recent years to support regular army operations. They are mainly Muslims, we know them as *harkis*.'

'Like those you just flew into Blida?'

'Yes. In discussing that subject, Major de Saint Marc asked me whether I would consider joining the group planning to take over military control. The purpose, as he explained it, was to make a military statement, not to interfere in the politics of the Republic. To show General de Gaulle and the rest of France the depth of feeling here.'

'And you say you only joined the group three days before the putsch. What about Major de Saint Marc?"

'I understand he only made up his mind a couple of days before me.'

'So you joined at his invitation?'

Henri knew he wouldn't in normal circumstances answer in the affirmative. Yet, Hélie was adamant he should do so.

'That's correct.' He didn't feel proud in saying that.

'Thank you, Major de Rochefort. That will do for the present.'

'Is there a possibility of me being released on parole until I am needed again, Monsieur Dubois?'

'I'm afraid not. At least two of the leaders of the putsch have already disappeared. We can't take the risk of anyone else going missing. I trust you understand the gravity of this whole matter. The charges will be treason against the Republic. The ultimate penalty for that is death.

A stony silence followed. Dubois then said, 'There's a representative of United Press International asking to see you, a Mademoiselle Mercure.'

'Thank you, I was expecting her to get in touch.'

'The authorities wouldn't normally permit any visitors under present circumstances. In this case, they're prepared to make an exception.'

They don't want to upset the Americans any more than they have already, thought Henri.

'The lady is here in the building,' added Dubois.

That's my Noelle, never miss a good story, happily the story's me this time. Henri nodded. 'If you could provide a room, I'd like to see her now, please.'

No embracing, Henri decided as he was taken to a room on the first floor. Keep it business-like. She would understand.

Their encounter was not emotional. Henri explained his position to Noelle, and how the interrogation went. The likelihood was he would be transferred to a prison somewhere in France, for further questioning. He needed to get a message to his sister in Paris, so that Françoise could find him a lawyer and let their parents in Bordeaux know what was happening.

Noelle handed him some personal things, and a small flask of cognac.

Very quietly, she said, 'My darling, I will stay as close to you as I can. UPI will understand. The *harki* story is a big one and you are part of it. Can't do any harm if your name is seen by the French authorities as a hero in the American press.'

'You're probably right,' he said. 'What news of the *harki* families Bill and I flew into Blida?'

'They should be okay. The Red Cross have them in hand. My contact there thinks they can arrange transportation to France.'

The gendarme came to tell them time was up. They were able to touch each other lightly as he was escorted out.

Henri suddenly felt overcome by her having to leave him, the uncertainty of what was going to happen to him. There couldn't be a future for their relationship if he was to be locked up for years. His life was imploding, and he didn't know how he was going to bear it.

23

UPI's office in Algiers

Noelle knew she would have to move. Henri meant a lot to her. Wherever he went, she wanted to be in striking distance, even though prison in mainland France looked a certainty for him. She was not going to let go. UPI should be understanding. With an important office in Paris, she should be able to relocate there.

She'd heard nothing further from the mysterious Jansson at the Hôtel Suisse. After his reference to her family's Communist leanings, she was wary of what he was up to. She needed help, she might not be able to manage her affairs and help Henri on her own. Certainly she had looked after herself since her brother's death, but things were now different. The feeling of having someone dependent on her was somehow comforting. She didn't want to ignore that. Who could help her?

Was the solution staring her in the face? That sudden call from Jacques Foccart, her bald-headed friend from the trip to Reggane. What did he say he was? He didn't, just claiming to be advising the Prime Minister. He wasn't a fraud, otherwise he wouldn't have been part of that select group admitted to France's atomic testing ground.

He sounded like someone with the right connections, who could get things done. Emotionally, he seemed to like her. There might lie the solution to what she was seeking. She'd watch him over the dinner he was proposing and, if he passed the test, she'd tell him Henri's predicament.

→❧❧←

They met like old friends, survivors of the expedition into deepest Sahara. Noelle congratulated him on his choice of the Auberge du Moulin, noted for its local dishes.

Noelle asked Jacques Foccart what would happen after the failure of the putsch. Adamant about General de Gaulle's intention to grant independence, he warned of serious trouble to come, from the OAS. Not only considerable bloodletting in Algiers, Constantine and Oran, but trouble in Paris. He spoke off the record about his direction of something called the SAC, short for Service d'Action Civique or Civic Action Service. The story was that General de Gaulle distrusted the secret services and set up his own paramilitary group to protect him and do his dirty work. That was to include confronting the OAS. Jacques Foccart was head of the SAC.

As they finished their delicious *méchoui*, Noelle judged the moment was right.

'The best barbecued lamb since I arrived here,' she said with conviction. 'Monsieur, I have something to ask you.'

He just smiled in his friendly way.

'I have a close friend in serious trouble.'

'Oh. How come?'

'He's an army officer with an impeccable record.'

'What's his problem, then?'

'He's implicated in the failed Generals' putsch.'

'Ah. That was a big mistake.'

'He became involved because of the threat to the *harkis*. He trained them as army auxiliaries.'

'And now he realises they'll be persecuted when the FLN takes over?' he said.

'Exactly.' She paused. 'He's locked up at police headquarters.'

'I see. He'll probably be transferred to the mainland to face trial.'

'Forgive me for asking, Monsieur,' said Noelle, 'but I thought you might have some advice on how Major Henri de Rochefort, that's him, could be helped.'

There was a long silence, as the waiter removed their plates and produced the dessert menu.

She knew Jacques Foccart's mind would be working overtime. Here was the arch dealmaker, deciding how to score from the opening she'd given him.

'Forgive me, my dear, but if I was to involve myself in your problem, I think I would ask for something in return.'

There it was. What would he demand in exchange? To go back to his hotel with him? Somehow, she didn't think that was his line of thought.

'I don't want to interfere with the independence of your reporting to the world's press,' he said. 'However, part of my mission is to turn the public against the OAS. Would your journalist's code of behaviour allow me to advise you on how to put that theme across internationally?'

Why not? Noelle wasn't fighting to keep Algeria French. She could handle his demand.

'I don't see why not.'

'Excellent. We're agreed. I'll think about what I can do for Major de Rochefort. Let me have a note of his background. I'll find out where they're sending him, what judicial process faces him.' He paused a moment. 'You said you were thinking of moving to UPI's Paris office. That should make our communication easier.'

After they parted company, Noelle could feel the relief running through her. Here was someone she could work with, someone she could turn to. She wasn't totally alone any more.

24

Kim carried several sheets from the teleprinter with her as she knocked on the glass door and walked into Art Buchwald's office.

'Kim, you've brightened my afternoon,' he said, looking up at her. 'Have a seat, tell me what's happening in this crazy world.' He poured her out a coffee from the glass container on a stand beside his desk.

'Art, this follows the Generals' putsch. It has just come in via UPI,' she said, putting the sheets of paper in front of him. 'It's written by one of their people in Algiers, a Noelle Mercure.'

'About the predicament of the *harkis* after the President has done his stuff, it seems,' he said as he scanned the text.

'Yes, a good story, and personalised. A French Foreign Legion officer taking a Dakota into the *bled* to rescue army auxiliaries, Muslims, and their families before they're slaughtered.'

'I can see that.' Perceptive as ever, he added, 'Do I detect you have some personal angle on this one?'

'Yes. You know I have a friend at the *piscine*. Well, this Legion officer is her brother.'

'Fascinating.' He paused, looking again at the UPI report. 'It says in here that the Gaullists have locked him up. He must have been on the side of the rebels.'

'I think he was. Anyway, I'm going to use it in tomorrow's edition. If he's in trouble with the French, but the American press thinks he's a hero, that could influence favourably the charges the prosecutors bring against him.'

Art Buchwald leant back in his chair. 'I wouldn't count on that. He'll need all the help he can get, they're a heavy-handed lot.' Then he laughed, saying, 'We Americans kill criminals with electricity. The French torture them with electricity, then cut their heads off with a guillotine.'

'Art, stop it. My friend Françoise is going to be in a terrible state. I must phone her this evening.'

⋄

Worried how Françoise would take the news about her brother, Kim dialled her home number that evening and was surprised when Françoise said she was already in the picture. It was the UPI correspondent out there who told her. She apparently knew Henri and visited him at police headquarters as soon as she heard what happened.

'Yes, her name's Noelle Mercure,' said Kim. 'I saw the UPI report she wrote and thought of using it. Apart from being a good story, it occurred to me that some publicity in the New York press might add to your brother's defence, but thought that I should check with you first.'

'Well, you're probably right. Go ahead.' There was a pause before Françoise continued. 'It's awful, Kim, I can understand his concern for his *harkis*, but I wish he'd kept out of helping the plotters.'

'I'll do what I can. I might be able to interest *L'Express* in a feature article on the whole *harki* question. It seems this was the motivation for both Henri and the commander of 1st Legion Paras, Major de Saint Marc.'

25

Theresa went for the phone as it groaned out its deep French ringing tone, exchanging a few words with the caller. Turning to Leo, she said, 'It's for you. Roger Trinquier.'

'More bad news, Leo,' came the voice from the other end.

'Can't be worse than the failure of the putsch,' said Leo.

'The President has given orders for certain units that supported the Generals to be disbanded.'

Immediately, Leo sensed what was coming.

'Your regiment, 1st Legion Paras, is one of them.'

Silence for an awful moment, then Leo said, 'I can't believe it. That's the finest formation in the French army.'

'I agree. The two Chasseur Parachute regiments have been disbanded also.'

'Outrageous.' Leo paused, trying to get a grasp of the consequences. 'I appreciate you letting me know, Roger. I'll have to consider my position.'

'Being at SHAPE, Leo, you've not been part of what just happened.'

'I know, but the Regiment is part of my life. If that's the way General de Gaulle rewards a military formation that has been wiped out twice in Vietnam, and come back to perform brilliantly in Algeria, I don't want to have any part in his army.'

'And another piece of bad news.'

'What's that?'

'Henri de Rochefort has been arrested. It seems that Major de Saint Marc persuaded him to join the plotters as logistics coordinator. Now they're both locked up.'

'Locked up where?'

'In Algiers, but they'll transfer him to a prison in northern France, before a military court hearing.'

'My God, poor Henri.'

'Leo, you'll have to consider what's best for you and Theresa if you're thinking of quitting the army. For me, I'm seriously considering that offer to go to Katanga, to help organise the resistance there. Remember what I said, I'd love to have you with me.'

'I appreciate that, Roger. I'll get back to you,' said Leo, putting the phone down.

Theresa was already there, pulling him to her, having heard enough to understand the impact on him. 'Take a very deep breath, darling. You're not responsible for what the Regiment did in Algiers. It's a political decision to close it down.'

'You're right. That bastard General de Gaulle is emasculating his army. He's going to stand back and let the FLN wade in. It'll be slaughter for those who've supported France and have nowhere to go.' He cursed, 'What a godawful situation.'

26

The invitation arrived out of the blue. For a moment, Leo couldn't place the name of the sender, Lieutenant Colonel Bertrand of Nord Aviation. Then it clicked, the train crash, the other passenger in their compartment.

Colonel Bertrand was coming to SHAPE to speak at a conference on new weaponry. Would Captain Beckendorf like to attend Jean Bertrand's session, and lunch with him afterwards? There was a covering note, reminding Leo of their conversation after the crash.

Leo replied at once, accepting, and saying he would book the restaurant. He checked the agenda in the catalogue of coming events at SHAPE and saw Colonel Bertrand was described as designer of the SS10, the world's first air-launched missile. Suddenly he remembered their conversation on the fateful day of the crash, the other's interest in the Alouette helicopter.

Lunch outside SHAPE would be better, he thought, booking them into a bistro nearby, with Theresa joining them.

Jean Bertrand's presentation the following week enthralled Leo and everyone present. No one doubted the revolution in warfare that launching missiles from aircraft would bring about. This was the man who invented it.

Leo congratulated him on his presentation as they drove the short distance to the restaurant. Theresa was waiting for them, stunning as ever in a smart blue suit, not on shift that day at her hospital.

'No delayed effects from the crash, Monsieur Bertrand?' asked Theresa as they re-introduced themselves.

'None, thank you, Madame. I was lucky, unlike your husband,' Bertrand replied, looking at Leo's arm, still in plaster.

'It could have been a lot worse,' said Leo. 'Just a complication, an infection.'

'They had to re-set it. The plaster will be off by the end of the week,' said Theresa.

Jean Bertrand hesitated, then said, 'Look, both of you, please call me Jean. After all, first names are the norm at SHAPE, aren't they?'

'Thanks, and you do the same,' said Theresa.

'I notice your accents in spite of the near perfect French, are you from Lorraine?' said the designer.

Leo explained that he and Theresa were originally from Germany, although he was now a French national.

'I understand. My family is from Lorraine, so I speak German as my second language. Must be why we're all drinking beer,' he said, laughing, as the waiter arrived to take their orders.

'How did you advance so quickly in the aircraft industry, Jean?' asked Theresa, clearly intrigued by the black-haired, tall and good-looking designer.

Jean Bertrand smiled. 'You flatter me. I'm the product of a classic Catholic education leading to the École Polytechnique, and then the ENA for Aviation. In the air force I became involved in the potential for missiles as an alternative to trying to shoot at the enemy with guns. I guess I have an inventive flair.'

They all laughed. The conversation found its way to the situation in Algeria, Jean Bertrand expounding his horror at what would happen now the President seemed determined to give self-determination to the country.

'General de Gaulle is two-faced,' he blurted out.

Leo looked surreptitiously around the other tables, hoping no one could hear.

The other continued. 'His arrogance is insufferable. He was invited back to be President again because he'd pronounced Algeria should remain French. Two years later, during which time the army drove the FLN back to the frontiers, he announces there must be a negotiated settlement giving them total independence.' He hesitated. 'He must be stopped.'

There was silence for a moment.

'There was a good chance of a military insurrection,' said Leo. 'The failure of the Generals' putsch put paid to that.'

Jean Bertrand calmed down somewhat, calling for more beer. 'We'll have to see. The public voted to follow General de Gaulle's policy. If he can be persuaded to amend it, they are obliged to continue to follow him, at least in theory. This man is key to the lives of several million white settlers and pro-French Muslims.'

'I'm not that well informed, Jean, and am not French,' said Theresa. 'Whatever one thinks of his policies, to me General de Gaulle is a brave, daring man, but he's also very stubborn. That sort of man doesn't change his mind.'

'That's what really scares me,' said Jean.

'My unit is the 1st Legion Para Regiment,' said Leo. 'We've been in the thick of it there for several years. Now we are being closed down. I have enormous sympathy for the Europeans and great concern for the fate of the *harkis*.'

'Then you understand me, we're of the same mind,' he said, showing his trust in them. On the spur of the moment, he added, 'Look, would you like to come down to our development base at Bourges? It's an easy trip from here. I can demonstrate to you why we're leaders in air-launched missiles.'

'I'd love to do that. We've been using the Alouette as an airborne command platform so the commander can direct attacks from above. There have been tests with your missile, against ground targets.'

'So I understand,' said Jean, clearly pleased with the response. 'I'll get back to you with a date.'

What a remarkable man, thought Leo. Clearly a brilliant and patriotic Frenchman, at the same time detesting the President.

27

Route Nationale 20, Versailles to Bourges

Leo's mind was on Henri as he drove south from Versailles. His old schoolfriend's involvement in the failed Generals' putsch was now two months ago. The President's televised speech after the taking of Algiers was the turning point. Powerful and threatening, as Theresa described it. Henri's arrest wasn't surprising. He remembered Trinquier's warning of Henri's likely involvement when they dined earlier in the year.

Heading first for Orléans, the Peugeot 404 thundered down between endless poplars lining either side of the road. Leo's mind switched to Jean Bertrand. His invitation to visit the Nord Aviation works was generous, given the man was clearly working flat out on his all-important missile project. Intense when in conversation, particularly on politics and General de Gaulle, Jean would be equally intense at his work, of that Leo was sure. Extraordinary that he was head of aircraft engineering at Nord Aviation, and yet only thirty-five. All that, and a wife and three daughters. He remembered Theresa's comment after the lunch with Jean that he showed signs of pressure, dark rings under his eyes and hands shaking. A nurse who'd spent a lot of time treating battlefield stress, she knew what she was talking about.

An hour after Orléans, the airfield and works lay before him on the edge of Bourges. There was Jean Bertrand at the barrier, talking to the guard.

'Welcome to the home of guided missiles,' he exclaimed, pumping Leo's hand. 'I'll take you for a wash and some coffee. Then we'll do a tour in the jeep.'

'Great of you to ask me down, I'm much looking forward to it.'

'Before lunch there's going to be a demonstration. I've told my team you're here to evaluate our latest development for the army. So, look important,' he said, giving his new friend the up and down. 'At least your Legion uniform will impress everyone. How's the lovely Theresa?'

Leo and Jean chatted about life at SHAPE. The conversation soon came round to Algeria, both of them agreeing that the only hope remaining was to convince the President to change his mind.

As they made their way to a makeshift grandstand beside the airfield control tower, a C-47 landed bearing Luftwaffe markings.

'Here come our German friends,' said Jean Bertand, explaining proudly that his firm was in negotiation with the Bundeswehr for the new SS11 missile to be purchased for the German armed forces. They all shook hands over drinks laid out in a tent alongside.

'Now you're going to see some impressive results of the SS11 development,' he announced to everyone. 'We'll start with an Alouette helicopter carrying missiles and destroying targets in the centre of the airfield. That will be followed by the SS11 being launched from a Mystère jet fighter. Please don't take pictures. We'll supply you with a pack containing relevant photographs.'

Leo watched Jean Bertrand closely during the action. To him, here was a man on top of his role, technically brilliant and displaying impressive leadership. Yet, he sensed there was another side to him. Was it to do with his political passions?

28

Françoise and Justine were together at their favourite meeting place, the waiters gliding between tables in their black waistcoats and long white aprons. The conversation jumped between the secret service and the political world.

'You know what,' said Françoise, 'that Legion Captain, Pierre Sergent who was arrested after the putsch, has escaped.'

'The one whose unit was first into Algiers?'

'Yes. He's gone underground, believed to have joined the OAS. It's given me an idea for helping Henri.'

'From what I've heard, the OAS are a load of terrorists,' commented Justine.

'We know Henri was flown to the mainland and taken to Fresnes prison to await the Military Court. Somehow we must avoid him being locked up for God knows how long.'

'I can see that.'

'Escape is one possibility, but would mean he'd have to go underground,' said Françoise.

'True. Probably better than a long prison sentence. Is there another way?'

'We have a problem inserting our people into the OAS because the secret service is split internally between those who back General de Gaulle's plan and those who can't accept an independent Algeria.'

119

'Yes, I take your point,' said Justine. 'You wouldn't be able to ensure secrecy and the safety of the agent.'

'Quite so.' Françoise paused. 'So here's what I think. Henri shouldn't be in the same category as the leaders of the putsch like the Generals Challe and Zeller.'

Justine felt herself tense up. What was coming next?

Françoise went on. 'Supposing we propose to the Prime Minister, or his Justice Minister, that Henri de Rochefort's court hearing be suspended in exchange for him agreeing to join the OAS as an undercover agent?'

Justine was speechless. This was coming from Henri's sister, so there was no need to point out he would be risking his life. 'I suppose it could work,' she whispered, 'if he accepted the challenge.' A pause. 'He doesn't have a wife and family to worry about.'

'No, but ...' Françoise hesitated before saying slowly, 'it would seem there is a woman in his life.'

'Oh?'

Françoise explained what she'd heard in a letter from Henri. How a certain Noelle Mercure was doing a lot behind the scenes to help him. That Noelle telephoned her yesterday, and was now in France and wanted to speak to Henri's parents in Bordeaux. She'd asked Françoise to tell them in advance.

'Noelle was someone Henri met in Cairo during the war,' said Françoise. 'They formed some sort of relationship, although that seems to have lapsed when he went into the desert.'

'How romantic,' said Justine. 'Do you know anything about her?'

'Yes. We've looked into Noelle Mercure. She's an interesting woman, quite a bit older than Henri. She's been working for United Press International, or UPI as it's known, for many years. She's French but with close ties to the States. Believe it or not her mother was a Nobel Prize winner for research into radioactivity. She and her husband were Communists, as was Noelle's brother, now deceased.'

'Good heavens,' was all Justine could say at first. 'The deal with the Justice Department would have to be dead secret.' She was thinking hard how it could work. 'In other words, there would have to be some sort of contrived escape?'

'Yes. To the OAS, he must appear to be a bona fide prisoner who has escaped custody and is making himself available to them.'

'You wouldn't fake an escape from somewhere like Fresnes. It would have to be during a transfer from one place to another, perhaps between Fresnes and the Military Court.'

'That's right. I hear the trial's likely to be at Vincennes Fort,' said Françoise.

'If he escapes with the government's connivance, how long would he have to serve as an agent, do you think?' asked Justine.

'Not reasonably for more than a year. When it was over, he'd be re-arrested and sent back to prison to make it look bona fide. After a few months he'd be pardoned. The deal would provide either for his army pension rights to be protected or for equivalent compensation.'

'It'd be the end of his army career, but that's going to happen anyway.'

'Yes,' said Françoise. 'We'd need to find a lawyer to establish the legal practicalities. The government department the deal is done with could put the agreement together. Henri would still need legal advice.'

Justine was thinking it through. 'How would all this be arranged, with Henri I mean? He's in detention, how do we get to him?'

'I think we should involve Noelle Mercure,' said Françoise. She seems to be able to reach Henri because of her special status as representative of an American news network. I wouldn't be able to do it because of my secret service affiliation. If someone tipped off the OAS, the whole plan would be blown.'

'You're right.'

'Look, I must get back to work,' said Françoise. 'What if I call Mademoiselle Mercure and arrange to meet her as soon as possible? The three of us could then get together?'

'Absolutely.' She looked at her watch. 'I must get back to the Assembly,' said Justine. 'I'll start thinking about how we approach the authorities, assuming Henri agrees to deal. My God, this is developing into a spy thriller.'

29

A message from Françoise was awaiting Noelle Mercure's arrival at her new office. It was a couple of days since their telephone conversation about Henri. Could she see Mademoiselle Mercure at UPI as soon as possible? Of course she could, and they agreed to meet later that same day.

Françoise would take her through the plan for Henri, mentioning she'd only discussed it so far with her close wartime friend Justine Müller who was now a deputy. Before that, she must assess Noelle. She must be sure she was the right person to propose the plan of escape and undercover work.

It became clear right away that Noelle was totally committed to helping Henri. All the vibes seemed right to Françoise. 'I'm delighted we understand one another, Mademoiselle,' said Françoise. 'You can do a lot of good to my brother in the long term, if we can get him out of custody and back into a normal life.'

'That's great. So, the next step is for me to see if he'll buy into what you propose. He might just say it's too risky. Not just for him, but with the family's reputation in mind. I'll see him again at Fresnes as soon as I can.'

'Now, how about something from UPI's cocktail cabinet,' Noelle said with a warm smile. 'I know there's a half bottle of Moët and some crème de cassis. Can I mix you a Kir Royal?'

'You certainly can, thank you.'

Noelle mixed the drinks, as Françoise walked across to the teleprinter that was starting to clatter in the far corner of the room.

'I see the Évian talks have broken down,' she said as she read the UPI message. 'The problem seems to be the Sahara.'

'Predictable, I guess. They'll reach a compromise over nuclear testing, I'd think,' said Noelle as she handed Françoise her drink.

'To Henri,' said Noelle.

'To Henri.'

30

That damp musty smell everywhere, the noise of shouting and clanging metal doors, the awful food. This place would take some getting used to. As the days crawled past, Henri began to lose hope. The only certainty seemed to be the Military Court and imprisonment.

What had he achieved by joining the Generals' putsch? Its failure provided the quick answer to that question, nothing. He'd followed Hélie de Saint Marc's example because he couldn't just abandon the hundreds of Muslim auxiliary troops that passed through his hands for training. They'd risked their lives for France, just like the fathers of some who had fought for the Allies in the Second World War, enduring the horrors of Cassino and that terrible last winter in places like Colmar. The few *harkis* he'd rescued with the help of Bill Lomberg, that was fine, but there were so many more left to suffer the atrocities he was sure the FLN were planning.

As usual through his soldiering career, he was forced to confront his conscience. The suspension of the moral law was inevitable in time of war. But did it need to happen in a struggle for independence as in Indochina, and now in Algeria? In warfare, morality took second place. The worst examples were driven by doctrine, as in 1941 during the German advance in the East with the starving to death of Russian prisoners of war and execution of thousands of

Jewish families. On other occasions, it was a regard for the lesser evil rather than a doctrine, but still a breach of the moral law. For instance, the forcing of information out of one captive so as to save your own men. Or the killing of civilians in bombing raids in the hope of destroying the enemy's industrial plant.

Then suddenly the boredom and disillusionment was gone. It was the words of the warder early one morning. His depression fell away, there was a new meaning to his predicament. Noelle Mercure was coming to see him. A vital link with the real world, here was proof that she cared, that she wanted to be with him. The sense of abandonment was gone, replaced by a new hope. Of what, he wasn't sure.

Outside you could see enough to know it was a lovely June day. The warder escorted him along the walkways, down the endless stairs and passages to the visiting hall. Would she be there already? The cubicles were mainly empty. He was let into one and the glass door locked. A small table and two chairs, that was all.

He waited. Others came and went in nearby cubicles. Suddenly, a turning of the lock and there she was. Tastefully dressed, her slender body in a blue linen dress buttoned up the front.

They were meant to sit opposite one another at the small table, nothing to pass between them that might be used in a break-out. He'd ascertained from others during exercise that the warders would turn a blind eye to an embrace. Importantly also, that the meeting space wasn't generally bugged. They were given half an hour.

He took her briefly in his arms. 'You can't stay in this place, my darling,' was one of the first things she said, looking out at other prisoners sitting in nearby glass cubicles with their visitors. 'I've moved to UPI's office in Paris, only an hour away.'

Henri couldn't believe it, hardly knowing what to say. 'That's amazing.'

'I've been in touch with your sister Françoise and your parents, and told them what happened to you, why you were arrested.'

'How did they take it?'

'They understood. I told them about the *harkis*, the rescue operation with Bill. They are proud of you, my darling.'

Noelle explained that Françoise spoke with a lawyer who believed the sentence would be at least five years, maybe even ten. That was in spite of the mitigating circumstances in Henri's case.

'How can I do anything but serve out the prison term?' was Henri's dejected response.

'Your case hasn't been heard yet. And we think we have a solution, or at least Françoise and Justine Müller do.'

'Justine Müller, the deputy?'

'Yes.'

'You're not serious?' A small glimmer of hope entered his mind.

Noelle took him through the plan they were proposing.

'Did they discuss that with the lawyer?' asked Henri, engrossed with the implications of what was being put to him.

'No. We felt we should get your reaction first.'

There was a long silence, Noelle reaching out to hold his hand when it seemed no one was looking on.

'I think I'd need a specific project, a mission to undertake. I'm not prepared simply to offer my services to the OAS, and be sent into town to shoot someone standing in line outside a cinema.'

'I understand, Henri.'

'And it would have to be on the basis of me passing information back to the authorities in advance, so as to prevent an atrocity. Not merely reporting on who was responsible for something that already happened.'

'Yes, of course.'

Henri added, 'If it was a major attack, say the assassination of a senior official and I stopped it at the risk of being identified as the mole, then I could demand to be pulled out. And protected thereafter.'

'Definitely. That makes absolute sense. Our thinking is that a memorandum would be drawn up between you and the Justice Department covering the rules of play, and also the basis of reward. In particular that your army pension rights would be protected.'

'So, I have to make up my mind now, I suppose. You can't keep coming in and out of here.'

Henri was trying to think through the consequences of what could be an irrevocable decision. To do nothing would mean a very public case in the Military Court with all the damage that would do to his family's reputation. It would devastate his parents. Not to mention the purgatory of a long spell in prison.

To go with what Françoise and Justine were proposing meant taking on a role for which he was untrained. An undercover agent inside the OAS was high risk. The retired career officers at the top of the OAS, he could work with. The more junior officers, some of whom had deserted their regiments, were another matter. They led commandos made up of hit men, some trained, some off the street.

'It's a big decision for me, Noelle. Either way it's hopeless from your standpoint. I've let you down.'

'I'm here because I love you, Henri.' She stretched out for his hand. 'I'm going to support you in any way I can. I don't want to encourage you into something which is too dangerous. On the other hand, if you do decide to take up the opportunity, Françoise, Justine and I are going to be behind you all the way.'

There was a long silence. His instinct was to think positively, he'd been brought up that way, at home and in the Legion. The risk was real, he'd live with it.

'Okay, darling, I'll give it a try. Anything's better than being locked up for years on end.'

'You're a good man, and a brave one,' she said. 'The next thing is for Françoise to meet with Justine, to see what Prime Minister Debré thinks. Justine's on special assignment to the Cabinet and is ideally placed to find out what's possible.'

'How are we to communicate?' asked Henri.

'Françoise and Justine have this friend who's a journalist at the *Paris Tribune*,' said Noelle. Her name is Kim Cho, a Cambodian educated in France. Justine and she have worked together on articles and stories for several years. There's a small section each day in the *Tribune* for personal messages, and the thinking is we have Kim make the insertions in the *Tribune* for you to read.'

'The *Paris Tribune*, so it'll be in English. Most of the papers are put in the recreational area we can visit once a day,' said Henri. 'The *Tribune*'s usually there, but it would be sensible to repeat a message a second time, a day or two later.'

'Good idea. Now, my darling, I suggest you be "H" and I be "N" in the messages. And that when read by anyone, it would appear the two of us are having an affair. Don't laugh.'

Henri did laugh a little, so did she.

'It's likely the escape will have to be when you're in transit between here and wherever the hearing is, probably

Vincennes,' she said. 'That's only twenty kilometres away. A typical message from N to H would state when and where the illicit rendezvous would be, and could include an instruction.

'It means the escorting gendarmes will have to be part of the escape plan. That's a big risk.'

'We'll have to find out. They could be trusted agents from the Sûreté. Those people hate the OAS and would keep their silence.'

'So what you mean is that they'd come and collect me here. Presumably they would drive me to one of their safe houses to be briefed?'

'That's it. The prison authorities would assume it was a regular transfer. You would make your own contact with the OAS. There are legionnaire deserters among them, you'd need to be told where they hang out.'

Henri thought it through. He knew two of the Foreign Legion officers who'd gone underground.

'That could work,' said Henri. 'You're the best, my darling.' He suddenly felt he couldn't lose her. She was about to go, he couldn't face being on his own again. 'We must be able to see one another, when I'm out?'

She reached out to him. 'I'm not going anywhere. I'm here in Paris. So are Françoise and Justine. You'll never be alone.'

'Thank God for that,' was all he could think to say.

'Okay, I'll see what can be arranged,' said Noelle rising and embracing him. 'Things might happen fast. Keep reading the personal messages section in the *Tribune*. Don't be surprised if you read about your transfer before the prison governor tells you.'

'My darling,' he said as he took the paper. 'I couldn't go on without you. Give my love to everyone.'

31

Paris, Hôtel Matignon

Justine was in no doubt as to the person she should see, the one with the power and insight to make their plan for Henri acceptable to Prime Minister Debré. That person was Pierre Messmer. Both Pierre and Henri were in the same Free French regiment, 13th DBLE, back in British 8th Army days. Now he was the Cabinet minister in charge of the armed forces and closer to General de Gaulle than almost anyone.

To Justine, the way to Pierre Messmer would be through her membership of the Prime Minister's special security committee. She agreed with him at the start of the following week's meeting that they would speak privately afterwards. Her approach was to refer to her friendship with Françoise de Rochefort, starting with their wartime training for British secret service operations. She reminded him of Françoise's brother Henri and their time together in 13th DBLE.

'I remember Henri de Rochefort well, a fine young officer,' he said. 'We were at Bir Hakeim together. He did well afterwards in Indochina. The fact remains that he's made a serious error of judgement in supporting the Generals' putsch last April.'

'I agree, Minister. However, his sister has come up with an intriguing idea that I felt you should be the first to pass judgement on.'

Justine explained what Françoise was proposing, while the Minister's face remained impassive.

Eventually, Pierre Messmer said, 'What does Major de Rochefort think about the idea?'

'He's positive. He's made clear that he's not willing to go out on the streets and shoot people for the OAS. He wants a specific project or mission.'

'Such as?'

'Justine decided to go all the way. 'He could be assigned to save the life of the President.'

Pierre Messmer stiffened. She thought he might leap from his chair. 'My God, how would he do that?'

'He would convince the OAS of his belief that the President was committing genocide in Algeria. I'm sure you know the arguments. He would involve himself in the planning for assassinations generally, but of General de Gaulle in particular.'

'Mademoiselle. I must commend you and Françoise on your creativity. It's not of course just OAS thugs who threaten the President's life. There are certain people of senior political and military backgrounds who are heading in that direction.'

Justine nodded.

He added, 'We must keep the matter dead secret. There are too many in government who could leak such a plan, clearly we must take no risk over whom we decide to share it with.'

Justine was jubilant that he was buying into the idea, but she didn't show it. 'Thank you, Minister. Is there a government legal official you could direct to work with me on the terms of the agreement with Major de Rochefort?'

'Yes, I'll make inquiries and let you know. Then we'll need to decide how to release Henri in a way that people will assume he's escaped. I think we'll wait until everything is worked out, before you and I put it to the Prime Minister.' He added, almost casually, 'If he really needs to know.'

32

Henri was impatient, now there was the chance of escaping the awful place. What if the real summons to appear in court arrived before Noelle and the others could launch their plan? Twice already a lawyer visited him to assemble the case for the defence.

Suddenly, there it was, staring him in the face in the *Tribune*. 'H. I've booked the Hôtel de l'Université for the evening of September 20. Longing to see you. N.'

That was in one week's time.

The day after Henri saw the notice, the head warder delivered a note from the Governor stating that transport would depart at 14:00 hours on the last day of July. His case was to be heard at Vincennes Fort.

The excitement of the escape flooded through him, and anticipation of what might follow. He must make this work. His few belongings were packed and ready when they came to unlock his cell and escort him down and out into the courtyard, where a dark blue Renault Estafette stood waiting. Bright sunlight flooded the scene. The driver and two other gendarmes introduced themselves. There was no indication whether they were agents of the Sûreté. The paperwork completed, Henri climbed aboard with them and the driver headed out through the gates.

'We have instructions to take you to an address in the sixth arrondissement,' said one of the two gendarmes with him in the rear of the van. 'Here, have some coffee,' he said, passing Henri a flask.

Great, this was confirmation that they were heading for the safe house rather than the Court.

'Hopefully more comfortable than the Fort of Vincennes,' muttered Henri, his spirits lifted by the sense of freedom.

An hour later, they were parking outside an innocuous looking apartment building in the rue du Bac. He was escorted inside, past an unmanned reception desk, up the stairs and into an apartment on the second floor. Entering a large salon, he saw that one wall was lined with books. Opposite were double windows overlooking a narrow court-yard. It was comfortably furnished with a small dining table, chairs and sideboard.

The two agents dressed as gendarmes remained in the room as another door opened and a middle-aged man in lounge suit entered, introducing himself.

'Welcome, Major de Rochefort. Maître Lacoste is my name, I'm from the Justice Department.'

'Thank you, Maître. It's a relief to be out of Fresnes,' replied Henri.

'Could I suggest we have a preliminary discussion over a drink?' the government lawyer said. 'All being well, this apartment will become your temporary home. I will intro-duce you later to Odette, the housekeeper. She comes in most days of the week.'

'I understand,' said Henri. 'Thank you.'

'Assuming we reach agreement on your role, Major, you'll be left alone here.'

One of the agents went over to a sideboard and produced a bottle of scotch and glasses. This'll be the best drink I ever had, thought Henri.

Maître Lacoste explained that they needed to be clear on the basis of Henri's release and the suspension of charges against him. There would be a memorandum of agreement to be entered into. Provided Henri undertook a one-year assignment as undercover agent for the protection of senior officials against terrorist attack, charges would be annulled and he would go free.

So far so good. Henri's relief must have been obvious, hard as he tried to appear nonchalant.

Maître Lacoste reassured him it was unlikely the army would ask for his return to active service, but his retirement rank of major and pension rights would be protected. During the assignment, he would receive a monthly allowance equivalent to his army pay, and would be reimbursed for reasonable expenses.

'That sounds acceptable,' said Henri. 'I would like my own legal representative to review the memorandum.'

'That's understood,' said the Maître. 'It goes without saying, your public status is one of escaped prisoner. The Governor of Fresnes prison is being informed that you escaped during the transfer to Vincennes, and that the escorting gendarmes are being severely reprimanded.'

'No press release, I presume.'

'Correct, but I think an appropriate leak will be arranged so the OAS and others will become aware that you are out, and on the run.'

'What about my identity?'

'I imagine you will be referred to by code name in the OAS, although some of them will know your true identity.

We'll provide you with a new identity for use in the outside world. That will require some induction into your new persona, which we'll arrange.'

Henri hadn't given much thought to that. Not only would he become a different person, what about his occupation? Would he make new friends, how was he to behave?

'Fine, I'll certainly need help preparing myself for a new way of life,' said Henri.

'You will. We'll also organise how you can communicate with us while in the field.'

'Can I make telephone calls from here to my girlfriend Noelle Mercure, and my sister Françoise de Rochefort?'

'I don't see why not, but please keep conversations brief. The shorter the call, the more difficult it is for an outsider to intercept. There is a scrambler for use when you have to reach me in a hurry. I'll show you how to use it.

'Oh, and there's the matter of armament,' the Maître added. 'It would be best for you to be armed by the OAS when working for them in the field. Failing that, I can arrange for our firearms expert to help you out.'

'I should be unarmed to start with,' said Henri. 'After all, I'm an escaped prisoner. In fact, I don't have any clothes worth talking about.'

The Maître smiled for the first time. 'There's a closet off the bedroom which contains some things which should fit you. Better that you don't have your belongings sent here from Algeria, at least at this stage.'

He ended the discussion by arranging to come the next day with a draft of the memorandum. They would cover then how the first contact with the OAS could be made.

Henri thought of two junior officers he'd known, both in 1st Legion Paras before the regiment was dissolved. 'On that subject, Maître, please could you see if there's any information on the whereabouts of Pierre Sergent and Roger Degueldre. Both were young Legion officers who disappeared after the putsch last April.'

33

Paris, rue du Bac

Maître Lacoste was back late the following morning, handing over a draft of the memorandum and rules of play.

'The two names you gave me, Major. Lieutenant Degueldre has remained in Algeria, running what the OAS call their Delta Force. Captain Sergent is more interesting. He's over here, chief of staff of OAS *métropole*. We think he's concentrating more on politics and strategy on the mainland, rather than terrorist action. He could be a good person to start with.'

'Sounds like it. Do you have any addresses where I could pick up a lead to him?' asked Henri.

'I'll try and find out.' He paused, making a note. 'While we're together, I'd like to list a few items of information we're in need of.'

'Certainly, go ahead.' This could be my first assignment, thought Henri.

'There was a serious attempt on the President's life recently.'

'Yes, I read about that. Somewhere on his route home, wasn't it?'

'Yes, east of Paris, at Pont-sur-Seine. A large bomb was exploded as his car was passing by. There was enough explosive to blow everything to kingdom come, except that only a small part of it went off. The larger part was affected by several days of humid weather, and didn't detonate.'

'A miraculous escape.'

139

'It was. Publicly, the OAS was blamed and they haven't denied it. Privately, we don't know who was responsible. Analysis of the unexploded components indicated the bomb was made in Spain.'

'Made in Spain,' Henri said quietly, then added, 'Whoever did do it is likely to try again.'

'Exactly. Next, we'd like to know how the OAS are funded. They were short of cash at one point. They started to rob banks in Algeria, but not here. We suspect they have someone funding them, a rich industrialist perhaps.'

'Okay, noted.'

'Now to the politics. The public in Paris are becoming jumpy over the OAS threat in the city. We've heard there's likely to be a trade union and student demonstration soon. I'll tell you when. Ideally, you should be there to see if you recognise anyone likely to be OAS. They might try to wind up the police who are on edge after what happened the other day.'

'The Muslim march from the suburbs.'

'Yes.'

'Okay, anything else?' asked Henri.

A slight smile from the Maître. 'That should be enough to start with. Go through the papers I've given you and consult with the lawyer your sister comes up with. Let's try to have everything agreed this week.'

'Fine by me.'

'I've organised a couple of training sessions here for you, tomorrow and the next day. Basic rules in espionage.'

'Understood. I might get some operational advice from my sister, if that's okay.'

'Absolutely. She was trained by the British, wasn't she? Probably still does undercover work for the *piscine*. You couldn't have a better tutor.' They both laughed, for the first time.

'You and I should meet here each Monday morning when it's practicable,' he said. 'When not, leave a coded message on the number I'll give you for emergency contact. Security is everything. You'll probably be followed by the OAS, at least in the beginning. Never let them discover this address.'

⟶⟨⟩⟵

The moment the Maître was gone, Henri picked up the phone and dialled the number of UPI's Paris office, asking for Noelle Mercure.

'I'm in Paris. Let's meet at eight tonight,' he said as soon as she came to the phone. 'There's a bistro called L'Échaudé in a small street of the same name, close to the Église Saint-Germain-des-Prés.'

'Yes,' she gasped, and he put the phone down. That was it, calls were to be kept short.

⟶⟨⟩⟵

The small bar faced him as he went in through the dark red door. Noelle was seated on one of the four stools, jacket and short skirt blending into the casual chic of the Left Bank. They embraced, and a scotch and Perrier was placed before him to add to the thrill of being with her again.

'Sorry for the abrupt call. That's the way it has to be.'

'Okay, but where are you staying, my darling?'

'Just round the corner, courtesy of the Republic of France,' he whispered in her ear. 'It's glorious to see you, looking as lovely as ever. You were brilliant, getting me out of that place.'

'Françoise and Justine did most of it, I was the messenger,' said Noelle. 'Now it's up to you not to get murdered for betraying the OAS,' she whispered in his ear.'

'I've still got to find them. Let's take our drinks to the table.'

Henri led the way down the steps into the dining area. They chose one of the plain wooden tables covered with a paper cloth. Taking the hand-written menu from the waiter, he said, 'My recollection is that the thing to have here is a *filet au poivre.*'

'Oh, Henri, I've been longing for this moment,'

'It's not Henri any more.' He pulled out a *carte d'identité* and passed it across to her.

'Frédéric Barnier? What an ordinary name!' exclaimed Noelle.

'You'll have to put up with it.'

'Françoise has found a lawyer for you, Monsieur Barnier,' she said watching him pour the house red from a brown *pichet.* Can I pick up the documents?'

'That means you'll be coming back with me after dinner,' Henri said pointedly but with the warmest of smiles.

'What? Me going home with a strange man?' Noelle looked at him in mock surprise. 'Oh well, when in the Latin Quarter, do as the –' That was the moment their steaks arrived.

34

After clever deviations on the way to practice throwing off any tail put on him, Henri knew he was on his own. One of several tricks of the trade he'd already picked up from his first training session.

The Sacré Coeur loomed in the background, overlooking the small square. This was where the artisans of Paris rubbed shoulders with the artistic. There was so much talent here, and long hard working days. He could see seamstresses through one window, heads bowed over their fine work, a hat maker adjusting his display in another window. He smelt the aroma as a waiter deftly negotiated a tray of coffees towards a small art gallery.

There was the bar. Going straight in, he chose a corner table. According to Maître Lacoste, the owner was called Louis and should be able to help him. He asked the barman to invite the Patron to join him for a drink. A few minutes later, out came a tall, middle-aged man, looking fit and energetic.

'I am Louis. What can I do for you, Monsieur?' the Patron asked.

'I need to get in touch with a Pierre Sergent.'

Louis gave Henri a suspicious look. 'Does he know you?'

'Yes, we were in the army together, but have not been in touch in the past year.'

'Captain Sergent used to drop by, though I haven't seen him recently. Someone comes each week to pick up his mail. You could give me a letter for him.'

Henri was expecting this sort of response. Pulling out a sheet of paper and envelope, he said, 'Okay, thanks, I'll write him a note and leave it with you.'

'I served in Algeria,' Louis said suddenly. 'We have to stop what is going to happen there.'

⇥⊜⊜⇤

Back on the Left Bank, Henri went to La Poste in the boulevard Saint-Germain to set up the poste restante address to which he'd asked Pierre Sergent to reply. Only four days later, there was a response. He was to go to an address in the avenue de Neuilly, next to the American Hospital, any weekday in the morning. The password would be 'Narvik'.

Avenue de Neuilly

The apartment cum office was furnished simply. Henri was shown into a room where Pierre Sergent was waiting for him, rising smartly from under the front window overlooking the broad thoroughfare leading from the Seine up towards the Arc de Triomphe. Tall and forever that boyish look, the jet black hair hanging a lot longer than in the Legion, not an ounce of fat anywhere in sight.

They shook hands.

'Great to see you again, Captain,' said Henri.

'Major, it's good to have you here in Paris, thank you for making contact,' said Sergent.

'I'm just out of Fresnes, you may have heard. I want to help in any way I can.' Henri paused. 'Since neither of us are serving officers any longer, I think we should drop ranks. Just call me Henri.'

'Very good, I'm Pierre.'

'You know my background, Pierre. I'm committed to making General de Gaulle change course, whatever it might take. I'm hoping you're of the same thinking.'

'Absolutely,' Pierre said, pushing a jug and cup across the table. 'Have some coffee. I heard about your escape, well done.'

Henri decided to be up front about his views. 'My belief is we have to reach the French people, only they can shift the President from where he stands today. Indiscriminate bombing will alienate the electorate. We have to be intelligent and efficient in the way we act.'

'Yes, that's my view. Not everyone in the OAS thinks the same way. Even though I'm chief of staff, I only rank as an army captain. That's how General Salan and Colonel Argoud see me. Then there's Georges Bidault.'

'*The* Georges Bidault, leader of the provisional government after the Liberation?'

'Yes, him, although now he's fallen out with General de Gaulle.'

'He was always a rock the General depended on.'

'Yes, but no longer.'

'Algeria?'

'Yes. Incredible, isn't it. Algeria is a fault line running through France.' Sergent paused, in thought. 'In fact, Georges Bidault has resurrected his old CNR, his resistance network, on the basis that we need another national campaign. He's keeping out of France, at present.'

'I don't blame him,' said Henri.

'He's just asked me to meet him in Rome. However, there's a more pressing issue occupying my time. It's proposed that we bomb the headquarters of the Communist Party here in Paris.'

Henri waited a second before replying. 'Why, for what purpose?'

'Two reasons. First, by attacking the Party here, we would be attacking the FLN's most powerful ally, the Soviet Union. Second, we'd put the government in an awkward position. Either it responds in force, implying support for the Communists, or it stands back and cuts itself off from the left.'

'The OAS should strike now,' said Henri, wanting to prove his credibility with Sergent.

'The plan is for a commando to hit the Party HQ in Place Kossuth, machine-gunning the façade. The attack will be on Thursday.'

In three days, Henri realised that would give him time to warn Maître Lacoste, and perhaps save lives. On the other hand, Sergent may be laying a trap to see whether he would do just that. He'd keep his powder dry.

'What sort of public reaction do you expect?'

'There'll be an anti-OAS demonstration,' said Sergent. 'It'll be interesting to see whether all of the left turn out, or just the Communists. We may succeed in splitting the left.'

'Pierre, you must tell me how I can help.'

The Captain seemed to be considering how much more to disclose. Running his hand through his hair, he said, 'I should explain that there's been disagreement over who's in charge in the *métropole*. I created the OAS in mainland France shortly after the putsch, last June. General Salan confirmed my appointment as chief of staff.'

'That seems clear enough.'

'Yes, so it was until a month ago when our positions were challenged by Le Monocle.'

'Le Monocle? Who on earth is that?'

'A code name. He's a businessman friend of General Salan, seems to operate between Paris, Algiers and Madrid. The General advised us Le Monocle would direct all OAS networks in mainland France. I protested, so he qualified this instruction by ordering me to continue to coordinate the networks.'

'Did that work?' asked Henri.

'No, Le Monocle seems unstoppable, ordering bombings to be stepped up across the country.' He paused. 'I feel I should be open with you on our operating problems.'

'I appreciate that,' said Henri.

'Now we're facing this student and union demonstration, in protest against the authorities' failure to neutralise the OAS.'

This wasn't news to Henri. Maître Lacoste already referred to the forthcoming clash with the police, stimulated by the unions and Communists.

'I could attend, and report back to you anything untoward.'

'Yes, that's what I was going to suggest,' said Pierre Sergent. 'Remember, the aim of the unions and others on the left is to whip up hatred against the OAS.'

'Is the date fixed yet?'

'Some time later this month, at Place Bastille. I'm concerned about what might happen. Maurice Papon and his police are on edge. Someone might take drastic steps to provoke them. Try and stay close to the action, and we'll meet here afterwards.'

'Right, I'll do that. Probably better at this stage we keep it between us.'

Seeming to remember something, Pierre Sergent said, 'I was thinking about a code name for you in your relationships with the OAS, how about "Camerone"?'

'Rather a grand title. Not sure I can live up to that,' said Henri.

'It means you'll never give up.'

'Yes, that's what worries me. Fighting to the last man.' They both laughed, thinking of that fight-to-the-death bravery shown by the Legion in that legendary Mexican battle.

On his way back to the rue du Bac, Henri thought about Pierre Sergent and how their first meeting went. He must stay close to him, win his confidence. Disclosure of the Communist Party HQ attack, and the Bastille demonstration, these were to test him. He mustn't feed anything back to Maître Lacoste until Pierre Sergent made up his mind to trust him.

35

'Your story about Henri de Rochefort and his *harkis* was picked up by the *New York Tribune*. I noticed you held it back here, Kim?' Art Buchwald said as he poured her coffee.

'Everyone's nervous. France isn't a police state yet, but I just didn't want to rock the boat.'

'Yes, since the putsch everyone in authority seems to be on edge. With these court hearings of those involved, we don't want to be accused of prejudicing the judgments. What else are you working on?'

'I'm thinking of a feature article for *L'Express*, on the whole story of the *harkis*. That's the magazine least afraid of publishing that sort of thing.'

'Those retired Generals and other plotters really misjudged it,' said Buchwald. 'There's now been so much media coverage, nobody's interested any more. Why not look for another dimension to the Algerian problem?'

'Such as?'

'He seemed to be thinking aloud, his creative mind exploring the landscape around the big story. 'What's going to happen in the Sahara?'

'Good question,' said Kim. 'In the final negotiations with the FLN, I guess General de Gaulle will try to retain rights to the Sahara and its oil.'

It suddenly came to Kim. 'And, I suppose, to the nuclear test sites. There's my story, perhaps. What if the FLN try to make a grab for them. The Russians would love to help themselves to secrets lying around there.'

'Spot on,' said Art Buchwald. 'Why would the French Communist Party be so interested in the FLN inheriting everything? So, its masters in the Kremlin can go on a nuclear treasure hunt.'

Kim was already thinking of whom she might approach for information. 'You know, we mustn't forget Henri de Rochefort himself. I heard a whisper that he was out of Fresnes and on the run.'

'You mean, he's escaped?'

'Yes, I suppose that's what I mean. I wish I could reach him. That would be a story in itself.'

Art Buchwald was looking out across the newsroom, his fingers drumming on his desk. 'Yes, but how do you find out where he is, do you have any friend in common?'

'I do, come to think of it. His sister, Françoise, although she wouldn't be giving anything away. And there's Justine, my friend in the Assembly.' She paused, then jumped up knowing what she was going to do. 'Thanks, Art.'

⟶◉◉⟵

Kim's mind was never far from Justine. Time was passing. That evening at Castel was embedded in her mind. They'd been companions for a long time, each helping the other in their professional lives. Where was their personal relationship going? Events must take their course.

Would Justine know anything about the future of the Sahara? She might even know about Henri's escape. A quiet head-to-head over dinner, that's the way to find out. Where better than La Petite Chaise? On the Left Bank, not far from Justine's work at the Palais Bourbon.

⇒▬◉ ◉▬⇐

Kim loved dressing to show the best of her slight yet beautiful body. She pulled out of the bedroom closet a green silk dress with plunging neckline. A pashmina scarf over her shoulders, she took a cab the short distance down the boulevard Saint-Germain and into rue de Grenelle. On time, she sat down at her table and surveyed the scene. Just a few hooped-back chairs and polished fruitwood tables. All very classic and typical of old Paris. Those already there were more of a middle-aged and older clientele, rather than young and touristic.

In came Justine almost at once, her height and slight swing of the hips carrying the narrow and very erect body as it would have on the runway at Schiaparelli.

'So good of you to join me at such short notice,' said Kim as they embraced.

'I'm in my working clothes, sorry, but it's mayhem in government right now.'

'You're helping Michel Debré, I heard. Working for a Gaullist prime minister when your political career has been on the left is unusual, Justine. You never cease to amaze me.'

They chose from the menu, both agreeing on a Pinot Noir from the Cévennes to accompany the grilled turbot. The conversation was the same as it probably was on the other tables. Trouble in Paris and trouble in Algiers, independence only months away. Rumours that the OAS were going to hit Paris.

Kim brought the conversation round to pending news stories. 'You know I occasionally pick up things that investigative journalists in the States are working on. Sometimes they ask me for information. The backdrop of the FLN taking over the Sahara is exercising minds.'

'The oil, you mean?'

'It's not just the oil. The know-how and equipment at France's atomic weapons testing site at Reggane could be put into play. The Russians would love to get their hands on whatever is there.'

'Interesting,' said Justine. 'There's been some discussion in government. It's not just the Russians, there's the OAS to contend with. Now that the Generals' putsch has failed, the OAS are running amok in Algiers.'

'Yes, terrifying, nineteen bomb outrages in one day.'

'You may not know, but a nuclear device was exploded at Reggane the day after the putsch.'

'Wow,' exclaimed Kim.

'Paris didn't want to take any chances of critical materials falling into the plotters' hands, so ordered a detonation to eliminate some of what was lying around.'

'It can't be easy to manage, the whole Algerian problem has so many dimensions.'

'It looks like General de Gaulle will have to let the Sahara go with the rest of the country. Personally, I think that's the only way.'

'You have to say that, you're in the government,' said Kim, laughing.

'My dear Kim, what other option does he have? The United Nations has voted for Algerian independence. The United States is pushing for it, and so are Russia and China needless to say.'

Kim nodded. She decided to move the conversation to Henri.

'Henri de Rochefort must know plenty about the Sahara. I heard that he was out of Fresnes.'

'You're well informed,' said Justine.

'That's the kind of answer which suggests you know something about it.'

'As a deputy, one hears about these things.'

'In that case, could you put me in touch with him.'

'You're asking a lot.'

'You're a very special person, Justine.' This was Kim at her most persuasive. She detected she was on to something.

The waiter placed the bill on a dish in front of her. She felt Justine's hand on her arm as it reached out to her, and heard the words, 'Come on, let's go somewhere together.'

They were at the corner of the rue de Grenelle and the boulevard Saint-Germain when the sound and shock of the first explosion made them freeze to the spot.

'That's from the quai d'Orsay,' shouted Kim dashing into the nearest café to telephone one of the *Tribune*'s photographers. 'We'll meet him at Metro Invalides. We can be there in ten minutes,' she said to Justine, 'Come on, race you, see who gets there first.'

They were both overcome by a mixture of excitement and doubt, as they tore along the sidewalks.

On the way several other explosions shook the area, and others more distant, across the river. 'There were rumours the OAS would have a *nuit bleue* here in Paris after the one in Algiers,' shouted Justine, breathlessly, referring to the night of explosions and violence over there. 'Sounds like tonight is the turn of Paris.'

Sirens were shrieking close by and far away, as the two of them met up with the photographer and made for the foreign ministry at 37 quai d'Orsay.

'No casualties here,' said the guard as they arrived, panting. 'Must be bad in other places,' he added as yet another explosion came from the Right Bank.

'Sounds like a blanket demonstration of firepower across town,' Kim said. 'There must have been twenty bombings, in ten minutes. Maurice Papon will have his hands full.'

'I'd better call the Prime Minister's office,' said Justine. 'There might be an emergency meeting of the security committee. Let's go into that bar over there.'

Both ordered coffee and cognac, Kim realising that Justine was looking at her in an odd way.

'You mentioned Maurice Papon. Do you know much about him, Kim?'

'Just that he dealt with that Algerian demonstration here in the most brutal fashion.'

'He's a brutal man, a criminal in my book.'

Kim could feel the passion in Justine's voice. 'He must be backed by the government if he's head of the police in Paris.'

'He has a past those people conveniently overlook.' Justine almost spat out the words.

'Oh,' said Kim. She sensed there was a story lurking behind her friend's evident hatred of this man. 'Wasn't he prefect of a department in Algeria?'

'Yes, the Constantinois department. He ran brutal counterinsurgency operations, using torture freely.' Justine paused. 'Then here the FLN-inspired march of Algerian families from the suburbs, three months ago.'

'I heard about it.'

'What you didn't hear was about the mass murders. Maybe two hundred were killed by the police. The story is that Maurice Papon was given carte blanche to teach the

Algerian Arabs in Paris a lesson. Bodies were being pulled out of the Seine for days afterwards.'

'My God,' said Kim, 'why didn't the press pick up on that?'

'There was a big cover-up.' Justine paused. 'Kim, I have to be careful what I say. There is more, going back to Bordeaux during the German occupation. I have information which would make a big story. You know I'm Jewish.'

'Ah, well, yes. We must talk all about that, another day I guess.'

'It's really late. That was a lovely idea, Kim, thank you. The next few days are going to be interesting, but that shouldn't stop us having a coffee somewhere.' They embraced, and Kim whispered, 'Take care of yourself, chérie.'

On the way back to her attic apartment, Kim was uncertain whether there was enough for an article on the Saharan nuclear facilities. Maurice Papon sounded interesting, depending on how much Justine would divulge. In the meantime, she would concentrate on tracking down Henri de Rochefort. It was time she called on this Noelle Mercure.

36

Such a friendly manner, on the phone and now face to face, was Kim's first impression of Noelle. After all, they were to some extent competitors, writing for the same readership. Meeting for lunch in a small restaurant near UPI's office, the older woman put Kim at ease from the moment they met.

'Strange that we've both been writing about the fate of the *harkis*,' Kim said.

'It's a big enough story for the two of us,' said Noelle with half a laugh.

The waiter came to take their orders. The place was crammed with office and shop workers, the conversation loud and animated.

They talked about journalism in the city, and the power of the magazine world. Eventually, Kim brought the conversation round to Henri.

'Françoise de Rochefort mentioned to me that her brother was out of prison and presumably in hiding. I suppose they'll try and sentence him anyway,' said Kim.

'We'll have to see what happens.'

Kim sensed that Noelle was being evasive, and said, 'A lawyer friend of mine speculated that some of those who supported the Generals' putsch might receive an amnesty after General de Gaulle gets his way on independence.'

'Frankly, I doubt it. The next few months will decide. The OAS is going full out to see he doesn't get his way.'

The mention of the OAS was what Kim was looking for. 'I've struggled to put a story together about the OAS,' said Kim. 'They're murdering and blowing up people everywhere in Algeria. Yet, here in mainland France, I couldn't put my hand on anything concrete until the bombings the other night.'

'There was that train crash, but that's old news, and the authorities still say it was just a derailment,' replied Noelle.

'The OAS say it was them. I know a couple who were on the train, friends of Henri actually.' Kim wasn't sure how much to say. 'He was in the Foreign Legion with Henri.'

Kim sensed that Noelle was trying to supress her interest, yet reference to Henri clearly lit her up.

'What do they say?' Noelle asked cautiously.

'That there was *plastique* on the track,' whispered Kim.

Silence for a few moments.

'What's his name?'

'Leo Beckendorf. His wife is Theresa.'

Noelle looked at her watch. 'We keep New York time at UPI, I'll have to get back in a moment.'

'I know what it's like, my deadlines at the *Tribune* have to fit in with our American partners,' laughed Kim. 'Look, I'll keep a lookout for anything that might be worth circulation by UPI. I've really enjoyed lunch with you.'

'Me too. Are you sure I can't contribute to the bill?'

'Certainly not. Let's meet again soon, Noelle.'

She was seeing Henri, Kim was sure, her intuition told her. First his escape, now what was he up to? She must find out. She could feel something big was in the making.

37

Justine was intrigued by a call from Françoise, asking if she could meet her at the *piscine*. In the past they'd met at the bistro nearby, or at the Café Flore.

Coming out of Metro Porte de Lilas, she walked along boulevard Mortier and soon found number forty-one. The building looked unimportant, no signs except one marked as visitors' entrance. No security guards, just a smart young man in civilian suit, who smiled at her and asked whom she'd come to see. 'Mademoiselle de Rochefort,' said Justine.

The young man said she was expected, walking with her into the small reception area where he picked up a phone and rang through to Françoise. All very low-key, thought Justine, other than the two black Citroën DSs parked outside.

'Lovely to see you, Justine,' called Françoise, approaching from along the corridor. The two embraced. 'I have a small meeting room booked.' Turning to the young man, she asked him to arrange for coffee.

'You won't be bothered by the press here,' said Françoise as they made for a ground floor room. 'It should be a relief after the Palais Bourbon.'

'What an honour to be invited to the *piscine* of all places,' said Justine, arranging herself at the table in the centre of the room. Looking around the walls, the only picture was a photograph of a much younger Charles de Gaulle sitting behind a BBC microphone.

'I saw your friend Kim the other day,' said Françoise, opening a leather-bound diary. 'Lots of interesting things to say, she really has her ear to the ground. For a Cambodian girl who started alone in Paris, she's really done well. The *Tribune* are lucky to have her.'

'Yes, Kim knows her way around.' Justine waited, then leant forward. 'So, why am I here, Françoise? Not many people know this place exists, let alone get asked to come in.'

Françoise reached out and touched her on the arm. 'Because you're special, Justine. Espionage is in our blood. Remember signing the Official Secrets Act in Britain? That training up at Arisaig, Mr Fairbairn showing us how to kill silently.'

'I haven't done that for some time,' muttered Justine, leaving unsaid whether she was joking or not.

'You did a great job with Pierre Messmer, getting Henri out of Fresnes.'

'I hope the OAS admit Henri to their inner thinking.'

'I'm going to stay close to what he's up to, if I can,' said Françoise. 'We must be ready to pull him out if there are signs they suspect him.'

Françoise hesitated before continuing. 'You're a deputy, Justine, with a network of influential contacts.' She paused for a moment. 'There are ways in which you could help us. '

Justine sensed excitement building in her, and with it danger. 'Why me? You already have Henri about to infiltrate the OAS. The secret service must have their moles in there.'

'You know something, we have a legacy problem.'

'What do you mean by that?'

'Secret service people come from different backgrounds and have opposing views and allegiances on Algerian independence. That's the need for Henri. He'll be an insider. We also need people like you, well-connected in politics and the trade unions.'

Justine wondered where this was going. 'What's the issue, Françoise?'

'The forces we're up against are complicated. Politics play a large part. But our objective shouldn't be political. It's about reducing risk.'

'That's intriguing. What's at risk?'

Françoise didn't hesitate. 'Put simply, the life of the President.'

There was silence between them.

Françoise added, softly, 'Assassination.'

The word carried a sense of finality, but it made Justine's senses alert for danger and excitement.

Françoise went on. 'You have the daring to ask questions, go places others wouldn't go.'

'You make it sound like 1942, going underground again. Who would I be working for?'

'I can't sign you up as one of us, Justine. You're a prominent politician, a public figure. The nation's split over Algeria. Only the President can bind it together. The natural instinct is for frightened people to fall back on their leader. They believe in the Republic, that it will protect them. And that means they believe in the President of the Republic.'

'Why would the nation become frightened?' asked Justine.

Françoise waited, seemingly choosing carefully her words, her eyes locking onto those of her long-time companion.

Justine said softly, 'You look disturbed, chérie. What is it you want to say?'

'Civil war.'

'Oh God, surely not?'

'Whatever your views on the President, one thing is clear. He's forthright and he's not afraid. He's the strong man, love him or hate him. In times of distress, the public will listen to him. This country is riven by the fault line of Algeria, but they listen to him. Without General de Gaulle, the nation would panic.'

'Dramatic words, Françoise. Am I expected to prevent that?'

'To help us to prevent it.'

Justine grinned. 'Let's get down to work then,' she said, reaching for a pad and Bic pen from the centre of the table. 'Who in the political world do you think I should get close to?'

'You have an affinity with the left. You're already close to PMF. He's no longer in government but should be a source of information. A more involved person, in the sense of the threat, is Georges Bidault. Do you know him?'

'Yes, but not well.'

'He's been close to General de Gaulle since wartime days, although he tends to the left. He now faces a watershed. Passionate about holding on to Algeria, he has broken with the President. I've heard he has links with the OAS. If you could get in with him, or one of his close associates, you might learn what he's planning.'

'That's interesting. Anyone else?'

'Jacques Soustelle, who was also close to General de Gaulle in wartime, and later became Governor General of Algeria.'

'I hardly know him. He was a deputy in the Gaullist Party, but was sacked from it because of disagreement when the President changed his position on independence.'

'Precisely. He's close to the OAS. Try if you can, to win his confidence.' Françoise paused a moment. 'Now, something more pressing, where you may be able to help.'

Justine waited.

'You know André Malraux's home in the Bois was bombed last night.'

'Yes, lucky he wasn't there.'

'Our information is that the OAS did it. Worst of all is that a four-year-old child, on the ground floor where she was playing, was seriously injured by the blast, in the face.'

'Oh my God.' Justine's faced showed her horror.

'There's going to be big trouble on the streets. The word is already doing the rounds that a student march is planned. The unions and Communist Party are part of it. They want more effective action to suppress the OAS.'

'That's worrying,' said Justine. 'The Paris police right now are capable of anything. Maurice Papon isn't my favourite. If he has half a chance, he'll start murdering protesters. You remember what happened to the peaceful march of Algerian Muslims into the city centre.'

'Would one ever forget?'

'Justine, if you could keep your ear to the ground, maybe watch the demonstration from a distance. If there's any sign of the OAS getting involved, I'd love to hear.'

'Okay. We're hoping Henri will tell us a bit more about how they operate.'

'That may take a bit of time,' said Françoise.

'I'll see what I can do, separate from your people. I took your point, some of your colleagues will be close to the OAS. God, what a mess.'

'Yes, it's a mess all right. Whatever you're tempted to do, watch out for yourself. Call me after the Bastille demo.'

On the way back, Justine thought it through. She'd see if Josephine Baker would come with her to the demonstration, she was streetwise in every sense. The support Josephine gave her when campaigning to be a deputy in one of the dodgy parts of Paris was spectacular.

38

They approached the square where the Bastille once stood, both intending to keep a low profile on a bitterly cold day. Justine was pleased to have Josephine as support, and for the Hasselblad she'd brought with her. They must be careful, given the ban on political meetings. The protest was against the OAS and its bombings, not a political demonstration.

There were students in the crowd by the look of it, as well as union members and Communists. She spotted a senior official of the CGT, and waved to him. He would pass on the word that she'd attended the demonstration. Organised by the unions, they would expect to see her there as a left-wing deputy whom they supported.

Some demonstrators carried large pictures of Delphine, the young child's face covered with blood from the bombing of André Malraux's apartment. Other signs were anti-government as well as OAS, reflecting anger that the authorities couldn't stop their attacks.

'Look at those police,' said Josephine suddenly, pointing at demonstrators cornered in a street cordoned off at both ends. 'They're beating them.'

'CRS, utterly ruthless. Nothing we can do. They won't pay attention to us,' said Justine. 'They'd beat us up as well.'

Then she heard it. That dull double crack of an army carbine, from somewhere behind her head. Justine wouldn't forget that sound, even years after the war. Josephine seemed not to be aware of it. Where was the target? One part of the crowd across the square was moving outwards to expose a body on the cobbles. She saw there was a policeman lying face down.

Josephine noticed. 'I don't believe it, a policeman's been shot.'

'What would you do if you wanted to create mayhem in a bad-tempered demo like this?' said Justine to her friend.

'Well, shoot a policeman, I guess.'

'Exactly. Probably the OAS. The shot came from behind us,' said Justine. 'A sniper in a building back there,' she muttered as she turned around to scan the buildings behind them.

'Oh my God, look down that street, those people pouring into the Charonne Metro to get out of the way,' shouted Josephine.

'I don't like it. Something's wrong. Look at those CRS tearing up the steel base plates around trees and metro vents. They're hurling them down on people on the steps into Metro Charonne. It looks like the entrance at the bottom is blocked.'

Shouts started to come back to them from the station, that the gates to the lines were locked and demonstrators were trapped on the stairs, pressure building up from those behind.

'We must call ambulances,' Josephine shouted. 'Let's get to the phone over there,' she cried out, pointing at a *tabac*.

'You do that. Then stay by it. I'll be about half an hour. Let me have the camera, please.'

Justine was looking for tell-tale signs as she entered the closest building behind them. No concierge in sight. She went up to the first floor, looking for evidence such as spent cartridge shells, the smell of cordite. The sniper would either leave the gun in the building, or walk out with it somehow hidden. If he had it with him, it would be in a suitcase or disguised as something else.

She scanned the area close by for someone who might fit the profile of an OAS killer, taking a few pictures with the Hasselblad. Suddenly she spotted a soldier in uniform with a kitbag over his shoulder. He was already some way away, walking towards a quieter corner of the square.

She must get close to him, position herself to take a picture before he disappeared down one of the side streets. Covering the ground rapidly around the perimeter, she was sure he would have disappeared by the time she got there. She stopped, stunned. He was talking to a policeman. Maybe they'd stopped him. She was just able to work her way around him and snatch a couple of shots of his face before the policeman waved him on, away and out of sight.

Back to join Josephine, where ambulances were removing bodies. Those arrested were being thrown into the backs of *paniers à salade*, the police vans carting them off to God knows where.

Françoise was thrilled to receive the film out of the Hasselblad, able to have shots of the suspect developed by the staff at the *piscine*. 'We'll see if there's a match with our records,' she said to Justine.

'Okay. The death toll is all over the newspapers. It makes you sick, those nine people crushed to death on the stairs or with skulls split by the steel plates thrown by the CRS.'

A few days later, Justine and Josephine were part of the massive crowd following eight coffins to the funeral. There were as many as a million mourners, some papers reported afterwards.

39

Paris, Café Flore

'You're a genius, Justine. We've developed those shots you took. Take a look,' said Françoise as she spread the photos out on the table. 'The soldier with the kitbag over his shoulder,' she said pointing at one of them. 'Was it he who shot the policeman?'

Justine looked hard at the photo. 'Yes, that's definitely him. He must have been carrying the carbine in the kitbag.'

'He matches with a legionnaire NCO who deserted when the putsch failed.'

Silence for a moment. Then Françoise added in a shaky voice, 'There was someone else.'

'What do you mean?'

'Look here, in the background.'

'Oh, who's that?' muttered Justine, looking again at the photo.

Françoise hesitated, then whispered, 'My brother.'

Justine looked up at her, a mixture of amazement and sympathy, reaching out a hand to grasp the other's arm. 'It looks like Henri's already acting for the OAS.'

'Probably at the demonstration to observe and report back,' said Françoise.

'Yes. At least that confirms he's been accepted, although they'll be watching him carefully to start with.'

Something else was bothering Justine. She looked around for a waiter.

'Let's order a sandwich, Françoise, I've got something else on my mind'

'Yes, here he comes.'

They ordered a *jambon beurre* each, a baguette with butter and ham, and two more beers.

Justine suddenly said, 'Something's got to be done about Maurice Papon.'

'Why him?' Françoise could see her old friend was upset.

'I'm not just talking about how he handled this demonstration,' said Justine, 'nor about all those Algerians killed in October. It's what I know he did during the German occupation.'

'Oh, I see. Wasn't he police chief in Bordeaux?'

'Yes,' said Justine. 'He deported two thousand Jews from Bordeaux to Drancy, and from there to the death camps.'

Françoise could see Justine was angry. 'I understand how you feel, being from Bordeaux's Jewish community.'

'Now I find myself working with the bastard, on the Prime Minister's security committee.'

'That's dreadful,' said Françoise.

'He leers at me. Perhaps he knows I have something on him.'

'The deportation of Jews,' said Françoise.

There was silence while the waiter served them. Then Justine said, 'Can't we frame Papon somehow, you must have stuff on him in your secret service files?'

'Justine, Maurice Papon has protection. The President awarded him the Légion d'Honneur last year. News of the killing of those hundred or more Algerians after the FLN march was stifled very effectively. Outside the Algerian community, no one knows anything.'

Justine was thinking. 'I agree. The moment to expose him isn't right now. To break through the news black-out, there'd have to be a powerful story, one sufficiently horrifying to hit the media overseas. Then the pressure would build for coverage in the press here.'

'What about your friend, Kim?' asked Françoise.

Hearing that, Justine sat up. Conceivably Kim could do just that. The *Paris Tribune* wouldn't risk printing it, but the *New York Herald Tribune* would if it was big enough. 'Good thinking, Françoise.'

'I know that when Maurice Papon was in Algeria as Préfet of Constantine,' said Françoise, 'he personally supervised an intensive campaign of torture.'

'There you are,' said Justine. 'Trouble is, here in mainland France it's only the intelligentsia who protest against torture. No one else wants to know.' She paused. 'Sorry, I had to get it off my chest. Attending meetings with the man is almost too much. I'll think about putting it to Kim.'

40

Paris, avenue de Neuilly

Henri found Pierre Sergent with his head in the newspapers, the events of Place Bastille plastered everywhere.

'You'll have read it all by now. I just thought I'd drop by to fill in around the edges,' said Henri.

'Ah, so you made it there,' the other said without looking up.

'Yes, it wasn't a pleasant experience. Could I ask you a question first?'

'I think I know what it is, about who shot the policeman?'

'Yes.'

'It was one of our men. I would have warned you in advance if I'd known.'

'Okay. Who ordered it?'

'It was Le Monocle. He asked one of his OAS friends to stoke up the police by shooting one of their own. They sent a legionnaire with sniper training, who deserted after the putsch. I didn't know until afterwards.'

'Ah,' exclaimed Henri. 'So that was it. It certainly drove the police into an even greater fury. Terrible things happened.'

'They did, and it won't have done any good to the public's view of the OAS,' said Pierre Sergent ruefully.

'I appreciate the problems you have. Something will have to be done about Le Monocle.'

Henri's mind switched to the information Maître Lacoste wanted. How could he encourage Pierre to share facts? He was aware of the pressures on him, that he was trying to strengthen the OAS organisation in mainland France while having to remain under deep cover.

'Pierre, we're agreed that things have to be done to bring government to a halt, make the public think again on the independence issue. One or two major events.'

'You're right. Bear in mind there've been some already, and not much has changed.'

'Did they fail?'

'Good question. The first was technically a success. The second wasn't.'

Henri waited, in the hope that the other would provide some detail.

'The blowing up of the Strasbourg to Paris express was spectacular. Trouble is, the government clamped down on the facts, just said it was a track problem causing derailment. The OAS was very new then, unknown in mainland France, and received no coverage at all. I was still with the Legion in Algeria when that happened.'

'And the second?'

Pierre Sergent paused in thought, then seemed to decide. 'The bomb attack on the President's car at Pont-sur-Seine failed. After a small part of the charge exploded, the driver accelerated through the smoke and debris. His quick thinking saved his precious cargo. The OAS were described as inept.'

'Oh, how much truth was there in that?'

'None. The fact is that we didn't organise it.'

There was silence for a moment.

'Do you have any idea who did?'

'Nothing specific. No names. The whisper is that the brains behind the Pont-sur-Seine attempt were to be found in the industrial world. Probably someone with the same thinking on Algeria as you and me, but who doesn't regard the OAS as a necessary partner.'

'With connections at the top, perhaps?' said Henri.

'Yes. I'm wondering whether those connections are with people like Georges Bidault and Jacques Soustelle,' he murmured. 'Anyway this someone will probably strike again. Maybe he'll ask for our help next time.'

'Perhaps I could help dig into it more easily than you can?'

'Possibly. I just heard what my sentence is. They're unlikely to stop looking for me so intensely, at least for the moment.'

'How long do they want to lock you up for?' asked Henri.

'Twenty years.'

'My God.'

'Now I have a question for you,' Pierre Sergent said.

Henri was immediately on the alert. 'What's that?'

'Just after the putsch, a woman from the American press agency UPI sought me out for an interview. She came out to Zéralda, was interested in me because someone told her I led the first Company of Legion Paras into Algiers on the morning of the putsch. She mentioned then that she knew you, and it stuck in my mind.'

Keep to the truth whenever you can. 'Yes, of course, Noelle Mercure. I knew her before, and she turned up in Algiers. Now she's here, at UPI's Paris office.'

'She's here?' He looked up in interest. 'What if we took her on board? As a neutral in terms of her press affiliations, she could approach people close to the top. What if we brought her in with us?'

Henri was amazed. What an idea. Did Pierre guess his relationship with her? Maybe it didn't matter. It would be risky for her, but she might accept that. He must get a grip of himself. 'I guess I'd have to tell her what I was up to.'

'Think about it, Henri. She's older than us, the type who would interest the likes of Georges Bidault, given her direct access to the American press. She could help us identify what those people are up to.'

'You may be right. I'll get back to you right away.'

'There are two other initiatives under way, Henri. First is I'm establishing a young people's OAS to be led by two lieutenants who just escaped from the prison at Mont-de-Marsan. We expect to have four hundred members, university and *lycée*, and will then launch an appeal across the country.'

'Sounds powerful, particularly with students of poor backgrounds,' said Henri.

'Secondly, there's going to be a political branch under the "CNR" banner, following instructions from General Salan. Georges Bidault will act as president of the CNR. I'm going to suggest that you, and Noelle Mercure perhaps, become the link with him in Rome.'

'That's interesting. I think you're right. I'll talk it through with her straight away, if you agree.'

'Yes. Go ahead, time is short.'

Rue du Bac

'Noelle, darling, I've just been with Pierre Sergent. He said he remembered you from that day in Zéralda when his regiment was ordered out of its barracks.'

'I'll always remember that. It was one of my most emotive reports for UPI, the legionnaires singing Edith Piaf.'

'He is suggesting you join me in some high-level work for the OAS.'

Her surprise was such that all she could do was cling on to him. She'd just arrived back from work, to join him at the apartment. 'Me, you must be mad, what on earth could I do to help the OAS cause?'

Henri explained it could involve trips to other countries. That there were powerful people exercising influence over OAS strategy from outside France. There was quite some politicking inside the OAS, and Pierre Sergent needed his own direct line to those people.

'I'm not sure I could add anything to the process, other than as a courier, even if I was ready to put my life in the hands of those people,' was Noelle's response.

'I'm not surprised at your reaction. I was surprised when he suggested it. The way he put it was that you're experienced in the media world. There's a communications department in the OAS, generating articles for right-wing publications, and submitting letters to the press.'

'I see,' she said.

He could sense Noelle was struggling with the concept of joining an illegal organisation, risking her successful professional life to put it mildly. 'You are quick to understand people and situations. That would help me.'

'Help you, how?'

'I'm going to represent Pierre Sergent with these people abroad, whom he needs direct contact with. If you were with me, it would make all the difference.'

'I'd only consider becoming involved, Henri, if it was to help bring you through this nightmare, get you back to a normal life.'

'Okay, let's meet him.'

⊰⊱

They had breakfast in the café close by Pierre Sergent's secret address. Outside, the early commuter traffic was pouring up the avenue de Neuilly. As they sipped their coffee, Henri could feel the motivation Noelle generated in him. The desire to look to the next day, towards a new life.

'What are you dreaming about?' Noelle asked.

'You,' he said, reaching out for her hand. 'Let's go and see what the chief of staff of the OAS has to say.'

He pressed the buzzer on the door, and spoke the password 'Narvik' into the speakerphone. There was a click, and they were in. Henri led the way to the office just as Pierre Sergent was coming out to greet them.

'Good to see you again Mademoiselle Mercure. Sorry I was so abrupt that time at Zéralda.'

'I was not surprised, given the situation you were in,' she replied. 'I hope you didn't mind me putting your picture and story in the world's press.'

'Not sure I ever saw it,' he said, laughing. 'Now let's sit down and talk about the future.'

Henri looked at Noelle, giving her a smile of encouragement.

Pierre Sergent explained his thinking that she could act as an unofficial media adviser to the OAS. There wouldn't be any contract, no paperwork except that necessitated by a project. She would maintain her existing role with UPI, and operate under her real identity. If she were on a mission with Henri, he'd be travelling as Frédéric Barnier.

'Clearly, the fewer OAS people who know about me, the better,' said Noelle.

Henri's pleasure couldn't be concealed. 'Do you have a first mission in mind, Pierre?'

'I've been asked to go to Rome, to meet with Georges Bidault. It's difficult for me to make the trip, I have to stay under deep cover for the present. I'd like the two of you to represent me.'

'We'll need a careful briefing,' said Henri. 'So will he. Why should he trust us, let alone talk about his plans?'

'Remember he knows who you are, Henri, and the part you played in the putsch. He's also asking us to raise public awareness of the OAS by improving relations with the press, and will recognise in Noelle Mercure someone with the experience and connections to achieve that.'

'He has his own resistance organisation to preserve French Algeria, doesn't he?'

'Yes, the CNR. It harks back to his Conseil National de la Résistance in '44. My impression is he regards the OAS, at least in the *métropole,* as part of his CNR.'

Noelle spoke suddenly, 'Should the authorities manage to catch General Salan, I guess Georges Bidault will become de facto leader of the anti-General de Gaulle effort.'

'Yes, you're right Mademoiselle Mercure.'

41

Noelle recognised the voice. Somehow Jansson sounded more Russian than when she first met him at the Hôtel Suisse before leaving Algiers.

'I heard you were now in Paris. So am I, and I need to speak to you.'

'Okay, where?'

'The Air France terminal at Invalides. Where the airport buses go from.'

'I know it. I'll be there at eleven tomorrow morning.'

⌖

In the Metro the next day, Noelle was uneasy about the man. Last time they met he was interested in her family's membership of the French Communist Party. She remembered the shock of blond hair and cold blue eyes. What was coming next?

When they were settled on a bench in a corner of the concourse, Jansson leant towards her. 'My friends in Moscow have read that report you did for the UN.'

Moscow. Now things were a little clearer. 'What I wrote after my trip to Reggane?'

'That's it.'

Surprising that they should find anything in that. 'Russia's nuclear weapons people must have known what was going on at Reggane.'

'Of course, but every extra piece of information, and from someone actually at the site, can help to put the technical jigsaw together. Anyway, it's you they're interested in.'

'Me?'

'Yes. They think you'll be sympathetic to the cause of the Soviet Union. At least that you would listen to them.'

'Why should I? I work for an American wire service. Americans don't like Communists.'

'They seem to think they can persuade you. They say there are things in your past, private matters that you would want kept private.'

They have done their homework. Mother was a Communist sympathiser when she was doing her research into radioactivity, so was my brother when directing the new CEA's research after the war. Maybe someone has talked about me to them.

'Think about it,' said Jansson. 'We'll call you soon and tell you where we should meet.'

Noelle didn't have to be back at UPI until later, and decided to walk the short distance to the river. The blossom was out, it was warm enough, and she could think better on her own as she made her way along the quai.

Jansson must be a go-between, or maybe a KGB agent himself. He'd asked her to think about a collaboration with his Moscow friends. Either he or someone from the Russian embassy would make contact. What was in it for her? Was there anything useful in involving herself with the Russians? They were into nuclear weapons like the Americans, it was a race that would end in the annihilation of millions. Britain and France were in the same business. There had to be an agreement between these countries to stop production of nuclear weapons. The UN was the obvious place to start working for a global deal, and she was already in with them.

She'd met someone from the Russian embassy years before, when her brother was running research at the CEA. A link with them could be useful in her desire to do something towards the peaceful use of atomic energy. But they were dangerous people. Perhaps they had something on her, would force her into some trap for their own devices. Did she have any option?

42

Rue du Bac

He was prepared when the buzzer sounded, followed by the voice of Maître Lacoste. It was Monday morning, time for Henri to present his first oral report.

They sat down in easy chairs in a corner of the salon, as the housekeeper Odette brought in coffee.

'I trust you have no objection to me recording our session,' said the lawyer, pulling a tape recorder from his briefcase. 'It avoids me having to take notes.'

'Go ahead,' said Henri as the tape began to revolve. 'I reached Pierre Sergent, chief of staff of OAS *métropole*. We've had two meetings so far, and I'll summarise where we've got to. Secondly, I was present at Place Bastille during the anti-OAS demonstration and have some information for you about that.'

Maître Lacoste nodded for him to continue.

Henri focused on the politics within the OAS organisation, the independent actions of Le Monocle, and Pierre Sergent's wish to have a direct line into Georges Bidault. Also, for Henri to represent him in discussions with the former Prime Minister, and for Noelle to act as unofficial media adviser to the organisation.

'That's good progress,' said Maître Lacoste. 'Confirmation that Georges Bidault's involved. Important because he's a big name and still influential. I've no objection to Mademoiselle

Mercure's involvement. I can see she'd be useful to them. She's experienced enough to judge the risk she'd be taking.'

'Okay, thanks,' said Henri. 'She's very much on my side and will keep me fully briefed.' Hardly necessary for him to say since he was sure the other could figure out the relationship between them.

'Where does the money come from for the trip to Rome?' asked the lawyer.

'Money doesn't seem to be a problem. There's a certain Maurice Gingembre who looks after that. He's a director of the Djebel Onk phosphate mines on the northern edge of the Sahara, and clearly has an interest in continuing French control.'

'Any information on who was behind the bomb attempt on the President at Pont-sur-Seine?'

'I asked Captain Sergent. He doesn't know, which confirms it wasn't an OAS initiative.'

Maître Lacoste was silent for a moment. 'That's an important point for you to pursue in Rome. Georges Bidault may know something about it.'

'Yes, understood,' said Henri. 'We must find out before it's too late.'

'What about the Bastille demonstration, did you uncover anything I should know about?' he asked. 'A policeman was killed.'

'Yes,' replied Henri. 'He was shot by a legionnaire deserter, a trained sniper. Captain Sergent wasn't told about it until afterwards. It was the work of Le Monocle. I think I spotted the assassin when he was making his escape, carrying a kitbag over his shoulder, presumably with the weapon inside.'

'It had the desired effect of whipping up the fury of the police,' the other said.

Maître Lacoste turned off the recording machine. 'You've made a good start, Major de Rochefort,' he said with the trace of a smile as he poured them more coffee. 'Your Rome trip could be very interesting if Georges Bidault accepts you as an insider.'

'I may take Mademoiselle Mercure with me, it might reduce suspicion when the authorities see me with her. I'll be travelling as Monsieur Barnier, of course. She'd be entering Italy as a UPI journalist and might even file a piece from their Rome office.'

43

A sense of foreboding flooded through Noelle as she entered by the pedestrian archway alongside the main gates of the Élysée Palace. Should she have allowed her friend Jacques Foccart to entice her into applying for the hot seat of press adviser to the President's office? A sudden telephone call, that he'd just heard she was in Paris, that he knew this job was being created and that it was perfect for her.

The uniformed Republican Guard smiled courteously and Noelle showed her *carte d'identité*. Inside the courtyard a number of shiny black Citroën DSs were parked side by side, a couple of chauffeurs in conversation, smoking and nonchalant. She was sure they would transform themselves into action men the moment a minister came out onto the palace steps.

An official in morning suit was evidently expecting her, moving forward from a visitor's entrance, ready to accompany her to her meeting. Was she really going to be interviewed by the Cabinet Secretary?

Noelle was determined to be her normal self.

The interior astonished her in its beauty and splendour. This wasn't just a reflection of ultimate power. It was surely to impress visiting heads of state.

Elegant was the only way to describe him. The Secretary rose to greet her, pulling out a chair at the ornate table of beautifully polished fruitwood. His manner was friendly, even warm, putting her at ease. From his questions it was clear he'd taken the time to read a detailed brief on her family background, education and career. Even the spell when she was a concert pianist wasn't missed. Her parents' and brother's Communist Party affiliations didn't prove a block, as far as she could see.

Noelle wanted him to take her for what she was, a senior journalist reporting on complex events in often hostile environments. When he probed her political thinking, she was able to respond fluently, stressing her conviction that General de Gaulle alone could save France at this juncture in its history. He asked for examples of her ability to speak in front of other journalists, and Noelle talked about the briefings she delivered when with UPI in Washington.

From his summing up of the interview, it seemed the Cabinet Secretary had bought into Jacques Foccart's idea that the Prime Minister needed someone of her seniority to promote internationally what General de Gaulle was doing for France. It would be a one-year assignment. She would have to stand back from UPI, but could return there afterwards.

When it was over, while having a coffee in the rue Cambon, she thought things over. What irony that she could be offered the job across the road, while she was playing a part in the OAS. Clearly she would need to extricate herself from the OAS and would discuss it with Henri. At least they would both have the same goal, to protect the President.

She'd do the Rome trip before starting at the Élysée, then see Pierre Sergent and tell him work pressure meant she'd have to withdraw from her OAS duties.

44

A message was awaiting Noelle back at the office, another call from Jansson. Would she dine at the Troika restaurant tomorrow night? He wanted to introduce her to a friend from Moscow.

Given that Noelle suspected the friend might well be a Russian agent, his appearance was not at all what she expected. The kindly face and gentle mannerisms of the fifty-something-year-old were the opposite of how she imagined KGB agents to be.

'I promised to introduce you to one of my Moscow friends, Mademoiselle Mercure. I think you'll have some interests in common.'

'I like to be called Evgeni,' said the Russian in a deep gritty voice, holding out his hand.

'I'm honoured to meet someone in the KGB, Evgeni,' she responded, hoping she'd guessed right.

Evgeni didn't deny it.

'I guess you've worked out why we think you should work with us, Mademoiselle Mercure,' he said after they'd settled themselves far enough from the violin player who was working hard at 'Midnight in Moscow'.

'Well, it could be connected with my brother,' she ventured.

'It was so unfortunate he fell out with that French Communist official after the Liberation,' said Evgeni. 'Just a policy difference. Moscow wanted data from experiments he'd conducted in secret during the war. In particular, they needed details of the cyclotron he'd constructed.'

'Yes, he knew you wanted to construct your own cyclotron. It was an essential step in producing plutonium.'

'And we had to have plutonium to make the atomic bomb.'

An honest Russian. At least he didn't beat about the bush. Noelle wondered what this was leading to.

'Yes,' she said. 'He discovered machine drawings of the cyclotron were missing, and assumed the French Communist Party official who watched over him was responsible. The official was about to fly to Moscow on a so-called goodwill mission, no doubt to hand over the drawings. It was straightforward for my brother to report him to the secret service.'

'To kill him?' said Evgeni. 'The Sûreté never worked out who did it.'

'Or were told not to work it out,' added Jansson, the suggestion of a smirk appearing on his mouth.

'My brother had nothing to do with any killing,' said Noelle. 'The victim was found dead in the Seine with no visible signs of what caused his death.'

'Which means he was poisoned,' Evgeni said. He paused before adding. 'Be that as it may, you would not want the matter re-opened.'

Noelle pretended to ignore the threat. The message was clear. 'Anyway, why do you want me?'

The two men looked at one another.

'We're worried about your President,' said Jansson.

'Worried about General de Gaulle?'

'We don't want him bumped off. He and our Mr Khrushchev see eye to eye on the future of Algeria.'

'So, what do you want me to do?'

'You are considering a new job in the Élysée, we hear.' He paused, allowing Noelle to recover from the surprise.

How on earth did they find that out? An aggressive response was the least they deserved. 'I am not here to discuss my career with the likes of you.'

'Think back to your visit to Reggane,' said Jansson. 'You met someone powerful and very close to the Prime Minister.'

Noelle knew immediately whom they were referring to.

'You must mean Jacques Foccart.' That was it. There was a link between them and Jacques Foccart. That doesn't mean Jacques is in with the Communists, let alone the Soviets. He just keeps the lines open to everyone. After all, his ultimate boss General de Gaulle isn't anti-them. He just hates politicians.

'Exactly. He's no way connected with us. He's just a friendly contact. Your name came up in conversation.'

Did he tell you the proposed role?'

'Press Officer.'

'I see,' said Noelle.

'Jacques Foccart explained that the Élysée wants someone with international experience to manage their press office. To help them tell the world that France is on the threshold of a new era.'

'What new era?'

Jansson interjected. 'That she's about to enter a post-colonial surge in economic growth, and take on leadership of the new Europe.'

Noelle's mind was racing to get around their motive for involving her.

Evgeni could see she was perplexed. 'The idea is, Mademoiselle, that from inside the Élysée, you can watch the President's back.'

'You mean spy out whether someone's out to get him?'

'We're suspicious of your secret service. Some in there want France to retain Algeria, others want her to get out,' said Jansson. 'There are fanatics in there.'

'We fear a conspiracy to eliminate him,' added Evgeni.

Noelle sat back, in thought. She believed in keeping her professional life watertight from her personal life. Involvement with the KGB would blur that objective. So far, it didn't seem they knew about Henri. There was the obvious risk that he would be dragged in.

'I understand,' she said.

Noelle looked carefully at them both. 'Okay, but I'm not becoming a KGB agent. I'll work with you because we both want the President to survive.'

'The same goes for the reputation of your brother,' Evgeni added mischievously.

'You may not be aware, I share my late brother's passionate belief that nuclear energy should be put to peaceful uses only. If you take me on as a collaborator, you have to live with that. It's fundamental to my make-up.

There was a heavy silence, until Evgeni said, 'I understand you, Mademoiselle Mercure. I'm sure we can live with a high-principled person like you.'

He gave every indication of being sincere. Of course he wasn't, he was KGB. At least both sides knew where they stood.

45

Work on the missile development consumed most of Jean Bertrand's time, but behind it lurked the despair that followed the collapse of the Generals' putsch. The referendum last January was about to be followed by another. It looked like giving to General de Gaulle the final backing he wanted from the people of mainland France. The ceasefire and beginning of the conference in Évian in April were confirmation that he was out to finalise a settlement with the FLN. Ratification by the public would reduce to nothing the efforts of so many brave people in Algeria.

What could he do? There was the OAS. The bomb killing the mayor of Évian just before the original talks started was a clear statement from them. He shared their view that General de Gaulle must be stopped, but wasn't comfortable with the way they were going about it. General Salan, in exile in Madrid, was its official head but there seemed to be little coordination of its murderous actions on the ground.

How about appealing for help at the top? His seniority in the aircraft industry made it possible to gravitate towards prominent anti-Gaullists like Georges Bidault and Jacques Soustelle. They were backing the OAS in the political arena. No doubt the authorities were watching them.

Jean Bertrand could offer himself to the two of them. They'd be impressed with his high-level industrial contacts, and the pressure that could still be brought to bear on the President.

He was not going to disclose himself to the OAS as a potential activist. He didn't trust them. If he could conceive of a way to stop General de Gaulle, and needed on-the-ground support, he knew how to find the firepower.

Operating on his own, he searched for a solution. At this late stage, the elimination of General de Gaulle seemed the only way to go. The question was how. He was torn between his successful career, still only thirty-five years old, and the fulfilment of a mission on which in moral terms he couldn't turn his back. His wife Geneviève and their three daughters were a crucial consideration. So was his religious background, and the compromise of taking a life in exchange for saving potentially so many others.

Could it ever be justified, such an act? In his mind, yes. The defence in the Pont-sur-Seine trial tried to plead the intention of the attackers was not to kill the President but to show he was not immortal and wasn't well protected. That line of defence failed. This time, the moral justification was there for all to see. Over a million *pieds noirs* and many overtly French Muslims including *harkis* would be made destitute, tortured and murdered. To him, the elimination of General de Gaulle was justifiable in terms of the moral law, now that the President's removal was no longer practicable under French law.

What about himself? For the sake of Geneviève and the girls, the challenge was to organise the operation without his identity becoming known. He needed support from someone else. Someone experienced in close-quarters combat, who was totally reliable. Someone who could help him escape. His contacts with the Sûreté confirmed the authorities were using torture as part of their counterinsurgency tactics, the *Gégène* had arrived from North Africa. He didn't fancy anyone's chances of refusing to talk when that was applied.

Suddenly an idea struck him. Was there a way to persuade Leo Beckendorf to help? Leo's concern over the Algerian drama, the consequences for the auxiliary troops and their families, was obvious. Coincidentally, both were strong believers in the same faith, Bertrand educated by the Jesuits, Beckendorf by the Benedictines. The difference was that Leo was only a Frenchman because of his commission in the French army. He was proud of it, but it couldn't be part of his inner self as it was in Jean Bertrand's case.

There needed to be something which would swing Leo towards his reasoning and intentions. Had he said anything to provide a clue? Their discussions during Leo's visit to Bourges, did they reveal anything? Leo mentioned his old schoolfriend in the Legion in Algiers, who was he? Yes, Henri someone. That he'd been arrested and could be charged with treason for involvement in the putsch. Then there was Leo's fury over his regiment being disbanded. Yes, these factors might sway Leo towards Jean Bertrand's thinking.

46

The train crawled into Termini station in the city's centre. Would there be a search on arrival? All had gone well at the border controls at Modane and Turin.

He spotted the Carabinieri on watch as they approached the barrier. Henri held his breath. Noelle showed her press card, and gave the ticket official a great smile, no doubt sensing how the heart of the Italian male would react. A smile back, and they were waved through.

Aware this was Noelle's first visit to Rome, Henri pointed out the remarkable architecture of the giant concourse with its glass walls and canted roof in aluminium. There'd been changes from what he remembered since last there in '44. Somehow Termini now illustrated the link between the eternal city and Italy's new thriving economy.

Noelle, calm all of the journey, bubbled over with excitement. Okay for her, she wasn't an escaped prisoner on the run. Henri must watch every step. They were booked into a modest hotel close to the Spanish Steps and the Via Condotti. 'I've heard of that street,' she said. 'Handy for my shopping,' and put her arm through his.

Their appointment with Georges Bidault was provisionally set for the following day, but they were to call and confirm. He could be reached at the Hassler.

Walking up the Spanish Steps after breakfast the next morning, they paused to look back across to ancient Rome, to the Forum, and just in front of it the iced cake effect of the Victor Emmanuel monument. Right in front of them was the majestic Hotel Hassler. The concierge passed Henri a message to go straight to the suite of Monsieur Bidault. A hotel attendant accompanied them up in the lift and to the sitting room of the suite, the service you'd expect when visiting an ex-Prime Minister of France.

'Come in both of you, this is a pleasure.' The great man was most friendly from the moment they appeared. Another member of the hotel staff poured everyone coffee as they settled in comfort in French Empire chairs beautifully upholstered in blue velvet.

'I remember your sister, Major de Rochefort, Françoise isn't it? She worked underground in Vichy for the British, and afterwards for General Koenig in Paris.'

It was obvious to Henri that Georges Bidault did his research. 'Yes, sir. You have a great memory.'

Then, to their astonishment, the former Prime Minister turned to Noelle, saying, 'Mademoiselle, I once met your mother. She was a hero of France for her work on radioactivity. Tragically it killed her in the end. The Nobel Prize has seldom been awarded to a person so deserving.'

Noelle appeared speechless for a few moments, before bringing herself together and thanking him.

Georges Bidault straightened himself. 'So, let's get down to work. Pierre Sergent has provided me with some background on you, Major. I respect the position you took on torture three years ago. And I read an article in the American press about the *harki* problem and the action you took. I share your concerns. You were stopped in your tracks by the failure of the putsch, and by your arrest.'

So far so good, thought Henri. 'Thank you, sir. I have an uncertain future, to put it mildly, but I'm committed to stopping independence without a safety net for those in Algeria who have supported France.'

'Quite so,' said Georges Bidault. 'Although you're technically on the run, I'm sure the French authorities are not as concerned about you as they are about Pierre Sergent. His effectiveness in the OAS is much reduced and I can see why he's asked you to stand in for him.'

'Captain Sergent has asked me to seek your advice,' said Henri. 'The question is how to strengthen the leadership he wants to exert as chief of staff, the role General Salan assigned to him.'

'So I understand from the note he sent me.'

'The underlying issue is how to determine our priorities. He believes that revenge attacks and bombing of civilian targets are turning the electorate away from the OAS.'

'I'm sure he's on the right path, Major. The fact is that there's very little time left.'

Henri decided to state the bald truth. 'You're right. That means drastic means have to be applied.'

The former Prime Minister said nothing, his penetrating eyes fixed on Henri's, waiting for what was to come.

'Any attack on the President himself should be planned by one or two people only. The police are everywhere, able to pick up the slightest whiff of rumour. Only just beforehand should the commando be assembled. That's why knowledge of who set up the Pont-sur-Seine attempt could be invaluable.'

Georges Bidault was silent before saying, 'That's going to be tricky. I'll make some inquiries in the hope I can give you a lead before you return to Paris.'

To Henri, that was an encouraging signal. This man must know something.

The ex-Prime Minister turned his attention to Noelle. 'Mademoiselle, I would like to discuss what could be done with the world press to promote the case for the President changing direction.'

'I'd be pleased to help, Monsieur. UPI is the right platform for the American press. I'm sure you know how to reach the media in Germany and Italy.'

'Indeed. I've asked Jacques Soustelle to join us for lunch today. He's in a similar position to me. Both of us were very close to the General for a long time, in fact Jacques joined him at the very beginning in London and set up the Free French intelligence service.'

Henri didn't like the reference to the security services. Would Jacques Soustelle still have links into the French intelligence world, and do a check on Henri? His cover ought to be watertight since only Armed Forces Minister Messmer and Maître Lacoste should know how he escaped from Fresnes. They'd kept the police and the *piscine* in the dark. However, he must tread carefully with Soustelle.

'It's our thinking that whoever was behind the bombing of the President's car at Pont-sur-Seine last September still has the same objective,' said Henri. 'That, offered the right support, he would launch another attempt.'

'That's a logical assumption,' acknowledged Georges Bidault.

'Currently, we have no idea who was the brains behind that attempt.'

In the silence that followed, Henri knew the great man was being forced to decide whether he and Noelle were what Pierre Sergent said they were. Could he rely on them? Was he in danger of giving away his own thinking and aims, which he would do if he followed the conversation to its logical conclusion? Henri was sure that Georges Bidault was wrestling with his conscience. The answer came abruptly.

'I'm ready to help.'

The restaurant was discreet, a separate alcove where they could talk in confidence and no one would overhear. Jacques Soustelle was already there when the three of them arrived. His jovial face and rimless glasses were disarming, and all four of them seemed relaxed by the atmosphere of a place far removed from the fraught conditions of France.

When they'd ordered their food and a crisp Sicilian white had been poured out, Jacques Soustelle said, 'Everyone, I'm going to drink a toast to France, and then I'm going to make a short speech.'

Georges Bidault laughed, 'Here we go.'

'To France,' everyone said.

'Now the speech.' Jacques Soustelle looked from one to the other. 'What I want to say is that all four of us are facing a judgement call. Each has to decide under what circumstances, if any, it is justified to end a person's life.'

Silence. The voices of other diners outside were just a background murmur.

'In the Second World War in France some of us would kill a French person if we believed he or she was passing information to the occupiers, that would put at risk the lives of our Resistance colleagues. Our war was a local war. A world war was raging in the background, but that's not why we killed French people.'

Jacques Soustelle paused, but no one was ready to interrupt him. 'Today, in France, we're faced with the certainty that thousands of French Algerians and pro-French Muslims are going to be maltreated and killed if the FLN have sole power after independence. General de Gaulle stands in the way of us preventing this from happening.

There was no doubt where this well-known personage stood.

Noelle was the first to speak. 'Monsieur Soustelle, it's stimulating for a journalist like me to hear someone of your standing state your mind so clearly. Of course, in terms of confidentiality this lunch never took place, but for me personally it has swept clear my mind.'

'I agree,' said Henri.

The conversation over the delicious meal provided Henri with useful material to take back to Pierre Sergent, their hosts confirming they would bring influence on General Salan to order cessation of bombings that put the public at risk.

Georges Bidault promised to call their hotel when he was ready to speak further. A message followed for them to meet him for breakfast the next morning.

⇥⇤

It was like out of a Federico Fellini movie, at least that was Noelle's observation when they joined the former Prime Minister on the terrace of the Hassler. Rome lay out below them in the clear air and sunshine.

Soft aromas coming from the warm rolls and silver coffee pots heightened the sense of euphoria that enveloped them. Deep chimes rang out from the bells of the innumerable ancient churches.

Georges Bidault asked how they spent the previous evening, and they described to him the two hours they snatched in the Forum.

'Jacques and I enjoyed the discussion yesterday.' He paused, looking round him. 'What I've heard about the Pont-sur-Seine attempt is that it was conceived by someone individually, without direct involvement in the political world, nor with the Organisation armée secrète. There were OAS people in the commando, but they didn't originate the attempt, nor plan it.'

'Is there any clue as to who this person is?' asked Henri.

The critical question. When the answer came, the reply was slow and deliberate. 'It seems he's a designer and engineer in the aircraft industry, young for his seniority. I don't have a name.'

Either Georges Bidault didn't know the person's identity, or wasn't going to disclose it. Nevertheless, what he'd said might be sufficient for them to track down the would-be assassin.

'I'm immensely grateful for your time and hospitality, sir,' said Henri. 'Captain Sergent and I will keep in close contact with you.'

'Thank you. Good luck both of you, and *bon courage.*'

47

Paris, Le Club Cercle Interallié

It was as though the porter recognised Leo from a previous visit. 'Good evening, Captain Beckendorf. Colonel Bertrand is waiting for you in the morning room, down the corridor, on the right.'

A lot had happened since the two of them first met, sitting dazed on the ground after the train crash. Here they now were in this inner sanctum of Paris society. He must tread carefully, not be drawn into something he couldn't control.

Generals and admirals of the Great War looked down from the walls as he followed the porter's instructions. Entering the room, the lighting was subdued as were the voices of members swapping news over their aperitifs. Jean Bertrand came forward to welcome him.

'Could I suggest we go straight in for dinner,' he said. 'We have much to talk about, and the tables are well spaced out.'

Both Leo and Jean Bertrand knew the pending demise of French Algeria was the burning issue, but tacitly agreed to leave it out of the conversation until the meal was over. When eventually the waiter presented burning wood tapers for them to light their cigars, pouring out the Armagnac, Leo sensed that the other was keen to express his views.

'We've talked in the past about the consequences of General de Gaulle's policy for independence,' the aircraft designer said quietly. 'Now that another referendum has ratified it, there are no legal means of stopping it happening.'

'We're both agreed on that,' said Leo, waiting a moment before adding, 'Knowing your creative mind, I'm sure you're not going to give up the struggle. Do I sense you have a proposal to make?'

There was some hesitation from Jean Bertrand, looking around the large room. When he spoke, his voice was firm and confident. 'Leo, I've decided what has to be done.'

Leo sensed what was coming next. What he'd learnt of his friend was that he was not a man of half measures.

'This person is about to commit genocide. He must be stopped.' Pausing, he then said, 'He must be stopped, whatever it takes.'

Leo waited a moment, then replied, 'That sounds extreme.'

'It is. I intend to go all the way. I have the people who will do it with me, but I need help in the background, help from someone I can trust. Someone with the experience of ambush and close-in fighting.'

Leo was expecting something along these lines, but now it came, he was shocked and stayed quiet.

'I want you alongside me, Leo.'

Conscious at once of the audacity of the challenge, Leo sensed conflict as well as danger. Aside from the moral issues, what about Theresa? His careful German mind searched for the detail behind Bertrand's request. 'What is it you want me to do?'

'I want your support and advice, using your experience of close combat. To tell me what you think of those I'm recruiting for the commando, and your views on how they should be organised. You'd be working with me only, they won't know who you are, won't even see you.'

'Okay. And what if it goes wrong? The target will be well protected whenever you strike. There's going to be a shoot-out. You need to have an escape route, an exit strategy.'

'Of course, but you'll have priority in getting away, Leo. Whether the strike succeeds or not. You're not to be part of the attack. I must get away also, and have my family to think about. But you must be able to wash your hands of your involvement. Should the worst happen and we are taken in by the authorities, I'll be the martyr. If forced to, you must point the finger at me. We must agree on that up front.'

Leo was more impressed than ever by Bertrand's passion and sincerity. 'I understand. We can discuss the detail later, that's if I agree to accept the challenge.'

'You told me about the offer you have to go to Katanga. That could be your exit strategy, should the need for one arise.'

'Maybe.'

Jean Bertrand smiled, leaning back in his chair. 'Leo, you need time to decide and to talk with Theresa. I can wait a day or two.'

'Okay, I'll think hard about it. What's your timetable?'

'That'll depend on the movements of the target. I have a source, and expect to have diary details shortly.'

Leo wondered who the source was. Someone inside the Élysée presumably, or with a line into the staff there.

'One other thing, Leo.'

'Oh, what's that?'

'I just had a visit from Le Monocle.'

Leo looked surprised. 'Who is Le Monocle?'

'A businessman. His eye was damaged in some accident, he wears a black monocle over it. The point is that Le Monocle is close to General Salan. Neither of them knows my plans but they seem interested in me.'

'Be careful,' said Leo. 'Raoul Salan is an immensely prestigious general who has links everywhere. He might even offer to arrange your escape overseas. But I'm sure he's watched closely. He's a marked man.'

⊹⊱⊰⊹

Late that night with Theresa, he explained it all to her. 'His reasoning is that General de Gaulle is going to commit genocide if he isn't stopped. That's how he reconciles it morally.'

Theresa was clearly shocked. 'And you, how do you reconcile it?'

'With difficulty. I respect Jean Bertrand, I like him. It boils down to whether eliminating the President of France will alter the politics of Algerian independence. That in turn depends on the people of mainland France. There's no doubt the *pied noir* voters would be delighted. They believe he's double-crossed them, which he has. Personally, I find his disbanding of my regiment and other fine regiments in the French army unforgivable.'

'You'll have to make up your own mind, my darling. You know me, I'm your camp follower. I'll go where you go, although I might draw the line at the guillotine. Talking of that, any news on Henri de Rochefort? I know he's escaped and is on the run. I'm so sorry for him.'

'Jean Bertrand thinks he might be able to help, he says he has friends in high places. Otherwise it could be a long sentence for Henri. That could change if General de Gaulle goes, of course.'

'What are the odds Jean and his commando can pull it off?'

'Too soon to tell. He's developing a detailed plan, and is ready to discuss it with me if I agree to join him.'

Theresa pulled him to her. 'Oh, Leo, I don't like it. Not being able to quantify the risk, I mean.'

'That's your German mind, darling. I think the same, even though I'm now meant to be French.' He tried to laugh but couldn't. 'I'm going back to Jean for a discussion on the detail, there's plenty more I want to know.'

48

'Jean, I need to get a feel for what you're planning and the make-up of the team. I'm supportive of what you want to do, but would like to quantify the risk, for both of our sakes. It's the German coming out in me.'

They were in a room behind a restaurant close to the Panthéon. Jean Bertrand said he'd used it before for entertaining customers. Several sheets of drawing paper were spread out on a large square table, as Leo was shown into the room by the maître d'. The place probably belonged to a *pied noir*, he thought, as Jean welcomed him with a warm handshake.

'I'm encouraged you want to know more, Leo. I'll take you through everything. First of all, the people. I'll use their code names.'

He placed a photograph on the table. 'This is Max. He'll lead the commando. From an old Breton family, he escaped recently from La Santé prison, having operated with the OAS. He's extreme right-wing and regards General de Gaulle as a closet Communist.'

'Any military experience?' asked Leo.

'Yes, lieutenant in the artillery.' He then placed the next photo on the table, saying, 'The Limp.'

'The what?'

'The Limp. He's an engineer, active in the OAS and lame.'

Another photograph. 'The Priest, at least that's what they call him.'

More photos on the table. 'These are Hungarians who escaped in the 1956 revolution and are manically anti-communist. The rest of the commando are *pieds noirs* living in mainland France. Here they are,' he said, putting more pictures on the table. 'They're out for revenge after what General de Gaulle's doing to their homeland, and the latest outrage in Algiers that they call the rue d'Islay massacre.'

'Yes, I read about it. How many are you in total?'

'Twelve including me, armed and on site, plus three look-outs on the route.'

Leo wondered about the mole Jean implied he had in the Élysée, but decided not to raise it.

Reaching for a large sheet facing down on the table, Jean turned it over to reveal the drawing of a crossroads.

'It'll be an ambush,' he said, 'in a suburb south-west of Paris. Based on what we know as of now, we'll aim to destroy the car taking the President and his wife from the Élysée to the airfield of Villacoublay.'

'From where he flies to somewhere close to his country home at Colombey-les-Deux-Églises?' said Leo.

'Exactly.'

'What protection will he have?'

'There's a second DS carrying three armed police and his doctor, plus Gendarmerie motorcyclists. Madame de Gaulle is usually beside him in the rear of his DS. Both cars are unmarked. To the public, only the motorcyclists would indicate anything unusual.'

'Any information on his driver?'

'Yes. He's had the same chauffeur for two years, Francis Marroux, a sergeant in the Gendarmerie. It was he who drove them through the smoke and away from the blast at Pont-sur-Seine.'

'He could make the difference, whether the President escapes or not.'

Jean took Leo through the whole operation as he saw it, from the lookouts telephoning him the progress of the vehicles from the Élysée to the point of ambush, to how the attackers would be positioned. 'I'll identify the convoy myself, as it approaches, and give the signal.'

'It won't take long for the police to pick up most of the team afterwards,' observed Leo. 'I guess you'll have a week at the most to get away before they force your identity out of them. How are you going to handle that?'

'I thought of driving into Germany. You might be able to help me in that regard. I'll tell Nord Aviation that I need a week there to work with our German air force friends on the missile project. I can watch developments in France. If the trail doesn't lead to me, I'll return. Otherwise, I would make for somewhere not friendly with France, maybe in South America.'

Leo was thinking. 'How about Israel? They could do with your expertise.'

'They would welcome me for that reason, but remember they buy arms from France, including aircraft. If the President survives, they will hand me over straight away. If a new administration takes over in France, the Israelis might protect me.'

'Theresa has friends in Israel.'

'Interesting, thanks.'

'And your wife and daughters?'

'They would have to wait at home, until it was safe to join me.'

Leo made some suggestions on layout and armament, saying reliance on MAT-49 submachine guns was problematic. Back-up with grenades and a medium machine gun would guarantee adequate firepower. He appreciated supply of those was a problem.

'Where would you want me to be?' asked Leo.

'I don't need a bodyguard,' Jean Bertrand replied, only half joking. 'It's for you to decide whether to be present, concealed at the ambush location, or not.'

49

Avenue de Neuilly

'How was the eternal city?' Pierre Sergent appeared more relaxed than last time they met, at least that was Henri's perception as he arrived to debrief the OAS's chief of staff on the trip to Rome.

'Glorious, and also productive. I have a letter here for you from Georges Bidault,' said Henri, handing over a sealed envelope.

'Thanks. Help yourself to coffee,' said Pierre Sergent, lighting a Gitane. 'Give me a summary of the discussions you had, if you don't mind.'

Henri described the initial meeting with Georges Bidault, the lunch when Jacques Soustelle joined them, and the breakfast session when the former gave him an indication of who was behind the Pont-sur-Seine attempt.

'The ex-Prime Minister seems to have taken you into his confidence. From what you say, we can expect General Salan's support and can concentrate on changing public opinion.'

'Yes. We'll need to be sure it gets through to Lieutenant Degueldre and his Delta Force. His revenge attacks and public bombings in mainland France have got to stop.' Henri paused, thinking. 'Equally important is that we identify this designer in the aircraft industry. Young for the senior position he holds, Georges Bidault said.'

'I don't know where to start,' said Pierre Sergent.

'Noelle Mercure knows a female journalist who took an interest in my efforts to protect the *harkis*.'

'What's the connection with the Pont-sur-Seine attempt?'

'She's brilliant at digging out people.'

'Okay. Tread carefully Henri, for your sake as well as mine.'

There was silence for a moment. Henri knew this was the moment he must come clean on Noelle.

'Pierre, there's something you should know.'

'Oh?'

'It's Noelle Mercure. She's been offered the job of press secretary at the Élysée Palace.'

The Captain looked as though he'd been drawn to attention on the parade ground, every muscle in his slim frame tensed up.

'Press secretary at the Élysée. My God.'

'She wants to accept, and asked me to tell you she must break her links with the OAS.'

'That doesn't surprise me. On the face of it she's changing sides. Can we make anything out of this, Henri?'

Having thought it through beforehand, the answer must be yes. Otherwise, Noelle's new role would compromise his own position in the OAS. Henri nodded, saying, 'It'll give us a potential source on the inside. She'll have to tread carefully.'

'She certainly will,' was all that Pierre said.

50

Rue du Bac

Maître Lacoste appeared on edge when he arrived the following Monday, clearly anxious for Henri's report on the trip to Rome and what leads it could give.

From Henri's standpoint, the burning issue was how much to tell him. If he triggered a search for the aircraft designer, at best they would frighten the man off whatever he was planning. If that happened, Sergent might well conclude that Henri was the cause, and his cover would be blown. The OAS had form for bumping off anyone who double-crossed them.

Maître Lacoste turned on his recording machine, announcing their names and the date and location.

Henri would concentrate on the meetings with Georges Bidault and Jacques Soustelle, their support for Captain Sergent as chief of staff, and agreement to persuade General Salan to stop OAS field attacks that endangered the public.

'They realise that drastic action is the only way to stop General de Gaulle,' concluded Henri.

'Did they give you any lead to the person responsible for the Pont-sur-Seine attempt?' The Maître was giving Henri one of his penetrating looks.

'Not directly. Both undertook to make discreet inquiries. They made it clear that if we find the person, then Pierre

Sergent and I should offer our help in any further attack on the President.'

Hopefully, that would satisfy Maître Lacoste for the present. No need to tell him about Noelle's new role at the Élysée. He'll find out about that in due course.

How could he track down this aircraft designer, before it was too late?

51

'Is that Captain Beckendorf, I'm Kim Cho, do you remember me?'

'I certainly do.'

'I was wondering whether we could get together, there's an urgent matter I have to discuss with you.'

'Okay. Could it be down here, near SHAPE?'

'Of course. Could you find somewhere private for us to lunch?'

Versailles

Seated in a secluded corner of a bistro Leo obviously thought would suit the purpose, Kim asked after Theresa and then came straight to the point, as was her way.

'Leo, if I could call you by your first name, I need help.'

'I'll do what I can, but we're rather off the map here in SHAPE, and spend most of our time on analysing the Russians rather than French politics, if that's what you want to discuss.'

'It's about Henri de Rochefort.'

'What about him?' Leo replied cautiously.

'I wrote an article about Major de Rochefort and the *harkis* for the *New York Herald Tribune* with whom we're syndicated. We didn't publish it in the *Tribune* here.'

'That makes sense,' said Leo. 'So, what's the problem?'

Kim felt comfortable with Leo. The chemistry was good. A tough guy, but not awkward, someone she could talk easily with.

'Henri de Rochefort escaped from Fresnes. He's presumed to be with the OAS.'

'Oh, that would surprise me,' said Leo.

'Why?'

'He's not the type, the last person to chuck bombs around. Henri's quiet and reserved, not a natural killer.'

'Oh,' said Kim.

'He's calm, almost gentle, although a fine officer. The Legion takes only the best, you know, generally top of the Saint-Cyr pass-out.'

'I'm impressed,' said Kim, with a slight tease in her voice.

'Although in times of emergency some are promoted from the ranks, like me,' he said with half a laugh.

Kim felt she should be honest with Leo. To her, a Cambodian, it didn't matter that he was brought up a German and fought on the other side. 'I'm interested in Henri, what drove him to support the Generals' putsch, what's going to happen now.'

'He must be bitter about his arrest, but he's not the type to exact a vicious revenge. I was at school with Henri, did you know that?'

Kim shook her head, surprised.

'We both had English mothers who wanted their sons educated by the Benedictines in the west of England,' said Leo.

'Why would he have joined the OAS then, if it's true?'

Leo was silent, evidently looking for the logic. 'Maybe he was made an offer,' said Leo. 'Perhaps his escape was part of a deal of some sort.'

Kim was surprised by Leo's remark. What sort of deal? Her inquisitive mind was now working overtime. Did Françoise say anything when they last met, or maybe Noelle the other day? Suddenly, the grain of an idea came to her, and she said, 'Could the authorities have done a trade-off with him? His freedom in exchange for some kind of undercover mission?'

'Anything's possible in France today, with this Algerian crisis. Let me think back. Henri told me he once worked undercover for the British in Cairo, for a short time during the war.'

'Like his sister, Françoise.'

'She was a professional spy,' said Leo.

'Maybe she still is,' muttered Kim. 'I'd love to know what Henri's up to.'

'So would I.'

Kim thought about Noelle. 'He has a girlfriend, I met her. I think she's helping him.'

'Oh, that's interesting,' said Leo. 'You know, it's too late in the day for the OAS to have any effect on Algeria. It doesn't figure that Henri would join them now.'

'So, it must be something else. Something big.' Kim's imagination was working overtime. 'What about an assassination attempt?' she found herself saying.

She was sure Leo flinched at that remark. German paratroopers didn't flinch. Leo knew something. She must tread carefully, but here might be a trail to a big story.

'I'm going to work hard on this one, Leo. If you come across any lead to Henri, would you consider calling me?'

'Certainly, Kim. Please do the same and let me know as soon as you find him.'

Kim said she would love to see Theresa again.

'She knows Paris well from her nursing training before the war,' said Leo.

'In that case, I'll see if there's something that she'd like to see and ask her to join me for the day.'

Kim headed back to Paris in the faithful Simca 1000. Turning over in her mind was the just perceptible reaction of Leo when she mentioned a possible assassination attempt. Was Leo mixed up in something? If so, he wasn't going to tell her. What about Theresa? Even if Leo wasn't giving her the full story, Theresa might. She must see her on a one-to-one basis. She had an idea.

52

'Come in, Lieutenant,' said General Salan, opening the door of the sitting room of his small suite. 'Colonel Arnoud is already here. Coffee's on the way.'

'Thank you, General,' said the powerfully built former parachute officer. Having risen through the ranks in Indochina, Roger Degueldre retired to the reserve list, to be elected a deputy from Algeria in the ultra-conservative Poujadist party.

They walked over to the small round table in the window, Antoine Argoud rising to shake hands. The three of them met regularly, yet the disparity of their ranks made for an inevitable formality in how they addressed one another. As founder members of the OAS a year ago, forced to go underground since the failure of the Generals' putsch, a strong bond existed between them.

'I want to talk about the *métropole*, in particular Paris,' said General Salan, picking up a letter from the desk close by. 'Georges Bidault has written from Rome. It follows a visit from Major de Rochefort.'

'Yes, sir,' said Roger Degueldre. 'I heard that Major de Rochefort escaped from Fresnes.'

'That's right. He went to Captain Sergent and offered his services. The Captain sent him to Rome to ask Georges Bidault to tell me a change of direction was called for. That we should concentrate on putting pressure on the President, and stop the bombings that are aggravating public opinion.'

'Sergent is a captain behaving like a colonel.' Antoine Argoud almost spat out the words. The other two knew there was no love lost between them.

'Be that as it may, Colonel,' said the General. 'I appointed Captain Sergent chief of staff because he is a thinker and a good organiser. We have to ignore differences of rank,' the most decorated general in the French army added.

Roger Degueldre, silent for a moment, suddenly said, 'I find it hard to accept that Henri de Rochefort has decided the OAS needs his help.'

'What do you mean by that?' asked the General, looking sharply at the former Lieutenant.

'Major de Rochefort's just not the person. He's devoted to his *harkis*, that's why he and Major de Saint Marc joined in the putsch. He's not a counterinsurgency man, wouldn't have his heart in the dirty business we have to get up to.'

There was silence, before Colonel Argoud said, 'In that case, what's he doing inside our organisation?'

Another silence.

Roger Degueldre looked at them both carefully. 'In my view, Major de Rochefort must have another motive for penetrating us.'

All three of them now saw the danger. General Salan spoke slowly. 'If there's a risk he's working for the government, we must find out.'

'I'm on my way to France tomorrow. Leave it to me.'

53

Paris, Pasteur Institute

'Kim, it's wonderful of you to give me the excuse for a day off to enjoy Paris,' said Theresa. 'What made you suggest visiting the Pasteur?'

'Two reasons actually. I knew the publicity manager here, who's just shown us around. Few outsiders can get into the place. Secondly, because your life is about fighting illness, and Pasteur must have helped that task immeasurably.'

'I knew he was famous for immunology and vaccines, like ridding the world of rabies, but he achieved so much else.'

'Yes, I'm Cambodian. Pasteur's work transformed my country.'

They were lunching in a small area of the staff restaurant, reserved for guests.

This was the moment Kim was waiting for. 'When my friend told us scientists here have won eight Nobel Prizes, I couldn't help thinking of Noelle Mercure and her mother who was a Nobel Prize winner.'

'Yes, Leo told me.'

Now the big question. 'Are Noelle and Henri de Rochefort close?'

Theresa looked a little surprised. 'I think so. She's been such a help to him since he was arrested.'

'Do you think Leo will find him? When we lunched the other day, he promised to let me know if he did.'

'I think he's making inquiries. The Legion has a great old boys' network. We heard a rumour Henri was treading on dangerous ground.'

'Oh, do you know why?'

'He's said to be undercover with the OAS, although Leo doubts that Henri would involve himself with them.' Theresa paused, she seemed to be concentrating her thoughts. 'I just feel there's something big being planned.'

'I wonder what. Any ideas, Theresa?'

'Leo doesn't want to discuss the subject, but I've been thinking about it. For instance, there's little more the OAS can do now to stop independence, unless they can change the President's mindset. Personally, I don't think he'll budge.'

'That only leaves one solution,' Kim said gently.

'Oh, what's that?'

'It could mean an assassination attempt,' blurted out Kim. Both of them took a quick look around the room.

'Oh God, I hope Henri's not involved,' said Theresa. 'Nor Leo, for that matter.' This time it was just a whisper.

'Is Leo spending time with anyone who might be planning something?'

Theresa was quiet for a moment. Kim knew she was deciding how much to say. To encourage her, she said, 'Both of us need to know what's happening, Theresa. You because Leo is involved. Me because I live off stories.'

'At least you're honest about it, Kim.' Theresa paused for a moment. 'This is strictly between you and me. He's been meeting with someone we both met some time ago.'

'Oh, who is this person?'

'He's a very senior aircraft designer. He came to SHAPE to give a talk on missiles.'

54

Paris, Panthéon

The call Leo picked up at home the evening before was terse. It was Jean Bertrand's voice. 'I have a date. Can you meet at the same address, soonest?' He'd answered, 'Eleven tomorrow morning,' and the call ended.

Driving into Paris, Leo watched in the mirror the cars behind him. He couldn't believe anyone would be following, but it was a good habit to get into.

Parking a couple of blocks away, he made his way to the restaurant they'd met at the last time. The mâitre d' took him through to the same room at the back.

Jean Bertrand looked business-like and alert, rising to greet Leo, then going straight to the point.

'I've heard from my contact who has access to the President's calendar of events. I have the date when the President and Madame de Gaulle will next leave the Élysée to connect with a private flight from the air force base at Villacoublay.'

'Okay, when's that?' said Leo.

'A week today.'

This is it, thought Leo. 'How does the commando look?'

'Max has them standing by, the same team I outlined to you when we last met.'

'Okay. Now, Jean, talk me through how everything's going to happen.'

Bertrand stood up and began to pace the room. As he spoke, his hands moved expansively. 'We'll intercept the convoy at a traffic intersection in Petit-Clamart on the Route Nationale 306, thirteen kilometres south-west of Paris. I'll take you out there today to look around.'

Leo just nodded.

'Let's start at the beginning,' said Jean Bertrand. 'Stop me when you have a query. I need all the advice you can give, it could make the difference between success and failure.'

55

'Art, sorry for crashing in on you.'

'I'm used to it, Kim. What's on?'

'I'm wondering whether they're going to assassinate the President.'

'What?'

'They could be about to kill General de Gaulle.'

'What's new about that?'

'This attempt is serious.'

'You mean it might work?'

This was Art Buchwald's scepticism at its best.

'Based on the characters involved, yes.'

'You know who they are? Tell me more.' He poured her a coffee, and lit himself a Camel.

'Strictly off the record, okay?'

He nodded.

'I've been following two sources. The first is Leo Beckendorf, or rather his wife Theresa.'

'The couple who were in the train crash?'

He doesn't forget anything, thought Kim.

'Art, Theresa thinks there's some plot being hatched by a top aircraft designer.'

'Someone who would never be suspected.'

'Exactly. A commando's been put together.'

'OAS?'

'Not as far as I can make out.' She paused. 'I still have to find the second source.'

'Who's that?'

'Henri de Rochefort.'

'Ah, Henri de Rochefort. From *harkis* to presidents via Fresnes prison,' said Art Buchwald with a broad smile.

'It seems that he has some deal with the authorities. He's undercover, and my guess is that, in exchange for his freedom, Henri's supplying information.'

'Why the President?'

'Because the only hope left for those still passionately *Algérie française* is to bump off General de Gaulle.'

Art Buchwald was leaning back in his chair, staring at his Cambodian friend. 'And you think Henri de Rochefort is feeding back information on the next assassination attempt?'

'Something like that.'

Kim knew what Art was thinking. 'I recognise there might not be much in this for us. We can't speculate on an assassination attempt on the President of France before it happens. After it happens, it might be too late.'

'True, but we'll be ahead of the competition in reporting on how and why it happened. You're smart, Kim. Don't get done in before you're paid your bonus.'

56

Paris, Café Flore

Kim rose to embrace them as they came inside. It was a beautiful mid-summer's day, and most customers were at the tables in the open, facing the boulevard Saint-Germain.

She needed to be alone with them.

'Justine, Françoise, thanks for joining me at such short notice.'

How would they react? These two were professionals. They would give nothing away unless presented with no option. She must shock them, make them realise this was the moment. That it might mean everything to Henri.

She hardly gave them time to sit down, looking first one then the other in the eye. 'If I'm correct, someone very close to you is in danger.'

They stared at her.

'Who is?' asked Françoise.

'Your brother, Henri, and his ex-schoolfriend Leo Beckendorf.'

Neither of them said anything. Kim looked around to make sure no one could overhear. 'I've been doing my job as an investigative reporter. I think there's going to be another attempt on the life of the President.'

Françoise looked at Justine, but still no comment.

'I've concluded that Henri escaped from Fresnes with the help of the authorities. His part of the deal is to penetrate the

OAS command and report back on plans for major outrages. He's taking a big risk but must have decided it's worth it.'

'That's a bold assumption, Kim,' said Françoise.

'It seems that Leo's involved with those planning the attempt, possibly advising in some way.'

Again, the other two looked at one another, then back at Kim. This time there was real surprise on their faces.

Justine spoke next. 'Let's say you're correct, Kim, and Henri and Leo are involved on opposite sides in a plot to kill the President. All France is split down the middle on Algerian independence. Most would be horrified at the killing of the President but would allow independence to take its course. To others, it would be the opportunity to wreak chaos.'

Françoise turned to Justine. 'Yes, Kim's point is that all three of us believe it would be a disaster for mainland France. It could lead to civil war.'

Kim continued. 'Yes, and more than that, Henri and Leo could be casualties in the attempt, whatever the outcome.' She wanted to put pressure on the two by opening their eyes to the danger the two men faced.

A heavy silence descended on them.

'What are you proposing?' asked Justine.

'I must reach Henri,' said Kim. 'I would like to help him. I might know who is organising the plot.'

The other two looked at her in amazement.

'I'm in this because it's my work to dig into events,' she said. 'Not only after they happen but sometimes before. I'm on Henri's side because he might be able to stop it happening. I think I have information that would help him.'

Both stared at her, they knew better than to ask her for more detail. Journalists didn't disclose their sources.

'I think I know who organised the attack at Pont-sur-Seine, in September last year,' said Kim. 'The assassin's going to try again.'

'I follow you,' said Françoise. 'As far as I know, no one at the *piscine* is on that trail. We're pretty sure the leader wasn't OAS.'

'I want you to help me,' said Kim. 'If you can connect me to Henri, I will tell him who's behind the attack on the President. That way, Henri can deliver on the deal he's done with the authorities. From what I understand, there isn't much time.'

Everyone was quiet for a moment, until Justine spoke. 'I can't promise anything, but I'll see what I can do. It's remarkable if you've dug out this information when the police and secret service have failed.'

Kim let that compliment pass. 'I expect Henri's operating under a pseudonym. Let me know what that is, and ask him to use it when he calls me at the *Tribune*.'

57

Place du Tertre

Roger Degueldre was wary of Captain Sergent. In the past year, there were differences of opinion on what the OAS in mainland France should be concentrating on. Now there was little they could do to stop independence going through, their scope for action was much diminished. He realised that the Captain would have his way, General Salan having accepted Georges Bidault's advice.

A back room in the bar run by Louis, where Pierre Sergent collected his mail, was not the safest place on earth but would have to serve as a meeting point on this occasion.

'Pierre, I'm aware you have Major de Rochefort working with you. I was with General Salan when he received a letter from Georges Bidault.'

'Yes, Henri de Rochefort came to me after his escape from Fresnes.'

'I don't want to question your judgement, Captain, but the escape seemed a little too easy for my liking.'

'I know, I was careful at the beginning and set him a couple of tests, but all seemed well. He certainly performed impressively on his trip to Rome.'

'We have eyes inside Fresnes. There's been some feed-back that he might be playing a double game.'

The Captain looked surprised.

'Well, if that's true, we'll have to deal with him. I'd like to know before you do anything drastic.'

'Of course. I'm just going to make some inquiries.'

The former Lieutenant's reputation for ruthless retribution left Pierre Sergent in no doubt of Henri's fate if he was found not to be clean.

'We took on his girlfriend Noelle Mercure as adviser.'

'Oh, have we?' said Roger Degueldre, showing his surprise.

'To help with press relations and our publicity material. Her day job is at UPI, the American news agency.'

'I guess we need to watch her also.'

'We do. Major de Rochefort just told me she's taking on a one-year assignment at the Élysée as press secretary.'

Degueldre looked incredulous. 'That makes me doubly suspicious.'

'I agree, but no strong-arm tactics, Roger, until we've discussed your findings.' Pierre Sergent wanted to avoid new tension developing between the two of them. At least Roger Degueldre's suspicions would keep him occupied.

58

Suddenly her phone rang.

'Kim Cho here.'

'My name is Frédéric Barnier. My sister suggested I call you.'

Kim's mind went into overdrive. Could this be Henri, using his pseudonym?

'I see. Why did she think of me?'

'Apparently she met you in Saint-Germain-des-Prés the other day.'

It was him. Must be, her breath tightening in her chest. 'Oh, fine.'

She paused a moment, thinking where they could meet. 'How about the Jardin du Luxembourg? We could meet at Metro Odéon. I'll be in a lightweight beige raincoat, carrying a *Paris Tribune*.'

A pause before the response. 'Fine, see you there in an hour.'

Jardin du Luxembourg

Kim saw him lift an arm as he approached. Good-looking, average height, the straight back of a soldier. Wearing the sort of clothes that wouldn't attract attention. She wondered what his cover story was.

'I'm Frédéric Barnier,' Henri said. 'Just a pseudonym,' he added quietly. 'I guess you know my real name.'

'Yes, Henri de Rochefort. I'll call you Monsieur Barnier.'

'Just as well to get in the habit. You never know when you might be pounced upon in Paris these days, Mademoiselle Cho.'

Looking around, Henri added, 'I don't think anyone's tailing me, but you can never be sure.'

'It's great of you to get in touch. Just call me Kim. I thought we'd find a park bench, like spies often do,' she added with almost a laugh as they walked into the gardens.

Safely seated away from anyone else, Kim explained how she knew Justine, and her recent encounters with Henri's sister, Françoise. Also that she'd written an article for the *New York Herald Tribune* about Henri's work for the *harkis*.

'I really appreciate that,' said Henri. 'I did hear about it. The more exposure America has to their plight as well as the problems faced by the million *pieds noirs*, the better.'

'Monsieur Barnier, I'm a journalist. I specialise in investigative work leading to big stories. I have information I think you want, which I'm ready to share with you. In exchange, I want an exclusive on your personal story.' She paused. 'It's as simple as that.'

'What kind of information? I must know where you're coming from.'

'I know who was behind the attempt on the President's life at Pont-sur-Seine a year ago.'

'You mean the organiser of the attempted bombing of his car?' he said.

She nodded.

Henri was silent for a long time. They both looked out from their bench at the wonderfully manicured lawns and tree-lined pathways. Kim knew he was balancing the opportunity for vital information against the risk of indiscreet disclosure that could lead him to disaster.

Kim liked him already, felt sympathy for his predicament, perhaps something more than that. She broke into his thoughts. 'Monsieur Barnier, I don't have to know how you escaped from prison. I want to help you, not just land a great story. I think you're in danger.'

'Henri turned to face her. Okay, I agree. I'll give you your exclusive, provided you show me beforehand what you're going to publish.'

'I'll certainly do that.'

'Now, your part of the bargain, Kim?'

Kim knew she must go ahead even though she wasn't sure she was right. It was a calculated risk.

Henri actually smiled at her, just at that moment. Why? To encourage her, no doubt.

'He's a senior executive with Nord Aviation, designs missiles.' There was a moment's hesitation. 'His name is Jean Bertrand.'

Henri looked surprised. 'The last person one would suspect,' he muttered.

'You're the only person I've told,' said Kim. 'We must keep his identity strictly between the two of us.' Not strictly correct, since she was led to the name by Theresa.

'You bet, we must,' said Henri. 'I gather you're not absolutely sure. We have to decide who's going to approach him to check he really is the person.'

'Yes. We have to be sure.'

'I think it should be me, Kim. If I tell him I'm linked to the OAS, I could offer my services in a new attempt.'

'Yes,' replied Kim. She was thinking hard on the next step. 'Assuming my information's correct and Jean Bertrand accepts your offer, what then? Presumably you will join his team?'

'Something like that.'

'I hardly know you, Henri – I mean Frédéric, I have to be sure you'll warn the authorities, even if it's at the last moment. I can't risk being associated with an actual attempt on the President's life.'

'I understand, Kim. I don't intend being an accomplice to murder either. I would do my best to stop it happening.'

Kim nodded. She was not going to share with him the other part of what she knew, that she'd learnt from Theresa that Henri's friend Leo was involved with Jean Bertrand.

'Here's a phone number you can reach me on,' said Henri, giving her the rue du Bac number. 'Only use it if you have to. Keep the call really short, Kim. Just tell me, in a simple code I'll understand, the time and place for us to meet.'

'Thanks. You already have my number at the *Tribune*. I'll wait to hear how it goes with Jean Bertrand.'

59

Henri let himself into the apartment, and said hello to the ever friendly housekeeper.

'How are you, Odette, any chance of some coffee?'

'But of course, Monsieur. There was a call while you were out but the woman on the other end rang off.'

'No problem, Odette.' He assumed she fed back all that sort of thing to the Maître.

Settling himself in a chair by the window overlooking the courtyard, he thought about his meeting in the Jardin du Luxembourg with Kim. What a woman, she was. How she could have dug out that information on the aircraft designer, he'd probably never know, assuming it was correct. He must check out Jean Bertrand right away. Even if it was, he wouldn't say anything to Maître Lacoste until just before the attack.

What about Pierre Sergent? He'd given his word to Kim not to speak to anyone. Even Noelle, strictly he shouldn't discuss it with her. Difficult, but something told him not to.

He must avoid making calls from the apartment. He'd walk down to the American library in the seventh arrondissement where they would have company directories and he could use the phone. How should he meet Jean Bertrand and put the question? He'd need a good excuse given he'd be identifying himself as Frédéric Barnier. Who was he?

He could say whatever would sound plausible. What about becoming an English professor in aeronautics, in Paris for the week, and wanting to talk about missile technology? He spoke the language perfectly, thanks to his English mother. He'd see if he could make a lunch date with Jean Bertrand.

It worked, they agreed to meet in a couple of days' time.

Seated together in Brasserie Lipp, a busy boulevard Saint-Germain outside the window, Henri realised he'd better not delay in disclosing who he really was. Pretending to be a professor in aeronautics to someone at the top of that profession would have made him look a fool in no time. He plunged straight in, explaining he was a Major in the Foreign Legion, arrested for his support of the Generals' putsch, adding a few invented words about how he'd escaped while being transferred between prisons.

'So you would be right to call me a fraud, Monsieur Bertrand. I'm in touch with the OAS but not an active member.'

Jean Bertrand looked surprised, to say the least. 'I have to say, you have my sympathy. However, I can't risk being associated with a fugitive from justice.'

Henri thought he detected a certain lack of conviction in the designer's reaction, and pressed on with the conversation.

'I wanted to meet you because someone mentioned you might have an answer to the terrible consequences of an independent Algeria.'

'You astonish me, Major. Certainly, I'm horrified by what is happening, but I don't have a solution. I wish I did.'

Again, Henri thought the reply did not sound sincere.

'Personally, I regard the actions of General de Gaulle as tantamount to genocide,' Henri said. 'He should be regarded as guilty of just that.'

He could see Jean Bertrand was thinking hard about what he'd just said.

'Major, could we continue this discussion somewhere more private?'

'I'd be pleased to do that,' said Henri, 'I'm free tonight.'

'Fine. I'm now going to enjoy the rest of this delicious lunch,' said the designer. 'This Alsatian beer is the best and reminds me of where I was brought up. Tell me about your military background, and we can return to the subject of the President at my club this evening.'

<hr />

Henri made his way to the Club Cercle Interallié, where the porter took him to Jean Bertrand, sitting in a corner of the members' smoking room.

It became clear from his opening comments that he'd used the afternoon to check out what Henri said at lunchtime. Evidently he was satisfied, as he launched into an impassioned plea to rid France of its President.

'What do you have in mind?' asked Henri, making sure there was no one who could overhear them. 'I agree with you absolutely. General de Gaulle must be removed before it's too late.'

Jean Bertrand looked at him with a penetrating stare, 'I have a plan to take out the President's car and escort party when he departs the Élysée Palace for his home. I'll be activating the attack when I see the convoy approaching. I could do with help to ensure the team understand my signals.'

Henri realised this was the moment. He must say yes if he was to learn the timing and location of the attempt. The authorities would have to wait until the last moment, if they were to catch everyone in the act. Arresting the suspects beforehand meant shorter sentences for the plotters, with no doubt some escaping the net.

'I'm ready to help if I can.' As he said it, realisation of the risk he'd be taking rushed up on him.

'There's to be a final briefing on Thursday,' said Jean Bertrand, 'With the leader of the commando we've assembled. His code name is Max. I'd like you to join the two of us.' He wrote an address on a sheet of the club notepaper. 'Keep your identity as Frédéric Barnier when you arrive. It's a restaurant, and the maître d' will take you to a room in the back.'

'How soon will the attempt be?' asked Henri.

'In five days' time. On the day, we should drive together to the site of the ambush, well in advance of when the President's car is expected. I'll show you the plan of attack when we meet.'

⟶▷◉◁⟵

Henri knew what he must do. He'd wait until the day before. It would take one short call on the scrambler to the number Maître Lacoste provided. Mention no names. Just the message, that there was to be an attempt on the President's life while he was being driven to Villacoublay airfield.

Making the call wasn't in itself a problem. In his book, taking a man's life for essentially political reasons was unprincipled. He had strong views about the likely consequences of Algerian independence, but that didn't alter the moral boundaries as he saw them.

The issue he was grappling with was how best he could preserve Noelle's safety, and his own. If the OAS were to learn that he deliberately prevented a carefully orchestrated attempt to end General de Gaulle's presidency, one likely to succeed, then the Organisation armée secrète would take its revenge.

Four days later, he reached for the scrambler phone.

60

Hôtel de Brienne, office of Pierre Messmer

'I have Maître Lacoste to see you, sir.' The secretary stood aside so that the lawyer could enter. The Armed Forces Minister rose from his desk, and they shook hands.

'I understand this is an urgent matter, Maître?' said Pierre Messmer.

'Yes, Minister. Agent Barnier, that's Major de Rochefort, telephoned me just now on the scrambler with a message.'

'Oh, yes. I remember. Our prisoner turned undercover man. What's the message?'

'There's to be an attempt on the life of the President.'

Pierre Messmer walked back behind his desk, waving to Maître Lacoste to take the chair opposite.

'Tell me about it, Maître.'

'Agent Barnier left a message on my secure line stating simply that there would be an assassination attempt tomorrow, when the President and Madame de Gaulle are driven from the Élysée to the airfield at Villacoublay, on their way to Colombey-les-Deux-Églises.'

'I see. What's the timing, and where will the attempt take place?'

'The President is due to leave the Élysée at 19:45 hours tomorrow evening. We don't know where the attack will be. The journey to Villacoublay takes about forty-five minutes.

It's likely the convoy of cars and motorcycles will have reached the suburbs before the attempt is made.'

'How reliable is the information, in your view?'

'Well, the fact that the notice is only twenty-four hours tends to indicate that the plan is firm and unlikely to be cancelled.'

'I agree,' said the Minister. 'I know well Major de Rochefort, from Libya in 1942. His record then and since is exemplary, until the putsch. If he says it's going to be then, we can expect it to happen.'

'Until we intervene,' said the Maître.

Pierre Messmer rose from his chair and moved to the window behind him, staring down into the courtyard. 'The President doesn't like his plans to be changed at the last moment. He's also an excellent tactician.'

'Can I ask what you mean by that, Minister?'

'Well, I'm now talking off the record, Maître Lacoste,' he said, turning to look the other directly in the eye.

'I understand, Minister.'

'The General wants to amend certain articles of the Constitution of the Fifth Republic. In particular, he wants the president to be elected directly by the people, by universal suffrage for a term of seven years.'

'And a further seven years if re-elected,' said the other.

'Yes. There will be a referendum to approve the General's recommended changes to the Constitution as early as two months from now.'

'I'm beginning to see,' said Maître Lacoste. 'If the President has just survived an attempt on his life, his chances of public approval of what he wants will be greatly enhanced.'

'Precisely, Maître. Of course, it would be inadvisable for him to take such a risk, but General de Gaulle is a fearless man and believes France has called him to office to lead it back to greatness. He needs the time to do that.'

'What about Madame de Gaulle?'

'She insists on being with her husband. She also is fearless.'

61

Colombey-les-Deux-Églises

Being aide-de-camp to the President and also his son-in-law placed him in a unique position. Colonel Alain de Boissieu picked up the telephone and listened. The relaxed aristocratic face changed from its usually happy demeanour to more of an ashen grey.

'How reliable is this?' he responded.

Having listened to the caller, he remarked, 'Not all the warnings and threats sound as reliable as that. I'll speak to the President,' he said, and put the phone down.

'What was that about, Alain?' said Madame de Gaulle. They were both in the kitchen of 'La Boisserie', the country home of the de Gaulle family.

'It's about our day trip to Paris tomorrow.'

'You look worried, Alain.'

'We've received information from an undercover agent in the OAS.'

'Oh?'

'There's to be an attempt on Père's life when we're driving back to the airfield tomorrow evening.'

'I didn't want to interrupt our holiday, in the first place,' said Yvonne de Gaulle, reacting nonchalantly as usual to that sort of news. 'Here, try this saucisse before we sit down to eat. It's from a local farmer.'

242

He never ceased to be amazed at the coolness in adversity of his wife's mother. Yvonne de Gaulle, medium height with her sleek black hair pressed down over the head, was utterly dedicated to her husband and their Catholic faith. When, after twelve years in retirement in the depths of the countryside, he told her of President Coty's persuasive voice in supplication for him to take over the reins of the nation once more, she hardly wavered. After their move to London in 1940, then to Algiers in 1943 and the threat to his Free French leadership from General Giraud, this was just another episode in their partnership of loyalty.

Just at that moment, the door from the back yard opened.

'This August heat gives you a thirst,' said the General. 'Alain, how about a bottle of Crémant de Bourgogne from the cold store?'

Alain disappeared down a stone staircase at the back of the kitchen, and was back in a flash. He wanted to be the one to tell the General about the call he'd just received.

The glasses were already on the table, and he poured out the sparkling wine, then turned to his father-in-law.

'Père, Pierre Messmer just called.'

'What does he want?'

'He says he has information of an attempt on you tomorrow.'

'Not another,' said the General as he finished drinking and put the glass down on the kitchen table.

'He says the hit is to be on the way back to Villacoublay in the evening. The source is reliable, he says. From a serving officer they have implanted in the OAS.'

The President said nothing for a moment, then looked across at his wife.

'We have to go up to Paris tomorrow, dear. It's an important Cabinet meeting, even though it's August. And a lunch you're invited to afterwards.'

'We could change the route back to the airfield,' said Madame de Gaulle. 'And the timing.'

'I don't like late changes in my arrangements,' said the President. 'In any case, our secret service is so leaky, the OAS would probably be tipped off even if we did change.'

'Yes, Père, I know you think that way,' said Alain de Boissieu. 'It's just that on this occasion, they will be determined to learn from previous attempts. Particularly if it's the same lot as at Pont-sur-Seine.'

The General looked hard at his son-in-law. 'We must be sure that everyone in the convoy is briefed on the possibility of an attack, particularly Sergeant Marroux. He is a master at getting us out of trouble.'

Alain de Boissieu wasn't going to argue about the skills of the President's chauffeur. Francis Marroux already proved he could handle the DS like no one else, coupled with his icy calm when in sudden danger.

'Well, I'm going to Fauchon after the lunch is over,' Yvonne de Gaulle said. 'To stock up for the weekend.'

Typical, thought Alain de Boissieu. He never wants to change, and she's happy to follow him, whatever.

62

Petit-Clamart, 10km south-west of Paris

Mist and rain made visibility unusually difficult for late August. Leo Beckendorf was in two minds where to position himself. The day before, when he and Jean Bertrand made their final reconnaissance, it was simple to see everything a full kilometre up the route nationale from Paris, down which the car and its escort would approach. Now you couldn't see clearly much beyond half that distance. Let's hope the new person he'd said would be with him would help.

The operation was well rehearsed. Half an hour before the President's convoy was due to depart the Élysée Palace, Jean would be waiting at the café by the traffic intersection for a telephone call from his lookout opposite the Élysée. As soon as he heard the President's car was under way, he would drive the short distance to the apartment building where Max and the team were waiting on the top floor. Having signalled to them to take up their positions, he would park his car up the road and stand on the sidewalk waiting for the convoy to appear.

Max and the Limp plus one other would climb into a Citroën ID. The Hungarians would pile into a yellow Estafette panel van, together with the *pieds noirs*. The Priest and two others would board a small Peugeot van to act as reserve.

The alert would be the wave of a newspaper from Jean Bertrand and his helper, a good way up the avenue de Petit-Clamart as that section of the RN 306 was known, as soon as the cavalcade came into sight. Leo studied it all with Jean, in the room behind the restaurant at the Panthéon, and on site. As rehearsed, all seemed close to fool-proof, at least to Jean. Leo wasn't so confident but was unable to improve the plan further, given resources and the timetable.

Élysée Palace

The two chauffeurs were running dusters over the wax polished bodywork of the two black Citroën DSs. A number of Gendarmerie motorcycle riders and their machines were parked close by. They were briefed of the possible attack, and the route via Porte de Chatillon and the RN 306 to Vélizy-Villacoublay was not confirmed until just before departure at 19:45 hours.

Colonel de Boissieu, aide-de-camp as well as son-in-law, came down the steps from the Palace entrance, accompanying Madame de Gaulle. 'Last opportunity to change to a different route,' he said in a fatalistic tone.

'Not a chance,' said the wife of the President. 'You know what he's like.'

The President followed. Still in uniform, the tallest of those accompanying him, the *képi* accentuating his height. At his shoulder was military doctor Jean-Denis Degos.

Gendarmerie Sergeant Francis Marroux, General de Gaulle's trusted chauffeur, opened the rear door of his DS for Yvonne de Gaulle to climb into the back, then went round the rear of the car to see the President into the seat beside her. Alain de Boissieu took the front passenger seat.

Suddenly there was a shout from the President's wife. 'La volaille. Did Fauchon deliver it, is it on board?'

'Yes, Madame,' replied Francis Marroux, 'it's wrapped in ice, in the back with the other things.'

The convoy moved forward, under the arch of the main gate, turning right into the rue Faubourg Saint-Honoré. The President and his wife relaxed in the comfort of the back seats, enjoying the immense legroom of the DS. After the drive to the airfield, it would be a short flight and then home. In the front, aide-de-camp de Boissieu was on full alert.

Few spectators saw them off. One person in an apartment high up and facing the gate, reached for the telephone and dialled a number.

⇒⟩⟩⟩ ⟨⟨⟨⇐

Leo's trained mind went over everything yet again. None of the commando knew about him. Whatever the outcome, he would be in his car and away as soon as the firing ceased, that's the way Jean Bertrand wanted it.

Max and his commando were all confident, that's what Jean told him in their last conversation. Let them be confident. His doubts persisted. The weather for a start. Visibility was an essential factor in managing an ambush. Today was typical of the northern highlands of Vietnam, wet foggy conditions. A determined, fearless adversary, including that chauffeur who'd driven his boss through the bomb blast at Pont-sur-Seine, that's whom they were up against.

Leaving his Peugeot further down the route from the traffic junction, he positioned the car up on the verge, out of range of light machine gun fire. Walking back, Leo found a loading platform from which he would have a clear line of sight when the action began.

Eight o'clock, the cavalcade should be on its way. No chance of seeing Jean up the far end of the road, not in these conditions. Could the commando see him? There was Max's Citroën ID in the side street, ready to pull out and block the escape. Beyond, the yellow Renault Estafette stood along the kerbside. Maybe they could make out Jean up the road, through their binoculars, in spite of the fog and drizzle. Hopefully, the new person would help.

The wait was the worst part.

⋅⋙◉◉⋘⋅

Henri didn't expect any presidential cavalcade to appear. Nevertheless, he must be ready in case his message to Maître Lacoste hadn't been acted on. Jean Bertrand was worried about the visibility when they arrived on site, and they agreed Henri would position himself closer to the commando and relay Bertrand's signal.

If the President did stick to the original plan, Henri knew that any delay in signalling to Max in these weather conditions would make the task of the commando harder. He would allow some interval between seeing Bertrand's signal and making his own.

⋅⋙◉◉⋘⋅

Colonel de Boissieu was encouraging Sergeant Marroux to get a move on. Where was it going to happen, or was it just a threat? You never knew.

Over Pont Saint-Michel, onto the Left Bank, they headed. It was unlikely any attempt would be made inside Paris. Outside, the lousy weather wouldn't help the attackers.

Through the Latin Quarter, along the avenue du Général Leclerc, then a right fork into the avenue Jean Moulin. High risk from now on as they drove rapidly down the route nationale. If it was going to happen, it would be in the next ten minutes.

It was still a shock. Just before the crossroads in the suburb of Petit-Clamart, a burst of gunfire from an Estafette van with its back open, other gunmen jumping into the road.

'Get down, Père,' the Colonel shouted, turning round to face his parents-in-law. They didn't even flinch. Suddenly he saw a Citroën ID approaching from the right, out of a side street. There was the thwack and zing of bullets hitting the car. A second shout from his son-in-law, General de Gaulle now pulled his wife down with him, just as a couple of shots smashed the rear screen into splinters.

Still travelling fast, Gendarme Sergeant Marroux wrestled with the steering wheel, the offside tyres blown flat by the shooting. The Citroën's hydropneumatic suspension was working overtime.

⋅►■◉ ◉■◄⋅

Leo spotted the lead car just before the shattering clatter of automatic fire burst out. There they were. Two black Citroën DSs appearing out of the haze, two motorcycles right behind them. He crouched down on the loading table. More shooting as the rear doors of the Estafette were thrown open. It looked like two *pieds noirs* jumping out, opening fire with their MAT-49's, the Hungarians firing from the rear of the vehicle.

The front DS was really travelling, the President's car pressing on dead straight into the intersection. It was going faster than they were expecting. The second DS was closing the gap from behind, as the gendarmes on the motorcycles went for their revolvers.

Leo could see Max pulling out, but the leader of the commando didn't make it in time. The President's car never let up. Still moving fast, it was just past him as the ID reached the centre of the road.

What the hell was that? A Panhard passed from behind Leo, approaching the convoy from the other direction. A family car by the look of it, parents in the front and children in the back. The President's DS started to swerve violently, almost colliding with the family coming towards it.

How did they miss one another?

Leo watched the DS hurtling towards him, its offside tyres flat, the steel belting of the Michelin X tyres hanging onto the rims as it kept coming.

Jumping down beside the platform, he saw Max's ID was following the two DSs. There was a burst of glass from the rear screen of the President's car, shattered by a revolver shot from the Limp as he leant out of the ID's front passenger window.

As the first DS swept past Leo, there were President and Madame de Gaulle crouched down in the back seat. Were they hit? Surely they must be after that volume of gunfire. The two gendarmes on their motorcycles had closed up on the DSs. The cavalcade was accelerating, must be doing 120 kph. That chauffeur just pressed on, regardless of the state of his tyres.

Max's ID was falling back, not having the pace of the DSs.

Time for Leo to pull out. As he ran to his car, he was conscious of a figure running up behind him on the other side of the road. Who was that, moving as though shadowing him? He looked familiar, somehow. Just as he arrived at the Peugeot, the other called out.

'Give me a lift, Leo.'

He thought he recognised the voice. It couldn't be, not in a situation like this, madness, it was an illusion. Henri de Rochefort, what the hell?

Leo saw Henri coming across the road, joining him as he was opening the car door.

'I've got to get out of here,' Leo heard his old schoolfriend say. He was too surprised to reply. They both jumped into the car, turning off the route nationale where Leo knew roadblocks would be set up, and headed back into Paris by another route.

'Put on RTF,' said Leo, as he gunned the Peugeot out of trouble.

The announcer was already interrupting the programme with news of the attempt on the lives of the President and his wife. The latest from the airfield at Villacoublay was that both General and Madame de Gaulle were unharmed after an attempt on their lives on the route national 306 as it passed through Petit-Clamart.

'Failure,' muttered Leo.

'I'm surprised it even happened,' said Henri.

Leo looked at his old friend with an odd expression. 'What do you mean by that?'

'I was expecting them to take a different route,' said Henri.

There was silence for a bit, while Leo navigated through wet side streets back into Paris.

'Were you part of the commando?' Leo suddenly said.

'I'll have to think before I answer that question,' said Henri. 'Were you something to do with it, Leo?'

'I'll have to think how to answer that, also.'

For the first time, they looked at one another, and grinned.

63

Élysée Palace

The deep-throated grunt of her office phone surprised Noelle, given how late in the evening it was. The Cabinet Secretary sounded agitated, telling her to wait for him, he was on his way. In the meantime, would she switch on the television in his office.

Although not surprised, she was still shocked. A failed attempt on the President's life. No casualties reported so far. Astonishing, that was her immediate reaction. Very quickly her mind moved to Henri. To what extent was he involved? If he knew about it, surely he would have warned the authorities. At the least, wouldn't the President's route to the airfield have been changed?

In no time at all, the Cabinet Secretary burst in, throwing off his raincoat. She looked up at him. Impeccably dressed in black tie and wearing his *smoking*. Evidently, he'd been torn away from some smart soirée where a dinner jacket was de rigueur.

'I'm so glad you're working late, Mademoiselle, we have a press release to prepare.'

'Of course, Cabinet Secretary.' She turned down the television.

'This story needs to be handled delicately. There's likely to be a referendum in a couple of months on General de Gaulle's proposed changes to the Constitution, and we should use his survival to best advantage in the French press.'

'Understood,' said Noelle. 'I suggest we highlight the President's and Madame de Gaulle's heroism.

'Definitely. How are we going to handle the rest of the world's press?'

'The wire services will be on to it already,' said Noelle. 'I'd like to speak first to my Cambodian friend Kim Cho, at the *Paris Tribune*. She has a direct line into the *New York Herald Tribune* and would use anything we give her in a more detailed piece for publication over there.

'Good idea. Play it carefully. She must understand we're giving her special treatment in exchange for a positive slant on General de Gaulle and his importance for the future of France.'

64

Kim joined her colleagues on the news floor, gathered around the teleprinters as they clattered out the story. The President and his wife were unharmed, a miracle given the number of bullet holes in their car. The chauffeur had excelled himself, again. No serious casualties and no bodies left behind by the attackers, all of whom escaped. An intensive manhunt was already under way.

No doubt Henri would call her when he could. It was for him to keep to his part of the bargain, giving her an exclusive on his side of the story. That would take time, weeks perhaps. Assuming he made contact with the organiser of the attack, following what she told him, why didn't he tell the authorities the attempt on the President was about to happen? Maybe he wasn't a double agent after all? Or perhaps they didn't believe him.

Her thoughts were interrupted, someone calling out her name.

'Coming,' she shouted, walking rapidly back to her desk.

'Hi, Kim, it's Noelle Mercure. I'm calling you from the Élysée, in my new job.'

'Yes, I heard, congratulations.'

'You'll have heard the news?'

'Yes, just now. Sounds like a miracle, he and his wife surviving unscathed.'

'You're right.' A pause on the line, then Noelle said, 'Look Kim, we'll be issuing a general press release tonight. Are you interested in something extra for the *New York Herald Tribune*? We want to promote General de Gaulle again in North America, this could be the opportunity.'

'Sounds interesting. I'll talk to them now. It's about teatime over there, so we have three hours to get copy to them.'

'Great. There's a café in rue Cambon, close to Chanel. Could we meet there in an hour's time? It's on my doorstep, and I can dash out and discuss the story with you.'

'Fine, see you then.'

65

Noelle drafted the general press release, and the Cabinet Secretary added some details she wasn't yet aware of. She told him she was about to meet Kim Cho.

'She'll want to write it as an investigative journalist would,' said Noelle. 'I'm going to feed her with our suggested content.'

'Give me a flavour,' he said.

Noelle consulted the notes in front of her.

'There'll be emphasis on the split in French public opinion over independence for Algeria, opposing views held passionately on each side. That the General is the one person who's been able to grip the issue, going the route the United States has pressed for all along. It's inevitable that the remaining weeks before completion are fraught with desperate action by the losing side. Importantly, French people are horrified by the brutality and widespread killings of the OAS, and have turned to the President of the Republic to protect them and lead them to safety. Finally, that the elimination of the costly Algerian war, together with firm government, will open the door to growth in the economy, employment and the value of the franc. I'll recommend she ends by highlighting the resolute style of General de Gaulle, that he is a brave man, and so is his wife.'

'Sounds good to me,' he said. 'Tell your friend Kim Cho that this text is not to appear tomorrow in the *Paris Tribune*. We can't risk the French press claiming that the *Paris Tribune* has preferential treatment over the French titles.'

66

Paris, rue du Bac

The buzzer sounded, it would be Maître Lacoste. He'd just called to say he was on the way round.

Henri let him in. Now, perhaps, he would hear why the President's convoy stuck to its itinerary in spite of the warning.

He could see the lawyer was in a good mood, one of those rare occasions.

'Major de Rochefort, congratulations. You delivered on your obligation to us. First you found out when the attack was to take place, then you warned us.'

'Thank you. But why wasn't the President's trip cancelled, or the route to the airfield changed?'

'My friend, we're not dealing with an ordinary man. General de Gaulle is fearless, so is Yvonne de Gaulle. He also distrusts the secret services, and probably the Justice Department. Pierre Messmer, Armed Forces Minister, knew it was for real. I went to see him right after your call.'

'So, didn't the Minister pass on the warning?'

'I'm sure he did.' Maître Lacoste stopped, evidently deciding whether to add something. 'Major, not only is General de Gaulle a brave man, he's also politically astute, even though he hates party politics.'

'Meaning?'

'His survival of the attempt on his life will improve his approval ratings across the French electorate, and that's particularly important right now.'

'Oh, why?'

'He's going to seek approval to change the election process for the President of the Fifth Republic. He wants the people to elect the president directly, for a period of seven years and a further seven years if re-elected.'

'Fourteen years in total if he is re-elected,' said Henri.

'Exactly. The General is dedicated towards re-building France and making it great again. He needs the public's support to give him the time to do so. He doesn't want his term of office to be interfered with by Parliament.'

'Yes, I see the logic,' said Henri. 'Dangerous logic, but now he's survived, I guess it will pay off.'

'Clearly he thinks it will, said Maître Lacoste.' A pause. 'It so happens that he's learnt about you. That could mean a pardon and return to a normal life.'

This was music to Henri's ears. He just nodded, smiling.

The other added, 'In the meantime, I presume your position in the OAS hasn't been compromised?'

'It shouldn't have been,' said Henri. Pierre Sergent knew I was on to something, that an attempt was being planned by an outsider. I can now tell him I was on the case, even though it was a failure.'

'All being well, therefore, you would look out for any follow-up attempt,' said Maître Lacoste. 'That raises an important point. The police believe they will pick up most of the attackers. If, under interrogation, they name the person behind the attempt, we'll be on to him. If they don't –'

Henri interjected, 'You will ask me who he is.'

'Yes. But I'm a realist, Major. That could endanger your position in the OAS.'

'Or worse,' said Henri, with thoughts that Roger Degueldre could be dispatched to eliminate him.

Henri felt he should mention something else. 'Maître, you may not have heard but Mademoiselle Mercure accepted an offer to work at the Élysée. I guess I should have told you before.'

'No, I hadn't heard. How could that happen when she's doing work for the OAS?'

'I told Pierre Sergent that she wanted to terminate her OAS relationship.'

'Oh, and what did he say?'

'No problem. No doubt he's hoping she might be a source of inside information.'

'Quite so.' The Maître hesitated for a moment. 'Watch out, Major de Rochefort. You and your friend will be walking a difficult path, be on guard all the time.'

67

Avenue de Neuilly

The decision whether to tell Pierre Sergent that he was present at the attempt kept Henri awake for much of the night. Now, as he spoke the password 'Narvik' and entered the building, he was still unsure. If he said he was, then he'd be asked for the brains behind the attack. If he didn't, he'd be seen to have failed to identify the mystery aircraft designer. The latter explanation wouldn't cover him in glory, but was the safest.

Pierre Sergent's table and part of the floor were covered with newspapers, as Henri walked into the room. Two days since the attempt at Petit-Clamart, it was clear that a massive manhunt by the police and security services was under way.

'Henri, come in, what do you make of all this?'

He helped himself to coffee from the flask. 'It confirms there's an assassin outside the OAS who wants the President done away with.'

'Yes. Are you any closer to finding him?'

'I was screening all senior people in the aircraft industry to arrive at a shortlist. The one we're looking for will be keeping out of sight while the hunt's on. Unless of course one of the commando identifies him to the police, and that'll be the end of it.'

'If that's going to happen, it's likely to be in the first couple of weeks.'

'I agree,' said Henri.

David Longridge

Pierre Sergent sat back in his chair, deep in thought. 'If they don't catch him, there's a good chance he'll want to try again.'

'Probably. The person concerned doesn't lack motivation. It's the execution that leaves something to be desired.'

'Must have been a close thing. My guess is the poor visibility had something to do with it.'

'And that same chauffeur, the gendarme from the previous attempt. Francis Marroux, he's their hero.'

'Did you read what happened inside the car?' Pierre Sergent pulled a copy of *Le Figaro* off the floor. 'The General's son-in-law, sitting in the front passenger seat, says he swung round and shouted to the President and his wife to get down on the floor. They ignored him until another attacking vehicle opened fire and the aide-de-camp shouted at them again. They did then crouch down just as bullets shattered the rear screen.'

'What about Yvonne de Gaulle's remark when they arrived at the airfield?' He paused. 'All she said was, "I hope the *volailles en gelée* in the luggage compartment are all right." They were from Fauchon.'

Pierre Sergent was not amused. 'Another bloody awful missed opportunity. How can he survive two such powerful hits? This can only boost his popularity.'

68

'Well done, darling, you've survived your first week at the Élysée.' Henri took Noelle's coat, and kissed her.

'What a week. I'm shattered.'

'There must have been panic when you heard of the assassination attempt.'

'They'd all gone home, but my boss came back. It could have been worse, the release went out to the French press and the wire services within an hour of the news.'

Henri still wasn't going to tell Noelle that he'd tracked down the assassin, nor that he'd been present at the attempt. No way she could be told that, now she was part of the President's staff.

Noelle helped herself to a drink and settled down beside him on the sofa. 'I've made friends with one or two of the Élysée staff. There isn't much tittle-tattle, everyone's on guard. But I did see something odd.'

'Oh, what was that?'

'I know it sounds ridiculous, but I read it in a scribbled note I saw on my boss's desk.'

'On the Cabinet Secretary's desk, who was it from?'

'Maurice Papon, passing on something the Sûreté picked up from an undercover source.'

'And?'

'That an official in the Ministry of Finance was collaborating with the assassin.'

'My God.' Henri thought fast. Jean Bertrand told him he had a mole somewhere close to the President. Could this be it?

'Everyone knows there are *pied noir* supporters embedded everywhere,' he said. 'That's not the same thing as collaborating with people out to kill the President.'

'You said it,' muttered Noelle, 'Maurice Papon didn't give a name.' She paused, remembering something. 'There was a codeword the person was known by.'

'Codeword, what was that?'

'B12'

Henri nodded. He didn't mention it, but that sounded like the format of code names he'd seen allocated inside the OAS. An OAS sympathiser in the Ministry of Finance? That didn't seem impossible.

69

Justine arrived at the second special meeting of Prime Minister Debré's security committee. The first was the morning after the attempt on the President's life, when it was too soon for any developments in the hunt for the attackers. Now a week after the attempt, everyone hoped there would be some news.

Michel Debré opened the meeting by saying he would ask Maurice Papon and Jacques Foccart for the latest information they had on the Petit-Clamart attack. He turned first to the head of the Paris police, Justine's eyes also falling upon the man she most disliked.

Maurice Papon shuffled his notes, then looked up.

'We're working on the assumption that this was the work of the OAS. The three vehicles used in the attack have been recovered, all were stolen. Five hundred police and detectives are assigned to the task. They are visiting every café and other establishment in the Petit-Clamart area, asking for suspicious activity and descriptions of people who came in to make telephone calls.' Maurice Papon paused, probably for effect, thought Justine. 'We already have a lead.'

The room went silent, except for the Boulle pedestal clock ticking away close to Justine.

'A Monsieur Perrin received a call forty-five minutes before the attack, in a café close to the crossroads where the ambush took place. He put down the receiver immediately and left the premises. This call was probably from a lookout at the Élysée. The name Perrin would be an alias, but is likely to have been used more than once.'

Justine watched for reactions around the table. The thought struck her. Could there have been an insider, someone at the Élysée passing information on the President's movements to the attackers?

Maurice Papon continued. 'We're bringing in known OAS associates for questioning. I would hope we'll start making arrests in the coming week. When the interrogations start, one arrest should lead to another.'

Next came Jacques Foccart, the Prime Minister's adviser and head of the SAC, General de Gaulle's own security service. To Justine, here was the antithesis of the previous speaker. Jacques was her closest confidant in the room. She bet he would have his finger on the pulse.

'I agree with Monsieur Papon that the attack has the hallmark of the OAS. However, the SAC's contacts with that world have heard nothing indicating it was organised by them. That doesn't mean there weren't members of the attacking force who have worked before for them. The impression I have is that the brains behind the attempt were those of an independent mind. We should remember that the inquiry into Pont-sur-Seine never uncovered who organised that attempt.'

Jacques Foccart waited, looking around the room. 'It could be the same person, and I have no idea who that might be.' He paused again. 'If that's the case, we're dealing with an utterly committed fanatic, who could try again. I'd expect that the highly competent investigators of the Paris police will find the would-be assassin, but it could take time.'

As he added that last sentence, he gave Justine a glance for long enough for her to catch in it the makings of a smile. She sensed he didn't like Maurice Papon either.

After the meeting, Jacques Foccart took Justine aside.

'I think we should have a conversation, Mademoiselle, about one or two things.'

'Fine, Monsieur Foccart,' said Justine.

'Could I suggest we fix a date for lunch, this week?'

'I can do Thursday or Friday.'

'Excellent. I'm a special adviser to the BAO, that's the Banque de l'Afrique Occidentale. I'm allowed to use their private dining rooms. I'll check when there's one free, and leave a message for you at the Assembly. It's in avenue Messines, number nine.'

It was amazing, the doors that opened to you when you became a deputy, thought Justine for the umpteenth time as she was welcomed by the security guard at the entrance to the bank. Inside, the walls of the banking hall showed scenes from commercial life in France's west African colonies. Accompanied to a private lift, Justine was happy she'd dressed smartly. The anthracite grey suit was Schiaparelli, a gift from when she modelled for them, the large black buttons down the front were by Giacometti.

Jacques Foccart was waiting for her in the small dining room. 'Good Lord,' he exclaimed, hands wide apart. 'Did I ever see such a beautiful woman so superbly dressed.'

'Oh,' said Justine, 'You certainly know how to flatter.'

They both laughed, as a waiter poured out a *coupe* of champagne for each of them, and Foccart started to talk about the BAO and banking in strange places like Bangui and Ouagadougou.

'I know very little about French West Africa.' Justine surprised him by saying her family was Jewish, that they'd fled from Berlin to Bordeaux in the thirties.

'I'm increasingly involved out there for the Prime Minister,' said Jacques Foccart. 'We have to protect our trade with these countries after they become independent states.'

Justine nodded, just a faint smile. What was coming next?

'Now, Mademoiselle Justine. Please take the following at its face value, no strings attached.'

She nodded again, watching him carefully, silent, waiting.

'You have a friend, Noelle Mercure, whom I met a few months ago in Algiers. She's now Press Officer at the Élysée."

'Yes, that's right.'

'Noelle Mercure is a very interesting person. I think highly of her. However, her close friend Henri de Rochefort is involved in some sort of undercover work I won't go into here.'

Justine was silent. Clearly, Jacques had picked up the trail on Henri from one of his SAC people, probably an agent embedded in the OAS.

'My information is that the OAS Delta Force commander has decided that both Noelle Mercure and Henri de Rochefort should be bumped off for double-crossing the OAS.'

'Oh God.' Justine shuddered at the realisation that Henri could be in such peril, and Noelle.'

'I was wondering whether you could warn her, I think it would come better from you?'

'Of course. Who is this Delta Force commander?'

'Lieutenant Roger Degueldre, a formidable character. He's wanted for murder, used to be in the Legion paras.'

'Do you know where to find him?'

'The police have a search warrant out on him. His base is Madrid, with General Salan. He's organised multiple murders in Algeria, and has started bombing targets in Paris.'

'Okay, I'll warn Noelle Mercure. I'm not in direct touch with Henri de Rochefort.'

'Quite so. They're both in the firing line. Let me know what help you need. The SAC has some hit men of its own.'

'The *barbouzes*. I heard about them. They gave the OAS a bit of their own medicine in Algeria.'

'It's been a ruthless struggle,' he said. 'Let's hope it's coming to an end.'

There was a pause while the waiter cleared their plates, and served a tarte Tatin.

Justine's mind drifted in another direction. She'd been searching for someone to share a sensitive subject with, a friend who didn't harbour anti-Jewish feelings. Jacques Foccart never expressed any to her, so why not him?

'Jacques, there's something else, totally different, something I'd like to take you into my confidence on.'

'Oh, what's that?

'Have you had much to do with Maurice Papon?'

He didn't answer the question directly, just saying, 'Well, we both have to listen to him on the Prime Minister's special committee.'

Justine smiled, 'I mentioned to you earlier that I have Jewish parents, that we settled in Bordeaux in the thirties.'

'Yes. I heard you. I was thinking, there must be a story behind that.'

'There's a lot of it, and I'm not going to bore you. I was caught in La Rafle, rounded up in Paris during that night in July '42. I was rescued from the Drancy transit camp by a British agent, a girl-friend from our days at the *lycée* in Bordeaux.'

'That sounds hairy,' he said.

'I wanted to ask whether you knew much about the deportation of Jews from France during the occupation.'

'I know something about it. It's still not a subject raised in general conversation in this country.'

'You're right' said Justine. 'There was the *épuration*, punishing the collaborators, but after that the General wanted the Communists, Gaullists, Socialists to work together towards a new future for France.'

Jacques Foccart just nodded.

'He chose those he wanted in the top positions in the civil service and military. Most were those who supported him through the war. Some were influential in the Vichy administration but had changed sides to join him.'

'Ah,' he said, 'maybe in that last category, you would put Maurice Papon?'

'I would,' Justine whispered.

'I'm not sure what role he played.'

'Let me tell you. At Vichy, Maurice Papon was in charge of transport and fuel rationing, as well as the confiscation of property and all matters concerning Jews.'

'I follow you.' Jacques Foccart's interest appeared to be growing, as he leant towards Justine, 'Presumably that's where you come in?'

'Yes. Because of my own experience, I've taken an interest in the deportation and who was responsible for it. I discovered that in Bordeaux alone, two thousand Jews including their children were shipped to Auschwitz and other camps.'

'That, I didn't know.' His face showed surprise.

'Maurice Papon was Secretary General of the Gironde prefecture at the time. It was his responsibility, his work.'

'My God. I see where you're coming from.'

'My parents escaped to England, with the help of the British.' Justine paused. 'Jacques, I'd like to see Maurice Papon removed from his post as police chief in Paris, at least as a first step.'

Jacques Foccart was silent, in thinking mode.

He then sat back, hands behind his head as the waiter poured out the coffee.

'I don't see how you can remove him, while General de Gaulle wants him where he is.'

Justine was ready for that response. 'I think he should remove himself. You don't have to go back twenty years. Maurice Papon committed a crime against humanity only months ago.'

'Oh, did he?' He seemed to be genuinely surprised.

'I belong on the left, Jacques, even though I'm with you on Michel Debré's committee. You remember that march of the Algerians from the suburbs, into the centre of Paris?'

'Of course. The FLN were behind it.'

'My union friends tell me close to two hundred of the demonstrators were slaughtered on Papon's instructions. Many bodies were recovered from the Seine in the days after.'

'I did hear rumours. Neither the OAS nor, I admit, the SAC wanted to know about it.'

'That's a good honest reply, Jacques.'

'Have you any ideas of what to do?'

Justine smiled. 'Not really. I don't think a public demonstration against Maurice Papon would achieve anything.'

'So?'

'I'm searching for a way of threatening to disgrace him.'

Jacques Foccart appeared to gasp, surprising Justine.

'You're being very open with your thoughts,' he finally said.

'I like you Jacques, I trust you.'

'Are you sure? Remember, I'm in charge of General de Gaulle's own secret service, that's what the SAC really is.'

'Be that as it may. I decided to bring you into my confidence. Bear in mind I'm a deputy with close contacts on the hard left. I could be useful to you one day.'

He smiled, remaining silent.

'Jacques, here's an idea,' she said, leaning towards him.

70

Paris, Troika restaurant

Noelle knew from Jansson's call that the Russians were on to something, and would be twisting her arm like before. The maître d' took her to an alcove in the far corner of the restaurant, like the last time she dined there with them.

'Mademoiselle Mercure, how lovely to see you again,' said Evgeni as he leapt up to greet her. Jansson also rose, although not with the same aplomb.

'A lot has happened since then, my friends,' said Noelle.

The first vodka of the evening arrived as the violinist started into a soulful 'Kalinka-Malinka'.

They exchanged news, the Russians asking about her new role at the Élysée Palace.

When they came to the attempt on the President's life, Jansson said sternly, 'We were greatly relieved that the attempt failed. You know that First Secretary Khrushchev and General de Gaulle have a strong working relationship.'

Noelle nodded, and smiled.

'Mademoiselle,' said Evgeni in his usual friendly style, 'We would like to raise a sensitive subject.'

'Oh, why not?' said Noelle, after wondering when he was going to get round to it.

'It's something no one in Paris talks about,' Jansson added.

'I'm fascinated to hear. In this city nothing is out of bounds,' Noelle responded, laughing. She loved sparring with these two.

Jansson's Nordic blue eyes were at their largest, dead still. 'One of our people has defected to the West.'

Noelle remained silent. Spies defecting to the other side happened from time to time, so what?

'During his debriefing by the CIA in Washington, the defector has implicated certain operatives in the French secret service.'

'Embarrassing,' said Noelle.

'The story is that President Kennedy has warned President de Gaulle who has dispatched a trusted official to cross-examine "Martel". That's the code name the French have given to the defector.'

There was a pause. What did this have to do with her?

Evgeni interjected. 'Information sourced from Martel by the Americans flows to Paris via the French head of station in Washington. We suspect that the station head is massaging the information so as to challenge General de Gaulle's policy on Algerian independence. You're aware, I think, that your secret service is full of *Algérie française* sympathisers.'

'So I'm told,' said Noelle.

'What is being implied is that Moscow has been helping General de Gaulle develop his policy on Algeria.'

'I see,' she said.

Evgeni continued. 'Nothing is further from the truth.' He paused, looking intensely at Noelle. 'Nevertheless, our fear is that the people implicated by Martel may be plotting another attempt to assassinate the President.'

Ah, that's no doubt where I come in. 'And you want me to get involved?'

'Mademoiselle, you are our only contact in the Élysée Palace. We want you to try and identify anyone who could have that in mind.'

'I doubt I would be able to tell who could fall into that category. Anyone with secret service links is going to keep quiet about their personal feelings on Algeria.' She wondered whether they knew something she didn't. Then it came.

'Mademoiselle,' Jansson said, almost in a whisper. 'We know you have a relationship with Major de Rochefort.'

Noelle was not surprised at this. By now, that fact should have been deduced by them.

Jansson went on. 'We also know that Major de Rochefort's sister is in the secret service, that she works at the *piscine*.'

So that was it.

'All we are suggesting,' said Evgeni, 'is that you use this connection to help find out who in government could be part of another plot to do away with your President.'

<hr />

First thing the following morning, the effects of the vodka worn off, Noelle thought through the direction the KGB were pointing her in.

Where would it lead her? If she was caught passing information to the Soviet Union, could she be charged with treason? She reached for her copy of *Larousse*. She was a French citizen. The test would be whether she was 'delivering to a foreign power information that undermines the fundamental interests of the nation and compromises the secrecy of national defence'.

Trying to prevent another attempt on the President could hardly be that.

Alternatively, would she be aiding and abetting the enemy?

She was tempted to argue that the USSR wasn't the enemy of France. But she wasn't that much of a fool.

Also, she was a state employee and committed to secrecy in her employment conditions. She could live with that.

What would Henri think of all this? No reason he should know, unless she was caught.

Noelle would invite Françoise to lunch, and seek her advice.

71

Paris, Brasserie Vagenende

The restaurant was close to the market in the rue de Seine where she shopped for Henri, easy for Françoise coming in from the 20th arrondissement. Décor was in the Belle Époque style, giant mirrors framed in dark polished fruit wood, the food traditional French cuisine. Noelle looked around the tables, some occupied by the older generation, probably regular clients, others by tourists fascinated by the ambience, above all the mechanical piano with its giant brass trumpets.

There she was, giving Noelle a little wave as she glided over to the table. They'd only met the one time before, when the plan was drawn up for Henri to escape from prison. They were twins and the likeness was easy to see.

Henri was the common thread in their conversation, Noelle expressing her appreciation for what Françoise had achieved with Justine in extricating Henri from Fresnes.

After the main course was cleared away, she edged her way towards the point. They were on the same side as far as the President's policy on Algeria was concerned. Whatever Henri was doing for the government, he would have the President's safety in mind after the attempt at Petit-Clamart. Noelle's work at the Élysée exposed her to some of the thoughts of her colleagues, in particular she was hearing about a Russian defector to the United States. It was thought the head of station at the French embassy in Washington might be

David Longridge

feeding back information on a conspiracy implicating secret
service people in another assassination attempt.

This was dangerous ground. Françoise might take offence
at the insinuation of treachery among her colleagues.

The contrary was the case. 'I know about the Russian
defection,' Françoise said. 'I can't think of anyone that close
to the President, who would be a party to anything like that.
Certainly, I have colleagues who are furious over what the
General is doing over Algeria. I will keep a sharp lookout,
especially towards those with links to the Communist world.'
She paused. 'Now, Noelle, I must raise something different.
Justine tells me you and Henri are in danger.'

'Oh, that's not news.'

'Maybe not. But in this case, I'm told someone who does
that kind of thing is out to kill you.'

Noelle was suddenly still, silent.

'His name is Roger Degueldre,' said Françoise. 'He heads
up an OAS unit called the Delta Force.'

'I've heard of him, real brute of a man.'

'I'm prepared to help you any way I can.'

'Yes, he did mention that.'

'I'm in touch with Henri, of course. I'll warn him, but I
wanted to let you know, directly.'

'Of course, I'll tell Henri, at once. It's great of you to offer
your help.'

72

Paris Préfecture, Île de la Cité

The lights were on late inside the department of Commandant Bouvier. It was ten days since the attempt at Petit-Clamart.

Maurice Bouvier sat with some of his criminal detection team, around a large table. Shirt sleeves rolled up, his large forehead and receding hairline glistened with sweat. August evenings in Paris were often hot, and today the atmosphere seemed intolerably stuffy. Other members of the team came and went with teletype messages from all over France. The largest manhunt anyone could remember was in full swing.

The first break came when a young subordinate approached the Commandant, with due deference.

'Excuse me, sir, our officers made some inquiries nearby the address of a female, a secretary, living where one of the cars was dumped. A neighbour remembered seeing a yellow Estafette parked close by, like the one used in the attack.'

Bouvier sat back in his chair, then said, 'Anything else observed?'

'Yes. The brother of the secretary uses the address for meetings, and one of the guys who comes round has a limp.'

Bouvier and the others working around him, all looked up. From the description, this could be one of the attackers. In the long list of suspects was one they knew of as 'the Limp'.

'It gets better, sir,' said the young man. 'The female told our officers she was due to meet her brother at the local library earlier this evening. The team staked out the place and just picked up the brother.'

'And?' said Bouvier.

'They found evidence on him, showing he was in the commando at Petit-Clamart. He won't explain himself, won't cooperate.'

'Okay, bring him here first thing in the morning,' said Bouvier. To his team, he said. 'Tomorrow could be a big day. Go home and get some sleep.'

<hr/>

Maurice Bouvier was right about the day ahead of them. As he walked into the department the next morning, he was met by an anxious assistant who'd just put the phone down.

'Sir, we just heard from one of the checkpoints set up on the routes out of Paris.'

'Heard what?'

'A man they stopped just started to talk, and kept going. He admitted being at the ambush at Petit-Clamart, and has given us the names of several of those in the commando.'

'Splendid,' said Bouvier. 'Any indication of who was the leader behind the scene?'

'He just said the boss was called "Didier" but didn't know his real name.'

'Right, let's get the whole team round this desk in half an hour. Top priority is to pick up all of those named.'

73

Hôtel Matignon

The Prime Minister asked Maurice Papon to update everyone.

Justine noted with distaste that the head of the Sûreté looked very pleased with himself.

'I'm delighted to report that we have commenced making arrests, and have five of the terrorists in the bag including the man who led the commando,' said Maurice Papon.

'Congratulations,' said Michel Debré. 'I understand that the brains behind the attempt is known by these people as "Didier". Is there any indication yet as to who this Didier is?'

'Not specifically, but a trail is opening up,' said Maurice Papon. Everyone's gaze was fixed on him. 'From those interrogated, we've learnt that Didier's in his late thirties, and is an officer working at the Air Ministry in boulevard Victor.'

Justine stopped breathing, probably everyone in the room did. Not a movement, not a sound. How could the would-be assassin be a serving air force officer?

'Commandant Bouvier, leading the criminal detection team at the Préfecture, pieced together a description and is identifying all those fitting the profile.' Maurice Papon paused, no doubt for effect, thought Justine. 'I hope to have more information by tomorrow.'

Something was stirring in Justine's mind. That day when Kim asked her and Françoise to meet urgently at the Café Flore. Kim told them she knew who planned the attempt last year at Pont-sur-Seine. That the same person could be plotting another attempt and Kim was wanting to contact Henri, to warn him. Did she do so? Where was he now?

Her attention was brought back to the meeting, Maurice Papon adding that when the likely culprit was known, there would be no disclosure of the person's identity until a charge was brought.

The Boulle pedestal clock chimed and, with a start, she remembered she'd arranged to meet her friend Josephine Baker.

74

Préfecture, Île de la Cité

The messenger stood before Commandant Bouvier, envelope in hand.

'Sir, the Air Ministry instructed me to deliver this to you personally.'

Bouvier took the envelope and reached for a paper knife lying on the table. He slit it open and out fell a photograph. That was all. The Commandant stared at it for a full half minute. He then raised his head to the messenger, 'That will be all, thank you.'

He need not have turned over to the back of the photograph, where a name was written in pencil. The moment he saw the picture, he knew who it was. He'd expected several suspects to fall onto his desk, but there was just this one. Anyone looking at the Commandant at that moment would have detected disbelief on his face. The person in the photograph was known to all of France, for his engineering brilliance and invention of the air-launched guided missile.

Maurice Bouvier wanted to be alone, uninterrupted for a few minutes. The shock of such a man conceiving, let alone implementing, an attempt to assassinate the President of France was beyond any normal person's comprehension. Taking coffee into a side meeting room, he closed the door and started to think it through.

He'd have to proceed with care. Jean Bertrand was a devout Catholic and ardent patriot, a graduate of the École Polytechnique. In addition to being a Lieutenant Colonel in the air force, his inventive skills put him at the forefront of the aircraft industry. His reputation stretched beyond France.

Commandant Bouvier determined on his next step. To obtain positive identification, he would start with those members of the commando already in custody. He would show each of them the photograph, individually.

None of the five claimed to recognise Bertrand. In fact, only the leader of the commando, Max, knew who he was. Although Max admitted the face in the picture was that of the organiser, in order to take the burden of responsibility off his team he refused to help the police further.

Immediately, Maurice Bouvier and a squad of police officers went to the address of Lieutenant Colonel Bertrand. The Commandant still found it hard to believe this was the most hunted man in France. How could a graduate of the École Polytechnique, the senior engineer in the French air force, someone known and revered by everyone, have committed such a crime?

Waiting until he came out of the villa, Commandant Bouvier and his men arrested Jean Bertrand, taking him back inside.

'We are going to search these premises, and I have questions to ask you,' said the Commandant.

'How dare you invade my home and behave like this in front of my family,' shouted Bertrand.

'We have reason to believe you were involved in the attack on the President two weeks ago at Petit-Clamart.'

'I have absolutely nothing to do with any attack on President de Gaulle,' responded Bertrand in fury.

The search of the house proceeded. No evidence was uncovered until one of the policemen found a newspaper on which the name 'Perrin' was noted down. The Commandant remembered the name from the police report that a man under that name took the phone call at the café close to the ambush.

Jumping into his car, he instructed the driver to find the café close by the ambush crossroads. Arriving there, he showed the proprietor a photograph of Jean Bertrand. The owner of the café identified the person in the picture as the Monsieur Perrin who'd taken the call shortly before the attack.

The Commandant had what he needed. He was back at the house in a flash.

'Sit down and listen to me,' he said to Jean Bertrand who was still berating the police officers.

'This has nothing to do with me, I demand that you leave me and my family alone,' said Bertrand.

'Take a look at this then,' said Commandant Bouvier, showing Bertrand the paper with the name 'Perrin' marked on it. 'This was found here in your home, and your photograph has been positively identified by the proprietor of the café at Petit-Clamart where you took a telephone call to a Monsieur Perrin shortly before the attack on the President's car.'

Already in a nervous state from the interrogation, Jean Bertrand broke down.

'I must see a priest,' he gasped. Shortly afterwards, he agreed to make a statement.

The statement contained a confession that he was the brains behind the attempt and that he'd been in overall charge. He claimed that it was not his aim to kill General de Gaulle, that his intention was to capture him so he could be tried by an independent panel of judges. Asked by Maurice Bouvier to explain the indiscriminate shooting at the President's wife as well as her husband, Jean Bertrand said that Madame de Gaulle accepted full risk and responsibility when she originally said she would marry Charles de Gaulle.

75

Versailles

The phone rang and Leo was first to it. A few fateful words, and the line went dead. He turned to Theresa.

'That was Françoise. They've got him.'

'What, who?'

'The assassin.'

'Who is it?'

'You won't believe this.' Leo paused, then said softly, 'Jean Bertrand.'

'Oh my God.'

'I know. A man with all that, and a wife and family.'

Theresa sat down slowly at the kitchen table, breakfast laid out. She was looking hard at Leo.

'How much did you have to do with this?'

Leo knew this moment would come.

'As I told you before, Jean asked me to advise him on the planning of the attack.'

'So, what's your position now, are we going to be arrested?'

'I met no one else, darling. The commando doesn't know of my existence, not even their leader, Max.'

Theresa still looked nervous. 'What about the interrogation? What are the chances the police will force Jean Bertrand to disclose your involvement?'

'He won't.'

'Will they torture him?'

Leo was wondering the same.

'I don't think so, simply because they now have their man,' he said. 'Unless there's evidence of another accomplice, I see no reason why they would search for someone else. His case is going to be a well-publicised process right up to the court verdict.'

The coffee percolator on the stove finished its gurgling, and Leo placed it on the table with a jug of hot milk. Theresa put two eggs on to boil, then fetched cheese from the larder. Neither said anything for a while.

Suddenly, Theresa blurted out, 'Why did the attempt fail?'

'A combination of circumstances. The visibility was poor, the hit team didn't see the convoy until the last moment, and not enough firepower. The French light machine gun used, the MAT-49, is a close-in weapon. Finally, the cars were travelling faster than expected. That chauffeur the President uses was brilliant.'

She said nothing.

Leo explained he'd decided to go and watch the action from further down the route, where he could look back at the convoy approaching through the traffic intersection as the ambush took place. As soon as the convoy broke through and passed him, he went back to his car and drove away.

'What about Jean Bertrand's escape arrangements?' asked Theresa.

'He and I discussed beforehand how he would get away after the attempt. The idea was to leave the country, and his wife and children would follow in due course.'

'But it was a failure.'

'He only wanted to discuss getting away after a successful operation.'

'Would he have wanted to try again?'

'He'd probably have started planning another attempt right away. Now he's been caught, he'll be lucky to escape with his life.'

'I think I told you when we first lunched with him after the talk he gave at SHAPE, there was something wrong. He was either suffering from over-work, or had a psychological problem.'

'Yes, I remember you saying that.'

'It couldn't be worse,' said Theresa. 'We must hope and pray they don't come for you.'

76

Paris Tribune *offices*

How should Kim react to the news that the man behind the assassination attempt just confessed? It would be all over the French media. Astonishment at who this potential assassin was. Disbelief that he claimed he wasn't trying to kill General de Gaulle, just to take him into private custody and send him for trial before impartial judges.

With most of those involved now arrested, something extra was needed if she was to go into print on the story. That was Henri's part of the deal. So far he was lying low. Not surprising that he would want to keep quiet on any part he played in the attempt.

She would build on the profile of Jean Bertrand, present her readership with the depth of complexity of his make-up. His background made him the most unlikely would-be assassin. There was little doubt that General de Gaulle would want him executed. Jean Bertrand might be arrogant, but clearly wasn't stupid. There was no knowing where he could have risen to professionally. Now he would be leaving a wife to whom he was devoted, along with three young daughters.

There was no doubt in Kim's mind that Jean Bertrand's passion for the pro-French population in Algeria transcended all else. He'd convinced himself that the balance of the moral argument went in favour of putting away someone who would otherwise be accountable for many thousands of deaths. He must be ready to die for that passion.

She decided to focus on Bertrand's independence. He denied he had anything to do with the OAS. The planning of the attempt was all his, and he'd undertaken it in parallel with his duties with Nord Aviation and the French air force. Was Jean Bertrand not the paradigm for all those in France convinced that de Gaulle's handling of the Algerian crisis had to be reversed?

Kim hauled together everything that she could find on Jean Bertrand, from his schooling through to the present calamity.

She realised also that these events threatened both Henri and Leo, whose friendship went back to their English school-days. What crime were they guilty of? She now knew Leo well, Henri less well. The common interest between them was Jean Bertrand. Somehow, a fatal fascination for this extraordinary man had brought them together. She felt a duty towards them. Was there anything she could do to keep Leo and Henri in the clear, out of the police investigation?

77

Roger Degueldre's suspicions were not unfounded. His line into Fresnes prison fed back that the gendarmes and police vehicle that picked up Henri de Rochefort were not what they appeared to be. His friends there made notes of all movements by OAS-connected prisoners and their visitors. A cross-check of the vehicle registration number with a contact in the Department of Justice showed that the vehicle was assigned to them.

That was enough for Roger Degueldre. Major de Rochefort had some questions to answer. First of all, he had to be found. Pierre Sergent was the obvious connection. Or what about Noelle Mercure, the girlfriend working at UPI that Pierre told him about? Now, believe it or not, she was working at the Élysée. He'd have the Palace watched. When she finished work, he'd follow her. She would lead him to Henri.

That evening, Roger Degueldre was in the café close to the exit from the Élysée Palace. When she came out, he took up position about fifty metres behind her. She led him, via the Metro, to the apartment building in rue du Bac. As Noelle pressed the buzzer, his hand was over her mouth.

Just a whisper in her ear, 'Behave normally.' As they climbed to the first floor, his gun was in Noelle's back. The door of the apartment was left open for her, de Rochefort must be in there. When he pushed Noelle into the hall before him, they came face to face with Henri coming out of the salon.

'Relax, Major, this is a friendly visit,' he said, turning to Noelle. 'I'm sorry Mademoiselle, it was the only way I could be sure of meeting with you both privately.' He kept the gun in his hand as he gestured to them to go into the salon.

Roger Degueldre settled himself in a chair, and waved them to sit down. The gun was still visible.

'I'm here, Mademoiselle Mercure, because I heard from Captain Sergent that you as well as Major de Rochefort were on his OAS staff. He also told me about your trip to Rome. Secondly, I received information that your escape from Fresnes, Major, was contrived and arranged by a government department.

Henri tried to keep his cool. He was only too aware of Roger Degueldre's reputation, of the ruthless executions by his Delta Force. Also, that he was close to General Salan in Madrid.

'I don't know how you obtained your information, Lieutenant,' said Henri. 'All I can say is that I'm on the same side as you and am devoting my time to the OAS, to preventing the President from finalising independence.'

'Be that as it may,' said the other, 'I'm warning you. If you are double-crossing us, the OAS will take its revenge.' He paused, then rose from his chair, adding almost as an afterthought, 'I'm in Madrid for a few days. We'll have another conversation when I'm back.'

With that, he was gone.

Henri moved towards the drinks cabinet. 'That's better,' he said after pouring themselves whiskies. 'Did that bastard hurt you, darling?'

'Only my pride. I was about to tell you I'd been warned by Francoise who'd heard from Justine, that we were in danger. He must have been waiting for me after work.'

'Trouble is, he now knows this address,' said Henri. 'I'll have to tell Maître Lacoste.'

Noelle suddenly said. 'Henri, I have to go to Madrid. Just a three-day trip. UPI have been in touch with my boss at the Élysée. There's a problem in UPI's office there, we've lost the lead journalist and I've been asked to do some interviews.'

'What, to Madrid at the same time as Roger Degueldre?'

'Why not? It's a big place, don't worry,' said Noelle. 'To be serious for a moment, I thought of trying to reach General Salan.'

'You're joking,' exclaimed Henri.

'I'm not. If he would grant me an interview as a UPI representative, it might convince him to tell Roger Degueldre to leave us alone.'

Henri was thinking fast. 'That does make sense, but you heard what he said, he's going to be there.'

'Not a bad thing,' replied Noelle. 'Maybe I'll be able to dissuade him, myself.'

'Watch out, darling, he's a killer.'

⋖⋗⋖⋗

Noelle knew what she was doing, this was too good an opportunity to miss. She would need help there for what she planned, and must get a message to her friend at the Russian embassy in Madrid, via Jansson and Evgeni. There was a morning flight from Orly each day. No time like the present, and Henri need never know the details.

78

Noelle and Vladimir, the KGB station manager in the Russian embassy, sat either side of a small bare table in Casa Paco, just off the Plaza Mayor. The locals said that the steak served there was the best you could find anywhere in Spain. Vladimir was a good friend of Paco, the city's inspector of slaughterhouses.

'This is such a welcome surprise, Mademoiselle Mercure,' said Vladimir. 'When I heard from Evgeni in Paris that you were paying us a visit, I tried to recall where we'd met before. Then I remembered, you were with your brother at a Communist Party soirée we hosted at the embassy in Paris.'

'Yes, what a night that was. The vodka nearly killed me.'

'We got on very well, I thought. Didn't we end up at Les Halles?'

'So that's where we went.' Noelle sounded relieved.

'Yes. Onion soup for breakfast.'

'What a memory you have, Vlad.'

'Part of the basic training in the KGB. My profession is all about memory.'

Not to be fooled around with was Vlad, Noelle worked that out a long time ago. At least there was still some of that rust-coloured hair on his head.

'He receives the best cuts, Paco does,' said the swarthy Russian, explaining the menu was always the same. A plate of *anguilas* still frying in oil, followed by a large filet on a baking dish so hot that when you sliced it down the middle with the wicked dagger of a knife, the pink meat continued to cook on the plate. A coarse red wine was drunk out of plain water glasses.

She looked around her. On the walls of the bar were posters of bullfights promoting the good and the great of bullfighting. A poster showing Manolete looked down on them.

'So, Mademoiselle Noelle, Evgeni tells me there is someone out to kill you and your friend in the French Foreign Legion?'

'Yes, I want to kill him, Vladimir.'

'You're not killing anyone. That's our business.'

'What do you mean?' Noelle was nonplussed.

'It's routine for the KGB. Your safety is paramount to us.'

'I'm flattered, Vlad. The problem person is an ex-French Foreign Legion Lieutenant. He's threatening me and my friend, a Legion officer and escaped prisoner.'

'You make some strange friends. How do you want to deal with your adversary?'

'I was going to ask your advice. Any ideas?'

Vladimir stared at the Manolete poster. 'How about enticing him into one of Paco's slaughterhouses?'

'You have an awful mind, Vlad.'

'What sort of man is he?'

'His name is Roger Degueldre. He's a giant of a man, ruthless, with a killer reputation. He and his OAS Delta Force have murdered several hundred French and Muslim officials. The authorities have been after him since the putsch.'

'Sounds like we need a platoon of the NKVD.'

'I'm not asking you to get involved. I was going to handle this myself.'

Vladimir gave her a look of surprise and scepticism.

'Where does he hang out in Madrid?'

'I don't know,' said Noelle, 'But he's due here any day now. What is clear is that when in Madrid he spends time with General Salan and Colonel Arnoud.'

'Ah, now you're talking. The Embassy keeps a close eye on those two.' Vladimir was staring into space. 'I think we should watch General Salan's hotel, identify your man when he appears, and call up a large heavy vehicle. When he comes out, we run him down and put a bullet in his head immediately afterwards.'

'Vlad, that's beyond the call of duty.'

'Not really. The Embassy and Moscow don't want the OAS interfering with General de Gaulle giving away Algeria. We also love you, Mademoiselle. Your mother Annette Mercure was not only a famous scientist, she was also a Communist.'

'Thanks for saying that, Vlad.' She paused. 'I'll tell you a secret.'

'I can't wait to hear it.'

'I am above all loyal to my late brother, and the principles which guided his research.'

'Into nuclear energy.'

'Yes. He was adamant that France's research and experiments into nuclear energy should be channelled into making the world a better place to live.'

'That was high-minded. It's not what's happening.'

'Correct. My personal mission is to change that.'

It was a wonderful evening. In spite of returning later to business, with Vladimir drawing out the killing of Roger Degueldre on the paper tablecloth.

'Do you have a gun?' Vlad suddenly asked.

'No.'

'I'll fix that. I need you with me. Your job will be to identify your Degueldre friend. Come to the embassy at nine o'clock tomorrow morning. You'll need some practice with the Makarov, just in case something unexpected happens. The trigger pull is heavy. It needs a strong squeeze.'

⋙ ⋘

She was there early the next morning. Vladimir stood beaming beneath a model of Sputnik 1, suspended from the hall ceiling.

'Good morning, Mademoiselle Mercure, welcome to our Iberian outpost.'

'Hello, Vladimir. You got there before the Americans,' she said pointing up at the satellite.

'Come, follow me. I'll take you to our little space in the servants' quarters.'

Arriving at the end of a long corridor, he showed her into a large but unassuming room, with two desks at one end and a wall map of the Iberian Peninsula at the other. Along the side walls she saw framed photographs of mostly wild-looking men.

'We don't bring Generalissimo Franco in here,' remarked Vladimir. 'You wouldn't exhibit these anywhere else in Madrid.'

'To do with the civil war?' asked Noelle.

'Yes. The leaders and generals of the Republican army,' said Vladimir.

'That war you lost,' said Noelle.

'Fascist bastards.' He spat the words out, as a secretary from one of the desks got up from her typewriter and walked over to introduce herself.

'I am Katrina, from Barcelona.'

Vlad added, 'Katrina is Catalan and proud of it. Her parents, the Morels, fought in the last stand of the Republicans before escaping over the Pyrenees.'

'With Russian rifles,' said Katrina.

'I might need one of those,' said Noelle, smiling and clasping the Catalan by the hand.

'Now, Mademoiselle Mercure,' said Vlad, 'we need to agree the plan of attack. I'll then introduce you to the armourer.'

<hr/>

The trap was set. An official from the embassy parked his car outside General Salan's hotel, clutching a photograph of the intended victim. Two days later, he recognised Roger Degueldre entering the small hotel, and signalled back to the embassy. Vladimir grabbed Noelle and they piled into the truck he'd organised. Just the two of them. He stopped the vehicle in sight of the hotel entrance.

It seemed to take for ever, visitors coming and going through the revolving door of the hotel. Every sort of person came up and down the street, mothers pushing prams and pulling along children, working men on bicycles with their tools tied up behind them.

She must concentrate. Suddenly, there he was, the bull-like head and shoulders of the target coming out through the door. In a few moments he would be down the steps and onto the street.

'That's him,' she said, pointing Degueldre out to Vlad. She tensed up as Vlad started the engine.

Slowly the vehicle crept forward, gathering speed. Noelle felt the door handle with one hand, the other gripping the Makarov. Roger Degueldre raised an arm to attract an empty cab. Slamming his foot on the throttle, Vlad went for him.

The truck swung into Roger Degueldre's line of sight. Instantly he seemed to realise what was happening and hurled himself sideways. It was only a glancing blow, knocking him off balance, throwing him sideways and face down onto the road surface.

Suddenly it was up to her. He was lifting himself from the tarmac, he would get away.

Noelle was out of the vehicle in a flash, throwing herself at him gun in hand, just as he was starting to pick himself up.

Inexplicably, Vlad saw Noelle plunge forward suddenly as she was stretching out the arm holding the pistol, about to shoot the Frenchman in the back of the head. The simultaneous crack of a weapon close to the truck could only mean one thing. Roger Degueldre had protection. They'd made a tragic mistake. Noelle was the victim, he was free.

Vlad had to get away. The Embassy couldn't be seen to be involved. The police would be on site any minute. First he must check whether Noelle was alive, even though they might shoot at him as well.

About to jump out of the truck, he heard a second crack and Noelle's head jerked sideways.

Vlad slammed the vehicle into gear, pulling the wheel in the opposite direction to where the shots had come from, and put his foot hard down on the throttle.

79

Henri sat waiting for Françoise, his sister having rung to say they must meet immediately.

She arrived with several newspapers under her arm. Behind her, rather to his surprise, came Justine.

'Henri, I have bad news,' said Françoise, 'I felt I should tell you face to face.'

'Oh, what's happened?'

'It's Noelle. She's dead.'

Henri felt the pressure in his chest, his breathing ceased for what seemed an age. 'Dead. What do you mean?'

'Our embassy in Madrid sent a teletype.'

It was that sudden trip on UPI business. And to see General Salan. 'Was it an accident?'

'Not exactly. She was shot. The Spanish press are saying she was caught in cross-fire, a shoot-out in a Madrid street.'

Henri's mind raced through the possibilities. Was there an OAS connection? Roger Degueldre was there when she was, there had to be.

'My God, how could that happen?' he whispered.

'I wasn't given any details, but it stinks,' said Françoise. 'I've been in touch with our intelligence people in the Madrid embassy.'

'What do they say?'

'OAS. It seems that this character Roger Degueldre was visiting General Salan. When he came out of the hotel, a truck hit him. Then, believe it or not, Noelle ran towards him with a gun in her hand, and was shot in the head twice by an OAS bodyguard.'

Henri was speechless, with grief and disbelief. It suddenly rushed up on him and he understood the truth. Noelle went there to kill Roger Degueldre, to protect him. He couldn't speak.

Justine tried to help him out. 'It's a terrible blow, Henri, we'll do anything we can to help you get through it.' She leant across and hugged him.

'I know you will.' It was a hoarse whisper.

'Henri, there's something else I've just learnt at the *piscine*,' said Françoise, 'Something else you'll find impossible to believe, but I have to tell you.'

Henri just nodded.

'Noelle was working for the Russians.'

'She was what?' Henri's face said it all. His world was falling in.

'Our people were playing it close, only the Russian desk knew about her,' said Françoise. 'In Algiers, she was in touch with someone who worked with the KGB. She'd been out to see the atomic bomb test site at Reggane, in the Sahara.'

'That's unbelievable.'

'I know.'

After a heavy silence, Henri said, 'So, Roger Degueldre's still on the loose.'

Henri recounted to Françoise and Justine the visit the Delta Force leader made to the apartment in the rue du Bac, having followed Noelle from her work.

'He suspects what I'm up to.'

'Hang on, Henri. There's a warrant out for his arrest. He has hundreds of killings to his name. It won't be long before our people catch him,' said Françoise. 'He'll go to the firing squad.'

'And I'll go and watch,' said Justine.

'And if he comes after me, first?'

There was silence for some time, before Henri said emphatically, 'I'll kill him before he kills me.'

80

Justine remembered the lunch with Jacques Foccart, and his advice on Maurice Papon. The impossibility of removing the head of the Paris police while General de Gaulle regarded the ex-Pétainist as one of his inner circle. She'd searched for a solution time and again. The challenge was to create a situation where Papon felt resignation was his only option. Threaten him with consequences he must avoid. At last, she believed she was on the right track.

Josephine Baker was by her side, her true friend in time of danger. Together, they were making a discreet visit to a long-neglected edifice in the heart of old Paris. During the great flood at the turn of the century, this site of the old royal palace was inundated. Close by, also on this island in the Seine, lay the Palais de Justice and the Préfecture, heart of law and order in the city. Not a place to commit a crime.

'You know that time was never wasted in reconnaissance, Josephine. This is where I've said I'll be tomorrow at midnight.'

'You'll have the list of names with you, the correspondence?'

'Just examples, not the whole lot. The master file is in the hands of a friendly lawyer so that if anything happens to me, he'll pass it to the press.'

'Do you think Maurice Papon will come?'

'Very unlikely, but he should send someone.'

'I can't help laughing, Justine, the two of us in all-over face masks, dressed as men. You, the ex-Schiaparelli model. Me, cabaret star past her sell-by date.'

'Josephine, Maurice Papon's hit men are ruthless. They'd have you floating face down in the Seine, given half a chance.'

'Now you tell me,' said Josephine, half in jest and half in terror.

<hr />

In darkness the following night, the two of them stood outside the Conciergerie in an alcove, in their disguise. Close by was the waiting room for the guillotine.

'So this is where Marie Antoinette spent her last night,' said Josephine.

'Before being transported to the scaffold at the Place de la Concorde,' replied Justine. 'Most of the aristocrats sentenced to death spent there last few nights here.'

Justine was thinking through what was likely to happen, one last time. Her message to Maurice Papon asked for him or a trusted representative to rendezvous with her at the Conciergerie at midnight on that date. It was anonymous, but she'd written enough for him to know the sender meant business.

The purpose of the operation? To frighten Maurice Papon. Her ultimate objective was for him to be tried in a French court for crimes against humanity. The first step would be his resignation. If he refused, evidence of his wartime record would be handed to the media.

'Trust you to dream up this place as the meeting point,' said Josephine. 'The departure lounge for the next world, courtesy of Robespierre and the Revolution.'

The letter Justine brought with her, typed on plain paper, contained a sample listing of certain Bordeaux citizens deported to the camps. It stated that the sender was in possession of the identity of two thousand such persons, as well as details of living family members with whom the sender was in contact. Further, that the families held Maurice Papon directly responsible for the deportation and death of their loved ones between 1942 and 1944.

'How many of his people do we have to contend with?' asked Josephine.

'Probably only one, perhaps covered by a couple of others in case of trouble. Remember, the Préfecture is on this island. You'd need General Leclerc's armoured division to compete with that lot.'

Justine looked at her watch. 'Josephine, why don't you disappear now into the darkness behind the pillars over there,' she said, gesturing towards the interior.

'Okay, I'll be covering you, but out of the line of sight of whoever turns up.'

'Yes, as we discussed,' said Justine. 'You told me you knew how to handle a pistol. Here's mine, and clips of ammunition.' She handed Josephine the weapon. 'If they rush me, come out and get their hands up, fast.'

'It's like the old days, Justine. When you were campaigning for the Assembly, in that rough nineteenth arrondissement. Except we weren't armed.'

'Should be all right tonight. I just want to get my message through to Maurice Papon, personally. That he either retires early from his job, or the families of the deportees will go public in the world's press.

They took up position and waited. It was a quarter past midnight when a shadow moved along the wall of the ancient building beside where Justine was standing. A figure appeared. She couldn't see the man's face, a scarf partially covering it, and his hat pulled down.

The man saw her, stopped, and came forward.

Justine addressed him in a voice pitched as low as she could. The padding of the mask helped the effect of a male voice.

'Who sent you?' asked Justine.

'The person you wrote to,' he replied.

It wasn't Maurice Papon himself, that was for sure.

'Do you have a message for me?' asked Justine.

'I'm from your correspondent's legal adviser.'

That would figure, but was it true? Would he try something, did he have back-up? If they could get her back to the Préfecture, she'd be recognised and charged. That would make a good headline, 'Deputy arrested for extortion'.

After a pause, he went on. 'I'm instructed to ask what you want, how much?'

'It's not a question of money, at this point.' Justine paused. 'The families of the deportees want a full admission and apology, and Monsieur Papon's resignation.'

The man looked hard at Justine, then suddenly made a grab for one of her wrists.

She was ready, back at Arisaig with Mr Fairbairn circling her in the crouched position. As he came for her, she thrust an arm under his, and over the back of his shoulder. One jerk and he was on the ground.

Suddenly, a second man materialised out of the darkness and advanced on her. There was the glint of a knife, something Justine wasn't expecting. At the end of her Arisaig training, she would have been confident enough to disarm him. That was a long time ago, when she was twenty-one years old and in peak condition. Trained the same way as the British commandos, and the Rangers from the US Army. That confidence wasn't there any more.

The first man, on the floor, was recovering. She must settle with the knife man first.

Smack, she felt the grit in her eyes. Her hands went up to her face, even though she knew what would happen. The plunge of the knife would be below her raised arms and into her abdomen. That's the way you did it. Once the knife was deep into the soft belly region and forced upwards, the massive discharge of blood would do the rest.

'Stand still, hands in the air,' shrieked Josephine appearing from the darkness, holding the Walther with both hands out in front of her. The two men froze, the knife dropping to the ground. Their arms went slowly up.

What should she do next? Stay calm, pick up the knife. Say what she'd intended to say.

'Here's a list showing examples of the names Monsieur Papon will be interested in,' said Justine, passing an envelope to one of them. There are two thousand on the master list held by my lawyer.' Justine kept her voice low, she and Josephine still face-masked and disguised as men. 'If you try anything like this again, he will release the list to the press.'

Josephine still held the gun, level from outstretched arms and pointing between the two men. She and Justine started to back away, melting into the darkness.

'Quick, our escape route,' said Justine, heading for the connection of the island to Pont Neuf. 'Let's get deep into the Latin Quarter before those two wake up the Préfecture. Well done Josephine, you saved me from being gutted.'

'What's that?' shouted Josephine, pointing at the stone wall above the river bank. Along it was written in graffiti '1961: Ici on noie les Algériens (Here we drown Algerians)'.

'Dozens of bodies were pulled from the Seine after the march of Algerian families into Paris a year ago,' Justine shouted back. 'That was Papon's business.'

81

Hôtel Matignon

Justine felt nervous, not usual for her. Entering the salon for another meeting of the Prime Minister's special committee, she must face Maurice Papon. Could he suspect her? Was there anything to connect her with the demand he'd received threatening disclosure of his part in the deportation of the Bordeaux Jews?

There he was across the table. The conceit of success written all over his face. Did she detect something else? Fear lurking behind that façade of contentment? Perhaps for the moment he was intoxicated with the glory of capturing the brains behind the attempt on the President's life.

Michel Debré came straight to the point on everyone's mind. 'You'll have heard that the person behind the attempt has been arrested. No doubt you are as astonished as me that it is Lieutenant Colonel Jean Bertrand. Monsieur Papon, please update us.'

The Préfet of the Paris police looked triumphantly around the table. 'Thank you, Prime Minister. Yes, we have in custody the organiser of the attack, and most of those who carried it out. Jean Bertrand was senior engineer of the aircraft industry, as well as an air force officer. He has made a full confession. The case will be heard before the Court of Military Justice.'

'Please pass my personal congratulations to Commandant Bouvier and his team,' said Monsieur Debré. He paused, then invited others to express their views.

Pierre Messmer raised a hand. The Armed Forces Minister expressed his surprise and concern that it was an officer in the air force who committed the ultimate crime. 'It's a lesson to us all that the passion over the future of Algeria and its citizens runs like a fault line from top to bottom of our society.'

Jacques Foccart added that Jean Bertrand was not a part of the OAS. This horrendous crime was nothing to do with them. It was conceived and organised by a brilliant but flawed fanatic. As he understood, there was no right of appeal to a decision of the Military Court. The only possibility for clemency lay with the President of the Republic.

There was a long silence. Clearly, no one wished to speculate on the outcome of the judicial process.

Justine's mind drifted sideways, towards unfinished business. What about B12, the mole inside government, the alleged source of information on the President's movements? Who was this person who may have been in direct touch with Jean Bertrand, aiding the assassins?

82

Café Flore

A couple of days after the drama of the Conciergerie, Justine and Josephine were having a beer together.

'So, Justine, what's the next step?'

'There's been no response from Maurice Papon yet.'

'It might stay like that,' said Josephine.

'Yes. He may just think he can bluff it out.' Justine was thinking. 'If nothing happens, I'll probably leave it for a few months. Right now, General de Gaulle is the nation's hero for surviving the attempt on his life. Maurice Papon is General de Gaulle's hero for catching the would-be assassin.'

'It's not like you to wait long, Justine.'

'The time will come when France wakes up to what it did to its Jews during the Occupation. Right now, we're a nation lacking the confidence to face the skeletons of yesterday.'

'I guess you're right.'

'The General's out to bring back France's pride, its standing in the world. Then will come the moment, but it will be a different President who makes us own up to such crimes against humanity. That's when people like Maurice Papon will be exposed for what they are and what they did.'

Justine was looking worried, cautious. 'There's something else.'

'Oh, what's that?' said Josephine.

'Do you remember me talking about Henri de Rochefort, brother of Françoise?'

'Vaguely. Wasn't he in the Foreign Legion?'

'Yes, in Indochina and Algeria. Now he's here, on a special assignment linked to the OAS. I can't tell you any more.'

'And?'

'Someone in the OAS is out to kill him.'

'That's dodgy,' said Josephine. 'Those guys seem to shoot and bomb first, and ask questions afterwards.'

'What would you do?'

Josephine looked hard at Justine. 'Well, let me see. I think I'd kill the other guy first.'

'The police have a warrant out for him, he's wanted for multiple murders. Trouble is, he's in deep cover, usually in Madrid.'

'Ah. Why don't you tie him to a post on a bull farm? Hang a sign on his chest, saying died while resisting arrest.' She chuckled to herself. 'Seriously, you should put pressure on those responsible, to find and arrest him right away.'

'They've been trying to do that. He slips back into Spain when things get too hot.'

'Okay, so pack him in the back of a car in Madrid and dump him outside the nearest police station in France.'

Justine loved her. This was the real Josephine Baker.

83

'Is that Kim?'

'Yes, sounds like Monsieur Barnier.' She felt a surge of excitement coursing through her.

'That's me. I have some interesting news, off the record of course.'

'Oh, tell me more.'

'Let's meet, and I can bring you up to date.' There was a pause on the line. 'In fact, I'd like to take you out,' said Henri. 'How about chez Madame Prunier tomorrow evening?'

Kim was short of words, not usual for her. Yes, she badly wanted to hear about the attempt on the President's life. But suddenly she realised she'd been waiting to hear from Henri for another reason, she just wanted to see him again.

'Monsieur Barnier, I would simply love to do that.'

'Great,' said Henri. 'Eight o'clock at Madame Prunier.'

Kim sat back in her office chair, thinking. She'd heard about Noelle's death, shot in Madrid. The news filtered through, although there was nothing in the French press. It smelt like a cover-up, there must be a real story there. Poor Henri would know.

So, at last, he was coming back into her life, at least across the dinner table.

⋯⋯

Kim took particular care with her coiffure. She never piled her sleek black hair up on top, although that seemed the style of the moment. Rather, she had it drawn back and swept into one large loop at the back of the head.

The emerald green silk of her dress suited the light tan of her Cambodian skin. Half on the shoulders, the fabric opened in the neck enough to reveal something of her small but beautiful breasts.

The cab swept her down to the Pont de la Concorde, over to the Right Bank, and up the rue Royale. The beauty and romance of the city enveloped her. She was on the way to the classic Paris fish restaurant, hiding in a narrow street off the Madeleine.

Once inside, a stern-looking female dressed all in black, took her cape. Remembering to ask for Monsieur Barnier rather than de Rochefort, she had a quick look in a large mirror, took a deep breath, and walked into the restaurant area where the maître d' was waiting. No sign of Madame Prunier, but Kim knew she could show up at any moment, nothing missing her critical eye.

Henri rose from a table half-way down the longish room, as she approached.

She was the first to speak. 'Hello, Monsieur Barnier.'

Henri kissed her first on the left cheek, then on the right, and she hoped the exotic scent she was wearing would work its magic.

'You have to call me Frédéric,' he said laughingly.

'Of course. I'm always Kim. I never change my name,' she whispered, with a cheeky smile.

Kim looked quickly round the room. In her world and in a place like Prunier, there might be someone she knew. Fortunately, there were no familiar faces. The waiter poured champagne into two *coupes* on a silver tray and offered her one.

'What do you think of my disguise?' said Henri.

She looked hard at him. 'Not sure I saw much of you when we met in the Jardin du Luxembourg. Your hair's growing, instead of the army crewcut, and that moustache is new. Not bad,' she said with a laugh.

Kim knew she must comment on the news of Noelle. 'Frédéric, I was horrified and so sad to hear about Noelle's death.'

Henri looked down for a moment, then into her eyes. 'It's terrible. I didn't know where I was when my sister broke the news.'

'You must lean on me for help. You're operating underground, so you won't have people you can easily turn to.'

'That's true, it's good of you to say that.'

'Aren't you taking an unnecessary risk, showing yourself in a place like this when you're supposed to be on the run?'

'You're worth it.'

'Monsieur Barnier, I love your explanation, but what if someone in the army recognises you in spite of the change in appearance?'

'I've been buried in the Legion overseas for all of my army career. I'd be very surprised if anyone recognised me.'

They sipped their champagne as they chose from the menu. Suddenly Henri looked up.

'Kim, when we met that day, we did a deal.'

'Yes. I gave you a lead into the brains behind the assassination attempt.'

'You turned out to be right. I found Jean Bertrand.'

'I thought you would. I hope you're still in favour with your government friends. After all, General de Gaulle is still alive.'

'I now have to deliver on my part of the deal.'

'Yes, but I'll be realistic, Frédéric. I know I can't publish your part in the story until you're clear and safe from the OAS.'

'Yes, I was going to say that. All being well, that might not be too long now.'

'Oh, I'm so pleased to hear that, Monsieur Barnier,' she said, reaching out and putting her hand on his wrist.

They started with oysters, presented on beds of ice. The turbot that followed was delicious, fresh like you could count on in Paris. Gradually through the meal, Noelle felt the two of them coming closer. Henri was attracted to her, that she could sense, yet was naturally withdrawn after what just happened to Noelle.

A slight chill of autumn air met them as they came out of the restaurant, intending to walk together a little. She saw the black DS against the kerb a few metres up on the same side of the street. They were beside the car in a few seconds, just as both the rear doors opened.

Kim felt Henri's arm grab her round the back as two men in hats and raincoats were on them in a flash.

'Into the back of the car, at once,' said the larger of the two, at the same time letting Henri have sight of the machine pistol under the flap of the coat.

She heard him whisper, 'Do as he says, I know him, he's OAS.'

84

Palais Bourbon

Justine saw the familiar figure of Pierre Messmer bearing down on her as she left the *hémicycle* after a late session of the Assembly. Behind him was another man who she guessed was a senior civil servant.

'Mademoiselle Müller.' The Armed Forces Minister seemed a shade breathless. 'They've taken Henri de Rochefort.'

'You mean the OAS have him?'

'Yes. As he came out of Prunier this evening, with a woman who works for the *Paris Tribune*.'

Oh God, that must be Kim Cho. 'How did we hear about it, Minister?' asked Justine.

'Jacques Foccart just called me. He said he knew you.'

Pierre Messmer turned to the other man. 'This is Maître Lacoste from the Justice Department, who's been our link with Henri de Rochefort. Jacques Foccart says one of his SAC people saw it happen and recognised Roger Degueldre.'

That made sense. Jacques was having Henri watched. He'd warned her that Henri and Noelle were in danger. They'd killed Noelle, now they would kill Henri.

'We've no time, we have to move fast,' said Justine. 'Did the SAC man follow the car?'

'He tried to, in a cab,' said Pierre Messmer. 'They took them to the Bois de Boulogne, and tossed out the journalist woman who ran off into the woods. Roger Degueldre's car piled on the speed and the cab driver couldn't keep up. It was a black DS, and the cabbie took the number.'

'Any time to have it checked?'

'Not yet but ...' He hesitated for a moment. 'The cab driver thought the number plate was in a series he'd seen regularly at the Richelieu Wing of the Louvre.'

'Isn't that the Ministry of Finance?'

The Armed Forces Minister hesitated, seeming to sense the implications of his answer. 'Yes,' he said, almost in a whisper.

Justine froze. There was a link somewhere. What was it? The insider, with the OAS code name of B12, was alleged to be in the Ministry of Finance. Could the mole be involved in the abduction?

'We've a call-out to all police units to look for a DS in that number series.'

Maître Lacoste spoke for the first time. 'De Rochefort's key contact in OAS *métropole* is Captain Pierre Sergent. There's a bar in the Place du Tertre where the Captain collects his mail. It's possible they will take Major de Rochefort there. As you probably know, we have arrest warrants out for Pierre Sergent and Roger Degueldre. I don't think the Captain would harm Major de Rochefort, but Degueldre could kill him.'

The Maître must know how Noelle died in Madrid, Justine realised.

'Roger Degueldre knows that when we get him, he'll be before the firing squad in weeks,' added the Maître.

Justine interjected. 'We must be ready for a shoot-out, in that case. There's no time. Where's Jacques Foccart?'

'Outside the back entrance, with two cars and four of his SAC men, *barbouzes*,' said Pierre Messmer.

'Good, we don't want the Préfecture involved.' No way was she going to have Maurice Papon in on this.

'Okay by me to close in on that bar in Montmartre,' said the Minister. 'I want to be kept in the loop on this, Henri de Rochefort's a friend. We and our mates held up Rommel at Bir Hakeim. This Degueldre type isn't going to defeat us.'

Justine was already making for the long corridor through the Palace, to where the SAC team would be. Over her shoulder, she said to Maître Lacoste, 'Find Kim Cho, please, and bring her to us at the Place du Tertre. She may be useful.' Justine didn't have time to find out how senior Lacoste was, but being a Maître he should know there were some women you didn't argue with.

<hr />

Jacques Foccart's two Peugeots were the large 404 *familiale* model, powerful estate cars with ample space for machine guns and ammunition where the children would normally sit.

He must have seen them charging out of the Palace and guessed what was on. Blue lights front and rear were being pulled out and fixed in place on both vehicles.

Justine saw the Minister having a quick word with Jacques as they were leaving.

She piled into the back seat of one of the Peugeots, next to Jacques. When the sirens came on they were the ambulance variety, three discreet tones rather than the two tone screech of police vehicles.

Out across the Pont de la Concorde, they thundered up the rue Royale. Over the wireless link between the two cars, Jacques Foccart talked to the leader of the SAC team about how the bar was to be approached and covered.

Justine's view prevailed. She was to walk in off the street, go to the bar counter and ask to see the proprietor. One SAC man would enter after her on his own, and go over to a table. His job was to cover Justine if she was threatened in any way. Two others were to find their way to the rear of the building and prevent anyone leaving. The remaining SAC agents were to remain in one of the cars parked in the square opposite, blocking the front of the bar and ready to move in if needed.

She felt ice-cold and detached from everything else. That's how it always was before a moment of danger.

What's that? A voice crackled in the driver's radio saying, 'The DS is parked just off the Place du Tertre.'

85

Blindfolded after they ditched Kim in the Bois de Boulogne, Henri sensed from the starting and stopping at traffic lights that they were heading back into the city. Roger Degueldre said nothing. After half an hour or so, he felt the DS pull up somewhere.

'Don't chance anything, Major,' said Degueldre as he opened the door and pulled Henri out. They walked down an alley, the back of a building Henri guessed, and in through a narrow door. He was pushed into a chair. As soon as they took off the blindfold, not only Roger Degueldre faced him but also Louis, the proprietor of the bar in Place du Tertre.

'We've met before,' said Louis, towering above him. 'Here's a beer to revive you,' he said, handing the glass to a very surprised Henri. The room was some sort of store, cases of beer and wine against the walls.

Roger Degueldre pulled a chair up. Even sitting down, the bulk of the ex-legionnaire dominated the scene, not exactly friendly but not behaving like an executioner.

'Major de Rochefort. There are one or two things I want to settle with you.'

Henri said nothing.

'First of all, what happened in Madrid was unfortunate. The fact is that your girlfriend was out to kill me. It was only because one of General Salan's bodyguards was fast off the mark that I escaped with my life. He shot your friend the moment before she would have shot me.'

Henri remained silent.

'I want to put a proposal to you.'

Roger Degueldre paused, and Henri wondered what was coming.

'Major, you felt strongly about General de Gaulle signing the death warrant of your *harki* auxiliaries, like we in the OAS did with his treatment of the *pieds noirs*. You supported the putsch by the Generals. We dealt ruthlessly with those officials and police responsible for implementing the President's policies.'

Henri just nodded.

'The FLN now rules Algeria. A million *pieds noirs* are left destitute, and the *harkis* and other French Muslims are at the mercy of the lynch mobs. You and I can no longer stop that. The next battle will be led by General Salan, Georges Bidault, and Jacques Soustelle, at the political level.

'I guess that's a fair summary,' said Henri, thinking he should sound supportive.

Roger Degueldre went on. 'The latest attempt on General de Gaulle's life failed, like others before it. You know Pierre Sergent and I strongly suspect you've been playing a double game, working in the OAS while at the same time feeding information to the authorities.'

Henri just looked the former Legion Lieutenant straight in the eyes, not an ounce of emotion showing.

'I could gun you down for that, right here and now.' Pausing no doubt for effect, he added, 'There is another way. Pierre Sergent and I have arrest warrants out on us and have to operate under deep cover. We suggest that you propose a deal with the authorities whereby in exchange for your release, we are permitted to exile ourselves in some overseas territory.'

Henri didn't respond immediately. Was there a real possibility of the authorities dealing with the likes of those two?

He was about to take a gulp of the beer when a waiter looked in through the door, calling out breathlessly to Louis, 'A woman is in the bar and wants to speak to you.'

The proprietor was gone for a few minutes only, returning in what looked like a state of shock.

'The woman is the deputy Justine Müller. She says we're surrounded by an armed security team and should exit the building immediately by the front entrance.'

Silence, everyone absolutely still for what seemed like an age.

Roger Degueldre reached out slowly for the machine pistol lying on a chair. Louis had his hand in a pocket, presumably on a gun of some sort. They looked at one another, then moved to the rear exit door, easing it open. A sharp burst of machine gun fire crashed out in the small space of the alley behind. They backed into the room in a hurry and slammed the door.

'Louis,' said Roger Degueldre, 'Go out into the front, see the woman and say that Major de Rochefort will be shot dead unless they allow me free passage to the Montmartre Metro station.'

Henri's mind was racing. That could be his death warrant. If government authorities were staking out the place, they weren't going to lose Roger Degueldre for the sake of risking his life.

Louis went out.

Henri contemplated overpowering the Legionnaire Lieutenant. It would be like Maurice Chevalier taking on Cassius Clay.

Suddenly the door was flung open, and Justine Müller was standing tall, glaring at the two of them.

Degueldre went for her, dropping the machine pistol to free both hands. In a flash, Henri's hands were around the weapon. At the same time, he was watching Louis, coming in behind Justine, pistol now in hand.

Justine's hands came up to just below her line of sight. Henri guessed her thinking. Degueldre was much more powerful, her only chance was to overload his mind. For one attempted move by him, she must put in several fast blows, using a hard elbow against his soft abdomen, a soft palm against the hardness of the head.

Her left hand went behind his head, her own head dropping to his arm, her right hand pushed hard against his face. Swinging her free leg around the back of his, she jerked him off balance and shoved him to the ground.

There was Louis, thrusting his handgun out in front of him to shoot Justine. Henri gave him a short burst with the machine pistol, aiming at the weapon. The man screamed, clutching at his wrist that started to spurt blood, the gun dropping to the floor.

Degueldre was almost on his feet as into the room burst the leader of the SAC team and one of his men. Going straight for the ex-Legion Lieutenant, they pulled him away from Justine and pinned him down until they had the man handcuffed.

Henri was over to Justine in a flash. Was she injured? From the way she picked herself up with his help, all seemed well.

'How did you manage that?' he said. 'Degueldre must be at least twice your weight.'

She grinned at him. 'Your sister Françoise and I were trained at Arisaig. Once through the course with Mr Fairbairn, you never forget how to do it.'

Roger Degueldre was carted out through the bar area, into the street. Louis was left moaning in a corner until an ambulance arrived.

⊶⊰⊸

Justine introduced Jacques Foccart to Henri.

'We'll hand Lieutenant Degueldre to the Justice people,' said Jacques. 'He needs the most secure lock-up that can be found. There can only be one outcome to his trial.'

A little cry came suddenly from a car drawing up across the road. The front passenger door burst open and, the next thing, Kim was throwing her arms around Henri.

86

Picnic in Versailles

Early autumn, and still warm. In the distance, the fountains played to music you could only just hear.

'Who's organised all this?' said Françoise, staring at the place settings, damask tablecloth and napkins, and crayfish on a large silver tray.

'German precision,' said Henri, poking fun at Leo and Theresa who were completing the laying up.

'How did you manage to bring us all together, Henri?' It was Justine speaking.

'Look over there, that broad-shouldered rugby player striding towards us,' said Henri. 'He gave me the idea.'

Justine was struck dead by the sight of Bill Lomberg. She and Bill rarely communicated, but between them there was a bond impossible to describe. It went back to the war and Buchenwald.

'That's Bill Lomberg,' Henri said to Kim. 'You're the only one who doesn't know him. He, Leo and I were at school together in England.'

'How come?' said Kim, her surprise showing.

'It was our English mothers. They thought the Benedictines of St Gregory's knew best how to educate the likes of us. Trouble was that as soon as we finished there, the war began.'

'And I was on the wrong side,' muttered Leo.

Bill arrived and they were all over him.

Tears appeared in Justine's eyes, as they embraced. 'Bill, I don't believe it. You're meant to be in Durban.'

Bill explained that Lomberg Air Transport's best client was now Tractebel, the Belgian engineering company. His aircraft were operating in and out of Katanga, the old Belgian Congo.

'How did you become involved in Katanga?' asked Leo.

'You remember Roger Trinquier in Indochina?'

'Of course. He did tell me he was quitting the army to work for President Tshombe.'

'Roger said he needed Dakotas for what he was up to there,' said Bill. 'At Leopoldville, or Kinshasa as they plan to call it.'

'Well, Bill. I've got news for you,' said Leo. 'Theresa and I are going to the Congo as soon as I'm released by the Legion. Roger told us about Katanga too, and wants us to join him.'

They looked at one another, astonished.

'That's not the end of it,' interrupted Henri, putting his arm around Kim. 'We're thinking of moving in that direction.' He paused as everyone stopped speaking. 'Kim has been offered a job with *L'Express*, to become their Central African correspondent.'

There was spontaneous applause, after which Leo exclaimed, '*À table*, everyone!' A clank came from the bucket he was carrying, holding champagne bottles on ice. That was the signal for the party to begin.

Nobody mentioned Noelle, although she was in everyone's thoughts except Kim's. Her eyes were on Henri who remained standing, smiling broadly and clearly about to announce something.

Clasping Kim, he said, 'My friends, my military career is in tatters. My private life is thriving. Je ne regrette rien.'

Aftermath

The assassination attempt as depicted in this novel is based on events surrounding an actual attempt at Petit-Clamart on 22 August 1962. The brains behind the actual attack was a certain Jean Bastien-Thiry who, together with all but one of the fifteen-strong commando, was arrested and tried before the Military Court. General de Gaulle commuted all of the death sentences handed down except that of Jean Bastien-Thiry. He was executed by firing squad on March 11 1963, the last such execution in French history. Several hundred of his supporters attended a requiem mass for him the next day at the Cathedral of Notre-Dame. There is a circle of followers of Jean Bastien-Thiry, who to this day commemorate this extraordinary person every year on the anniversary of his death. The background to the brilliant aircraft engineer, who designed the first air-to-ground guided missile, is an enthralling story in itself. As one commentator wrote, how could a man, endowed with profound Catholic convictions and a strong cultural upbringing, end up in this way?

The mysterious insider within government, code-named B12 and alleged to have supplied the would-be assassin and the OAS with information on the President's movements, remains an enigma. Suffice to say that a source within the OAS, and Jean Bastien-Thiry himself in his trial testimony, identified B12 as Valéry Giscard d'Estaing.

Maurice Papon, Prefect of the Paris police during the period this story covers, became president of Sud Aviation, later Aérospatiale, manufacturer of the first prototype Concorde jet airliner. He went on to serve in the French National Assembly, and in the Cabinet of Raymond Barre under President Giscard d'Estaing. He was eventually brought to trial in 1998, found guilty of crimes against humanity, and remained in prison until finally released due to ill health after his petition was refused three times by President Chirac.

Jacques Foccart was in charge of African affairs for both President de Gaulle and his successor, Georges Pompidou. He led the structuring of France's influence in its former colonies across Africa, only losing his role when Valéry Giscard d'Estaing took office. He was an octogenarian when brought back to the Élysée Palace by Jacques Chirac.

Pierre Sergent was sentenced to death *in absentia*, having escaped to Switzerland. He benefited from an amnesty in 1968, returning to France. Entering politics in the Pyrenees region, he was elected deputy in the National Front party. He later contributed to de-demonising the NF, now known as National Rally and led by Marine Le Pen.

Roger Degueldre, commander of the OAS Delta Commandos, was executed by firing squad later in 1962.

Raoul Salan, five-star general and the most decorated soldier in the French army, was arrested and condemned to death *in absentia* for treason, later commuted to life imprisonment. Having escaped to Switzerland, he was pardoned in 1968.

The *harkis*. As predicted by Hélie de Saint Marc and our fictional friend Henri de Rochefort in this story, France's recognition of Algerian independence in July 1962 triggered the persecution of the *harkis*. Gouging out of eyes, castrations and crucifixions were widely reported. Thousands died of disease and starvation in forced labour camps in the

Sahara. Some managed to escape to mainland France where initially they were incarcerated in camps in appalling conditions, reflecting abandonment by the French authorities in spite of their service as auxiliaries in the armed forces. To this day, many *harkis* in France continue to live in humble conditions, while the survivors in Algeria are refused higher education. President Chirac was the first to recognise their plight nationally, making September 25 an annual day of homage to them.

Hélie de Saint Marc was sentenced to ten years' imprisonment after a trial in which he strove to have his legionnaires exonerated from the blame that he accepted, in respect to their participation in the Generals' putsch. He was pardoned after serving four years of his sentence. Ten years later his full military rights were reinstated. After a civilian career in the metal industry, he wrote a number of successful books and spoke at conferences around the world. At 89 years of age, President Sarkozy awarded him the Grand-Croix of the Légion d'Honneur, the highest level of the order. This was fitting recognition of de Saint Marc's extraordinary life-time contribution to his country, which started in the Resistance and led him to near-death in the V2 rocket bomb tunnels of Dora, followed by his service in the French Foreign Legion in Vietnam and Algeria.

The song 'Non, je ne regrette rien', made famous by Édith Piaf, was adopted into the heritage of the parachute regiment of the French Foreign Legion, and was sung by the legionnaires at the funeral of Hélie de Saint Marc.

Historical note

Why was the Algerian crisis so different? Let's go back to May 1945, almost to the day when the war in Europe ended. At that moment, the movement among the Arab population of Algeria for independence from French rule exploded into conflict. The flashpoint was the town of Sétif, the Arab capital of the country. Hunger after months of drought and long-time expropriation of the best farming land by white settlers, melded with a belief that now was the moment. The United Nations was about to come into being, and the issue of independence was forcing its way into the headlines from India to Malaya, Tunisia to Morocco.

The horror of the attacks on the non-Arab population in Algeria was met by the authorities with widespread repression and organised humiliation of the peasant classes. The aim was to leave the rural population in no doubt as to who was in control, and would remain so in the long term. After all, Algeria was not another French colony. It was part of France, divided up into departments with their deputies sitting in the National Assembly in Paris.

Crushing poverty and illiteracy amongst the rural Arab population remained the norm for the next ten years, while the political movement for independence, the National Liberation Front or FLN, steadily grew its organisation and membership. Its military wing, the ALN, began to receive arms from newly independent nations including Egypt.

On All Saints' Day, November 1 1954, the FLN issued a declaration listing the elements and objectives of a new Algerian nation. Shortly afterwards, it organised a revolt of peasants in and around the city of Philippeville. Photographs circulated mainland France of the horrific deaths matching those of Sétif nearly ten years before. From this point on, the FLN/ALN went head-to-head with the French armed forces.

During six years of guerrilla warfare, France committed a substantial part of its professional and conscript army. With the aid of counterinsurgency experts who had learned their trade in Indochina, the rebel forces were driven back to the frontiers with Tunisia and Morocco. By 1960, the French armed forces considered the battle won. But by then, the FLN had gained the support not only of Russia, China and emerging Third World nations, but also the sympathy of the USA. The struggle transferred to the floor of the United Nations.

So what characterised the Algerian crisis, differentiating it from the bloodshed of revolution in other colonies fighting for independence? France regarded Algeria differently from Tunisia, Morocco and its other African colonies. It was part of France. Uniquely, the mass of its population didn't only consist of an indigenous Arab population. Its wealth was in the hands of a large population of white settlers, French citizens whose ancestors were from across southern Europe, and a Jewish element important to the country's commerce. Whereas in most colonial emergencies, the government and army were up against a single force for independence, here they faced two groups fighting with conflicting aims. Neither would accept the solutions proposed by successive French administrations, from political integration with France through to self-determination and declaration of a new nation state.

A succession of short-lived governments in Paris failed to solve the problem. On May 13 1958, a coup d'état was launched in Algeria by leading political figures and General Massu, commander of the 10th Parachute Division. They took over Corsica, and threatened insurrection in mainland France. The President, René Coty, decided that only General de Gaulle could prevent civil war. Charles de Gaulle, who led the fightback of the Free French after France's capitulation in 1940, and then steered the country to Liberation, had retired in disgust over the party politics that followed peace in 1945. After twelve years living quietly at his country home in Colombey-les-Deux-Églises, he stated his conditions for returning to power. He demanded approval to rule by decree for a period of six months, that is to govern without Parliament, and to draw up a new constitution. In spite of the Socialists being split down the middle, and opposition from the Communists, Parliament approved and voted him in as Prime Minister. During the six months, an incredible volume of legislation was introduced including a new economic plan and important educational reforms.

By September 1958, the new constitution was drafted. A referendum was called to seek the public's approval and to elect General de Gaulle as President. They did just that, with the help of the Algerian white settlers who had the vote, but not of the Arab population most of whom did not. The ineffective Fourth Republic was dead. Under the Fifth Republic, which lives on to this day, the President's powers were greatly increased and reforms enacted to bring more stability to the government.

As this book shows, General de Gaulle steered a course through the minefield of opposing interests towards the first discussions with the FLN on Algerian independence. The mayor of the town of Évian, where the talks were to take place, was murdered before they began. The OAS was baring its teeth, as it had done with the crash of the Strasbourg to Paris express train. Finally, on March 19 1962, a ceasefire came into force and the French armed forces were obliged to stand back while widespread atrocities were committed in the towns and cities along the Mediterranean coast of Algeria. As the riot police intervened at great risk to themselves, the OAS continued to recruit and gun down anyone they fancied from officialdom to ordinary civilians walking the streets. The SAC and its *barbouzes* hit back, wiping out OAS commanders in the field. The Europeans, now referred to as the *pieds noirs*, started a general strike in Algiers and began to flee the country in their thousands. Ports were jammed with families desperate to reach Marseille after abandoning their homes and businesses. On July 3 at 10.30am, President de Gaulle declared Algeria to be an independent nation state.

The years that followed did indeed witness a period of exceptional investment, economic growth, and recovery of France's standing in the world. Then happened the events of 1968, *aux barricades*, but that's another story.

Acknowledgements

For me, the culmination of war in Algeria and the consequences of that nation's independence seem as if they happened yesterday. I was living in Paris at the time; the occasional OAS outrage still in evidence including the bombing of a restaurant that I occasionally frequented. My employer sent me to Algeria to spend time with an American oil company in the depths of the Sahara where one of their wells pumped more oil than at any other oilfield in Africa. Had I not turned down their offer of a job in Algiers, I might have had the time to write novels earlier in life. Suffice to say, researching the material to write *Fracture* evoked memories of those exciting times.

I was most fortunate to have the help of three persons younger than me but with strong historical affinity to France in that era. Sir Francis Richards contributed his invaluable skills in identifying what in my fictional story was appropriate and possible and what was not. Ann Buxton brought into play an intimate knowledge of how French people reacted to the real events and pressures of that time. The third person is my wife whose university education was in Pau, close to the home base of military units in which French Algeria was part of life. Anna's know-how and encouragement meant everything to me. Finally, Simon Murray agreed to read the finished manuscript and validate its authenticity from the viewpoint of someone who was actually serving in Algeria in 1961–62, when this story unfolds. My sincere thanks to all of you. In truth, *Fracture* would not have been worthy of its readership without you.

For source material, I referred to three books in particular: *Algeria: France's Undeclared War* by Martin Evans; *A Certain Idea of France: The Life of Charles de Gaulle* by Julian Jackson; and Alice Zeniter's remarkable novel *The Art of Losing*, translated from the French by Frank Wynne. I thoroughly recommend these books to anyone wishing to learn more of the historical background.

Tom Witcomb of the Literary Agency reviewed the manuscript when the book was little more than half finished, but was able to help me with the ever present challenge of bringing fictional characters alive to the reader in a historical context. Kim McSweeney at Mach 3 Solutions Ltd and Graham Frankland were as understanding and skilful as ever in handling the typesetting and proof editing respectively, and Ian Hughes's brilliant cover design speaks for itself. Thank you.